JOURNEYS OF THE MIND

*The Amazing Adventures of
Ethel and Willy*

by
Carol Edler Baumann

Order this book online at www.trafford.com
or email orders@trafford.com

Most Trafford titles are also available at major online book retailers.

Printed in the United States of America.

ISBN: 978-1-4269-6056-7 (sc)
ISBN: 978-1-4269-6055-0 (e)

Library of Congress Control Number: 2011904425

Trafford rev. 03/25/2011

 www.trafford.com

North America & international
toll-free: 1 888 232 4444 (USA & Canada)
phone: 250 383 6864 ♦ fax: 812 355 4082

Table of Contents

*Originally published in *IMPRESSIONS/EXPRESSIONS* – Spring, 2003 as *Journey of the Mind*, first place winner in the Wisconsin Press Women's 2002-03 state-wide contest.

INTRODUCTION

Ethel Matson is a sensible, semi-retired professor whose life up to this point has been concerned with the pursuit of rational, tangible knowledge and experiences. Then she starts having both strange encounters and incredibly lucid dreams. In these supposed dreams, Ethel and her enigmatic and unruly companion, Willy (whom Ethel's husband regards as a figment of her imagination), set about exploring the core essences of ideas she'd only mildly wondered about before, like the interdependence of faith and science -- and life and death. Is her subconscious mind suddenly springing to life, or is there something more going on?

Journeys of the Mind: The Amazing Adventures of Ethel and Willy, by author and retired professor Carol Edler Baumann, brings us twenty-seven interconnected episodes in the unusual experiences of Ethel Matson. As we delve into the conscious world, the subconscious world, and the world that lies between, we are faced with the questions of what is real and what is imagined, and whether reality actually matters if in the end we discover truth and everlasting love.

THE ISOLATION TANK

Ethel shivered as she began to disrobe, but her chill was due less to the penetrating cold than to her own apprehension. The elongated black box which looked like a coffin crafted for Frankenstein and the eerie half-light of the dank basement only served to heighten her unease. She stepped hesitantly into the tank, hunkered, and finally slid down on her back in the water as the lid bumped down shut above her.

Ethel had not really wanted to try out the isolation tank, and now, floating inside in complete darkness, she wondered why she had agreed. Her daughter, Chris, was writing about sensory deprivation and was visiting one of her friends who had built an isolation tank in his basement. When Ethel arrived for a short stay, they both spoke excitedly about their "out of body" adventures, and Chris had insisted that Ethel take advantage of the opportunity to experience it.

"The water and air inside the tank are exactly the same as your body temperature, Mom -- so you don't know where your body ends and where the air and water begin. There's no light, or sound, or smell. You're just there -- alone with your inner being." Some tanks, Chris said, were used for language instruction, facilitating rote learning by concentrating all of one's attention on the words and phrases piped in, with no other sounds or sights to distract. Some experimentation with hypnosis and thought control had also been done by the Defense Department, but Chris hadn't been able to ferret out much information about that.

But to do it as a lark? Ethel thought. Or to try to "plumb the depths of one's innermost being" and feelings? She wasn't quite sure about that. A sensible middle-aged professor, Ethel Matson didn't spend much time on introspection or self analysis. She thought of herself as rational, realistic, and driven by common sense. Stepping naked into the tomb-like isolation box in a damp basement, with her daughter nodding her head in encouragement and her boyfriend looking the other way, did not at all fit with her self image. But she was also open to new experiences, and she had to admit that what Chris had told her about her own exposures to the tank had intrigued Ethel enough to try it.

As she began to relax in the silky soft velour of total blackness, Ethel paddled her hands once or twice to feel the motion of the water against her skin. Chris was right; if she lay perfectly still, her body seemed to merge with the surrounding elements and she couldn't tell where it ended and everything else began. Her breathing now slowed to a deep and even rhythm and she knew that her initial apprehension was gradually fading away. From what Chris had said (and some reading she had then done on the subject), Ethel thought that perhaps she would simply indulge in a sort of Virginia Woolf "stream of consciousness" -- letting her mind float to wherever it wanted to go. But to lose herself in this contraption? No, that just wasn't her style.

She had become a water lily. Her stem was anchored below her, but her upper torso swayed gently in the water. Her leaf-arms floated weightlessly beside her and her head had become a beautiful golden lily with wide open petals reaching up toward the sun. She couldn't see the sun -- she only felt it on her flower face, warm and soothing. How absolutely comfortable and relaxing it all felt. The muddy bottom of the pond enveloped her roots up to her ankles, and the water and air around her stem and leaves and flower head caressed her gently in their embrace. It was so peaceful and quiet that she didn't even want to open her eyes to search for the sun.

Then she became a fish -- a golden fish with long, wispy fins and a tail that flowed far behind her in undulating waves. Her mouth gaped open and shut as her wide round eyes peered into the blackness to seek the tiny bits of plant life that swirled around her. When the shark approached, she wasn't afraid because she understood the ways of the sea life that sustained them all. She would pass through the shark's body like the water through her gills and become one with the dirt and silt below. Then -- over time -- her protean pieces would nourish the water lily that sprouted from that muddy bottom.

Ethel opened her eyes to the black interior of the coffin tank and tapped firmly on the lid. It opened immediately and her pupils contracted against the dim light of the basement bulb. Her daughter smiled as she lifted back the top and helped Ethel out. "Well? How was it?" she asked. "You were in about twenty minutes. Anything happen?"

"Oh, I sort of pretended I was a water lily." No. She had *become* a water lily. "And then a golden fish." But she hadn't pretended that, either. She had *been* that fish and had strained the oxygen from the water with her fishy gills -- and she had been swallowed by that shark. And then ... and then she had awakened. Yes, that was it. "I don't know," she mused aloud as she was dressing. "I didn't exactly pretend I was a lily or a fish. I must have dreamed it, I guess."

Since both Chris and David wanted to talk at length about the tank and their own experiences in it, Ethel was spared the pressure to go into greater detail. Still uneasy with her seeming transformation, she wanted to have more time to think about it and come to her own conclusions. "It's kind of like deep meditation," Chris was explaining. "You can get to the same stage by meditating, but it takes longer. The tank allows you to really concentrate on what's going on inside. Not in your head, y' know, but at a spiritual level."

"What's this spirituality all of a sudden?" Ethel smiled at her oldest daughter. "I thought you didn't buy that kind of stuff."

"No, you missed the point." Chris was not going to let it pass as casual humor. "I never said that I didn't believe in the existence of a spiritual self or in spiritual power. I just don't believe in 'God' as you have chosen to define him -- or her. I don't think that the early Christian prophets had any monopoly on religious knowledge or insight. People today can find their own versions of God without the Bible to guide them."

"Oh, come on, lighten up." Ethel shook her head as they went upstairs. "I was only kidding, Chris. I know you believe in the spiritual forces or powers that we all have -- perhaps more than I do. What I'm not so sure about is whether you have to go into a state of meditation or lie in an isolation tank to experience or use those powers." She reached for the two books by John Lilly which her daughter had given her. "That session really tired me out. I think I'll rest a while and get started on these books. Which would you read first?" Still annoyed, Chris shrugged, but pointed to *The Center of the Cyclone.*

John Lilly had been an early guru of the late sixties and early seventies -- he had experimented with LSD and had written about it extensively. He was particularly known for his work with isolation tanks. Ethel read, *"What one believes to be true, either is true or becomes true in one's mind, within limits to be determined experimentally and experientially. These limits are beliefs to be transcended."* She paused to digest that. Lilly continued, *"This is the situation when one is freed up from one's environment, from one's surrounding reality, and all of the usual forms and patterns of stimulation are attenuated to the minimum possible level."*

So, she thought, the tank removes the stimulation of sight, sound, smell -- and feeling (as long as you lie still) -- and your mind then becomes free to find -- what? The truth? Or what one believes to be the truth? And how does all that relate to her becoming a water lily -- or a fish, for God's sake?

The next morning Ethel climbed into the tank with a mixed agenda: on the one hand, she wanted to again lose consciousness, or gain a new consciousness; on the other, she was reluctant to lose control, to let herself go. The confining box seemed stifling at first, and the darkness oppressive. Her breathing was labored and her heart thudded irregularly in her chest. Why was she doing this? Chris had given her an easy out by saying that it might be better to absorb fully her first exposure to the tank before embarking on another immersion. But Ethel had become fascinated by Lilly's book and theory; she was determined to explore it further on her own. She forced herself to take slower, deeper breaths. It made no difference whether her eyes were open or shut -- either way, the black abyss yawned open before her.

This time she became a little girl -- not just any little girl, but herself when she was two or three. She didn't like the "nice gookie" her mother was feeding her. It was a soft-boiled egg with a runny yellow inside. Not all of the white was hard, either, and the clear slimy liquid looked like the stuff that came out of her nose when she sneezed. She shoved away her mother's hand and the spoon fell to the floor, soon followed by the dish which she defiantly pushed off her tray. Her mother would have let her get away with it, but her dad had seen the whole thing and was not in a mood to humor her. He grabbed her from her highchair, slapped her behind, put her back in the chair, and said firmly, "Now eat that egg!" She choked as she tried to force the egg down her throat, while the tears poured from her eyes. Her Daddy had spanked her. It was the first -- and last -- time. After twenty minutes of her crying, he had lifted her gently from her highchair, and had carried her back and forth, back and forth -- for three hours -- until she finally sobbed herself to sleep.

He was dying now. He had been in a coma for some ten hours and the nurses said he wouldn't last the night. Ethel's two little daughters had said goodbye to their grandpa for the last time and while Roscoe took them home she sat with her mother -- waiting. Her mother would occasionally get up from her chair at the foot of the bed, walk over to her husband, pat his hand, and then walk slowly back to wait some more. They comforted each other by saying that at least he wasn't suffering now (he was dying of cancer), but it didn't help much. When he finally exhaled that rattle breath of death, it all passed so fast that it seemed

5

like anticlimax. While her mother hurried down the hall to call the nurse, Ethel cried by her father's side, "Oh, Daddy, we loved you so." And they did.

Her eyes were wet with tears when they opened the tank lid. She just shook her head when they asked her what was wrong, and both Chris and David instinctively understood that she didn't want to talk That afternoon Ethel went to her room and again picked up *The Center of the Cyclone*: *"...what one believes to be true either is true or becomes true within certain limits .... These limits are beliefs to be transcended. Hidden from one's self is a covert set of beliefs that control one's thinking , one's actions, and one's feelings. The covert set of hidden beliefs is the limiting set of beliefs to be transcended. To transcend one's limiting set, one establishes an open-ended set of beliefs about the unknown."* Heavy, Ethel thought, as she closed the book and rested her head back against the pillow.

When her father died, what had she believed? Ethel was a practicing Christian -Lutheran by upbringing and church going by routine. But her dad had not been a church goer -- "the pews are too hard," he had said -- nor had he believed in any life after death. "When you're gone, you're gone," he used to say. He was given a Christian burial and was buried in the Protestant cemetery outside the small town where they had lived. "Was that it?" she had wondered. According to church doctrine, one was supposed to be "saved by grace through faith." But if that faith wasn't there, as in her father's case, then how could he be saved? She never pushed this to its logical conclusion, nor did she speculate much on matters of this sort, but somehow it did manage to bother her -- when she thought about it.

Ethel was still mulling this over during dinner that night when she realized that David had asked her a question. Unable to focus on the conversation, she had simply stopped listening. "What? I'm sorry, David, what did you say?"

"David was saying that sometimes it helps to go back into the tank right after a particularly profound encounter -- like you seemed to have. Right, David?"

"Well, I just thought that since you're leaving tomorrow afternoon, you'd only have the morning for another session -- unless you want to go back in tonight?"

"Thanks, David. I think that's exactly what I'd like to do. If you two don't mind?" Ethel hadn't planned on another immersion, but maybe that was what she needed to do to rid herself of this confusion, these nagging doubts about what she really believed.

At first, her mind wouldn't slow down. She couldn't stop her rational thinking. If Lilly was right, she asked herself, was her own quasi-fundamentalism (her university colleagues could never understand her seemingly naive acceptance of these out-of-fashion beliefs) -- the "limiting set of beliefs to be transcended?" If so, then where might she find and how might she develop that more "open-ended set of beliefs about the unknown?" Was the sensory deprivation of the isolation box a possible way to free her inner spirit from the narrow constraints of long-ago learned "truths" and unchallenged "beliefs?" Or was she being lured by the fantasy dreams of a former drug addict to question the very bedrock of her faith?

"What do you mean -- former drug addict?" She was sitting at a bar, and the man who looked like the picture of John Lilly on the book cover frowned at her over his glass of beer. "Don't believe everything you read, Ethel. You ought to know better than that!" He had introduced himself as Lilly's younger brother, Willy. "Willy Lilly?" she had blurted out and then laughed hysterically. "That's just too much!"

She tried to put this absurdity completely out of her mind. "Well, I was just thinking ..." Ethel hardly uttered the words , when she was interrupted. "That's the whole problem, Ethel. You don't mind my calling you Ethel, do you?" Willy didn't wait for her reply. "You see, if you're really going to transcend those limited beliefs of your childhood

7

teachings, you have to clear your mind of them -- you have to open your self, not just your mind, to a deeper level. And you can't do that by thinking!"

She took a sip from her glass of Scotch and ventured a shy smile. "I suppose you're going to say that I can only do it by living the rest of my life in this aquatic box?"

He smiled back. "No, Ethel, not the rest of your life. But if I were you, I would give it one more chance." Ethel glanced up at the passing waiter to ask for some snacks. When she turned back to address her persistent companion, he was gone.

"Mom, are you sure you want to go into the isolation tank again today?" It was Chris the next morning who noticed her mother's tired eyes and her only partially stifled yawns. "No, I'm okay, honey. I just got hung up on John Lilly's book last night and didn't finish it until about three this morning. But I do have to leave this afternoon, so if I want to try the tank once more -- and I do -- I'll have to do it now." Ethel wasn't quite sure what the tank would open up to her this fourth time, but she was determined to find out. After all, she had been advised to do so by the very best of authorities.

The gentle air and water seemed to welcome Ethel in their warm embrace. She floated effortlessly and weightlessly, her body absorbed in the amorphous nothingness of the elements that held her. She let her thoughts wander, but nothing came. Slowly, little pinpoints of light emerged all around her. Ethel knew that nothing was there, but whether open or shut, her eyes told her otherwise. The pinpoints expanded and merged together in a Milky Way of light, swirling around a black tunnel in the center. She knew that this happened when people died – "the light at the end of the tunnel" -- but as soon as she began to think, the lights receded. Once again she relaxed and the lights returned.

This time when the tunnel appeared, Ethel let herself drift into it -- slowly at first, and then more quickly, until finally she was catapulted through its darkened void. When she emerged on the other side, all she could see was light -- all around her was light -- and she was part of it. As she grew accustomed to the brightness, Ethel realized that all the light was coming from the swirling stars that had formed the tunnel on the other side. She too had become a star. She was somehow joined with all the other stars in a huge heavenly display of light and music.

At the very core of that light, forming the center, was the love of God. Ethel remembered the teaching that "God is love," but for the first time she now understood what it meant. It was an all-embracing love, not condemning or excluding, not narrow and confining, but so broad as to include all mankind -- and the water lilies and fish as well. Laughing and crying at the same time, she now danced with the other stars in total abandonment. But then it was time for her to go home.

Ethel decided not to talk about it until she herself could absorb it more fully. She wanted to think through this profound mind-changing hour she had just experienced before she even attempted to share it with others -- even her daughter. She hugged Chris as she said goodbye. "Well, honey, it was a good visit, as always. And I did enjoy your isolation tank -- and my voyages within it." Chris nodded her agreement. "I only wish you would tell us more about what happened, Mom. It must have been some wild ride to first bring you home crying and the next time laughing. Any word for the wise?"

"Belief, I guess. But a belief that's more open-ended than what I had before, less limiting. Here, wait, let me read you something from Lilly: *"The something to believe in -- somehow, somewhere, within inner space or without, in outer space ... must be positive and whole. ... The search for the something cannot be done before belief that something exists. Something to believe in. The something to believe in is greater, somehow, than one's present self. It, something, can be future self, changed. ... It can be something out there, among the planets, the stars. It can be something everywhere ... inside and outside. Something far beyond Man."*

Ethel handed the book to Chris. "My belief was just never big enough, that's all. But it is now. It goes all the way up to the stars -- and back."

WHEEL OF FORTUNE

The short, professorial-looking woman heard the announcer introduce Pat Sajak and Vanna White, as the audience went wild with whistles, clapping, and shouting. Unable to remember how she got there, Ethel was befuddled and anxious as Pat approached the wheel and began to talk to each of the contestants. The young man at the far left worked for an insurance agency and liked to ski out in Colorado; he had his own cheering section near the front of the filled auditorium. The chic black lady standing in the middle was of indeterminate age -- perhaps in her mid-forties. She was an executive secretary to the president of a large aerodynamics company in California and the mother of "three wonderful children."

It was Ethel's turn next. She said that she was a Professor of International Relations; had two talented daughters and five darling grandchildren. She added that she loved to travel and had done so extensively. No one seemed to be too interested in her, she thought, including Sajak. Although he had begun to give the instructions for the first round, Ethel couldn't concentrate. She kept wondering how she had been selected, and when, and how she had gotten here. She was dressed in a nicely tailored slack suit, but suddenly saw to her horror that she was wearing her white tennis shoes. Ethel could remember all the unkind remarks made about "little old ladies in tennis shoes" -- and here she was one of them!

Pat said that the puzzle was an "old war-time song title" and the other lady, Ruby, had drawn the first turn. There were eight words (_ _ _ _ _ _   _ _   _ _   _   _ _ _ _   _ _ _   _   _ _ _ _ _ _), a couple with two letters each. Ethel would have opted for an "N," but Ruby went with "T." There wasn't a single one. That was unusual, Ethel thought, but so be it. It was her turn next, so she shook off her lethargy, grabbed the wheel, and spun it around as hard as she could. It landed on $500 and she yelled out "N!" Sure enough, there were five "N"s and she was credited with a nice, round $2,500! Knowing it was smart to buy some vowels, she spent $200 on an "I" and an "A," and the board now looked like this: _ _ _in_   in   _n   a   _in_   an_   a   _ _a_ _ _.

Well, there was no way to guess that one, so Ethel spun the wheel and hit the "lose a turn" space. She swore inwardly, but managed a weak smile as Colin (the insurance man on the end) took his turn. Ethel kept thinking, "don't say 'S,' don't say 'S'" -- but he did. How lucky can you get? There was no "S!" Next up, Ruby hit a $300 space and guessed "R" correctly; there were two, so she earned $600, though Ethel was still far in the lead. Ruby bought an "O," got two of them, and spun the wheel again. This time she landed on the $1,000 space, asked for an "M" and got it. She was now up to $1,600, minus the $100 she paid for the "O." Her next spin landed on "Prize," but she missed that one -- no "L." The board now showed: _omin_   in   on   a   _in_   an_   a   _ra_ _r.

It was Ethel's second turn. She spun the old wheel with gusto and landed on $400. She had been pretty sure of the "G" she called for, but hadn't expected two of them. That brought her up to $3,100. Spinning again, the wheel landed on the $1,000 space. The audience went wild. Vanna was waiting for the letter, while Pat urged her on: "A letter, please."

Ethel checked the board another time and finally shouted out, "A 'C,' please." "Yes, there's a 'C,'" Sajak responded, and Vanna tapped the card. The big board now read: "coming in   on   a   _ing   an_   a   _ra_ _r." "You're up to a total of $4,100," said Pat. "What will it be, Ethel?"

She spun again to the $1,000 slot and won it with a "W." Ethel knew the answer now, but she felt she was on a roll, and tried one more spin. She agonized as the wheel approached the "bankrupt" space, slowed down and hovered at its far edge, but then slid over to the $900 spot. "P," Ethel shouted, and upped her total to an even $6,000. She decided not to be greedy.

"I'll solve the puzzle," Ethel stated in her best professorial tone: "COMING IN ON A WING AND A PRAYER!"

The screaming of the audience now came from the other passengers as the pilot's voice crackled over the whirring of the jet engines: "It's going to be a crash landing -- fasten those seat belts and hold on tight!" The plane careened off the dusty sand far before the approach to the tarmac and then, veering to the right, it headed directly toward the mountain foothills that bordered the airstrip on both sides of the narrow valley. Ethel could see the ugly boulders draw closer and felt the wrenching rip of the wing as it tore away from the body of the huge airliner. She grasped the tiny golden cross that hung from her neck and murmured, "Oh, dear God, don't let us die; please don't let us all die!"

The smoke was gone now, though its acrid taste lingered in Ethel's throat. Unconscious, she must have been thrown free of the wreckage, and now found herself wandering down the sandy surface between the foothills on either side. Her tennis shoes were brown from the sand and dirt, but her clothes were not torn and, as far as she could tell, she had emerged from the wreck unscathed. There was no one else around. Her eyes searched in all directions for some sight of the plane, the airport, or her fellow passengers -- nothing. Where had they all gone? Where in hell was she?

The gorge curved gently to the right and then divided into two separate paths, each widening into broader plateaus some miles ahead. The one sloped down sharply -- stony and obstructed in places by huge rocks. The other, though slanting upward, was more inviting and gradually led toward a green vista which Ethel could see in the distance. She took the upper path.

Ethel's eyes refocused on the spinning wheel. It was the second game and Pat Sajak had just informed them that the seven blank spaces on the board formed a "same name" or "common word" puzzle -- two people having the same last name or two phrases joined by the same word. Colin landed on a $500 space and led off with an "S" -- there were two of them. His next spin just eased past the "lose a turn" sign and landed on $800. "L" he shouted out, and was rewarded by Vanna touching the corners of two of the cards. He bought an "A" and got one. Spinning again, Colin landed this time right on the "bankrupt" space; he wasn't able to control his frown, but he clapped his hands dutifully. Ruby came on loud and strong with her "Big Money! Big Money!" chant, but it didn't do her much good, as she landed on a $250 spot. She tried for a "T," but there were no "T"s.

Eyeing the board carefully, Ethel spun the wheel to a $400 spot and said "N" in a slightly questioning tone. "Yes, there are two 'N's," Sajak grinned, now getting into the mood of the moment; he liked the winners and Ethel was starting to look like one.

She bought an "O" (three) and an "E" (four), and spun again. This was the big one: $5,000. "Y," she called.

"Two 'Y's," Pat confirmed, as Vanna tapped the cards. The pattern that emerged was: _o_ _ _een _as _y _alley o_ _e_ _s_on. With the additional two "W"s that Ethel won at $600 each, the two "I"s that she bought, and a "D" at $500, she was able to solve: HOW GREEN WAS MY VALLEY OF DECISION. $12,200 for that round alone! The crowd was now with her, roaring its encouragement, and she was raring to continue. But it was break time.

The path widened into a parklike entrance leading up to what looked like a Disney World palace -- towers, gates and all. Ethel thought that maybe the crash had given her a serious concussion, though her head didn't ache or throb. Her limbs were all working reasonably well, she told herself, considering the tiring walk up the winding path to the plateau spread before her. She approached the gates haltingly, looking about for any signs of human life. The birds of this strange place had seemingly recovered from the noise of the crash and the black fumes which had risen from the wreck. They twittered in an almost idyllic symphony of soft music, while little squirrels and gophers, and even a rabbit or two, dashed in and out between the trees. "Hello?" Ethel finally called. "Hello, there -- is there anyone around?"

"Well, here we are, back at our third round. We have only one winner so far, but the game is far from over. Let's see what our contestants can do with the following phrase of four words. The category is book title. Your start, Colin." Colin just wasn't lucky. He landed on a nice healthy $600 spot, but there were no "S"s. This time Ruby hit some "Big Money," though, with three "T"s at $1,000 each. She bought an "E" and got four of them, selected an "H" for $300, but then lost out when she asked for "L." The puzzle was emerging as follows: _ _ _ _ he_e t_ ete_ _ _ t_.

Ethel's spin landed on "Prize" (an all-expense trip to Los Angeles valued at $4,000) which she won with an "F." She bought two "O"s and then flubbed on an $800 space when she repeated the "H" which had already been called. Colin missed again when he asked for "C." This time round Ruby went all the way. She correctly guessed three "R"s at $900 each, an "N" for $350, an "M" for $500, and an "F" for another $1,000. But Ruby wanted it all. She landed on the "Dude Ranch" space for the estimated value of $2,500 and won it with the last letter, "Y." She correctly called out, "FROM HERE TO ETERNITY," and secured a grand total of $7,050 -- less than half of Ethel's $18,200, but a good haul for one round.

The wizened and bearded old man approached the gates with a quizzical look and asked, "What are you doing here, Ethel?" She peered at him intently, but didn't recognize him. "I was in that crash back over the hill. You can still see a few wisps of the smoke. Didn't you hear it?" she asked with a frown. Not bothering to answer, he shook his head and scanned the scroll he was holding in his left hand as he patted her shoulder through the gate. "Yes, there it is. I thought I was right. You're not supposed to be here for twenty-six more years, Ethel! You took the wrong path down there, that's all. Yes, that's it, you just took the wrong path. Why don't you go back down the way you came, Ethel. You'll find your way all right, won't you?"

She felt a little bit like Dorothy, following the yellow brick road in Oz. But the old man wasn't the Wizard and she wasn't Dorothy. She tried once more to protest, but he had already disappeared as suddenly as he had come. Her head did ache slightly now, as she walked slowly over to the grass and sat down next to a stately hickory tree, resting her shoulders against the rough bark of its trunk. A tall hickory tree had dominated her back yard when she was a little girl, and in the fall after the first frost she and her brother had scurried about under its branches, gathering the white nuts that had fallen on the lawn from their shells above. What a strange time to be nostalgic, she thought, yawning softly and inhaling the slightly sweet-scented air as her eyelids closed.

It was the final round, and Ethel was surprised to see that her winnings had risen to $25,200, while Ruby's had also grown to $14,500. Poor Colin was still at zero -- but of course he'd get some of those fabulous prizes at the end! The one word puzzle was "Occupation" and Ruby had already guessed one "T," an "R," and had bought an "A." But there was no "S," so it was Ethel's turn. The rotating wheel and flashing lights had made her a little woozy, she felt, as her spin lacked the strength of her earlier efforts; but the pointer landed right on a $500 space and she called out the "G" that she somehow knew was right. She bought the four "E"s that she also knew were there, as Vanna brought up the letters and the board took shape: gate_ee_er. Ethel knew that it had to be "GATEKEEPER," but she decided to chance it to the end. She got her "K" at $450, but ended with a roar of audience approval as she landed on the $5,000 space and shouted out the final "P." She thought she saw the old man smiling at her from the front row.

Pat commiserated with Colin over his poor luck, congratulated Ruby on her "Big Money" winnings of $14,500 ("a nice job"), and then escorted Ethel down to the winners' circle with her grand total winnings of $31,050! There were several possible prizes, Pat announced: An all-expenses paid, two-week stay at Nassau's Paradise Beach, a luxury appointed Grand Am GT convertible, a visit to the Himalayas from Nepal to Tibet, a number of $25,000 envelopes, and of course the grand prize of $100,000! After having just missed winning "From Here to Eternity," Ethel fervently prayed that she wouldn't draw "Paradise Beach," but she wasn't at all worried about Tibet (in fact, she had wanted to go there ever since seeing Ronald Coleman in *Lost Horizon* years ago). She spun the wheel, picked up the folded card where it stopped, and handed it to Pat.

"Place," said Pat, while Vanna pointed to the three blank words on the board. "As usual," he continued, "we'll give you five consonants and a vowel to start with. You can then choose three more consonants and a vowel; you'll have ten seconds to solve. The consonants are: R, S, T, L, N, and the vowel is an E. Let's have the letters, Vanna." Vanna touched the edges of five letters: t_e _ _ _ _ e_rt_. "Well," said Pat, "I don't know if that's enough for you to solve it, but you have three more consonants and a vowel to choose. What will they be?" Ethel stared at the board and said quietly, but distinctly, "H, M, C, and O." Vanna tapped three more cards: the board read, "the _oo _ e_rth." "Now, you're a good puzzle solver," Pat encouraged her. "You have ten seconds to solve. Sound it out. It's a place."

"The wood ---? The something earth? The wood earth ---? No, THE GOOD EARTH! That's it! That's it! THE GOOD EARTH!!" Pat hugged her and she hugged Pat and for the umpteenth time the audience shrieked and cheered. "So, what will it be?" grinned Pat. "Shall we take a look at what you've won?" He slowly opened the card and now Ethel shrieked as she saw "The Himalayas -- from Nepal to Tibet."

The white sleeves came down toward her and strong hands clasped her under her arms. Ethel felt her legs protest in agony as she was pulled upwards from her seat. "Here's one alive!" The tone of the voice was like a shout, but it sounded far away to her, as if coming through a long tunnel. "Here, give me a hand. Her legs are in bad shape, but she's breathing steady and her pulse seems okay." Another pair of arms encircled her waist and supported her legs as her body was carried off the plane to the waiting truck. Was she on her way to Tibet when the crash happened? Had she ever really been on "Wheel of Fortune?" What about the gatekeeper at the entrance to the Disney palace? Where was she -- and where had she been?

As the truck jerked down the steep descent she saw the other path that she had taken when she was there before -- or had she? In the distance she caught a glimpse of the gatekeeper waving at her through the gates. Gates to where? Shangri-La? Ethel vaguely remembered a story about a Chinese man and a butterfly -- it had ended with a riddle: Had the Chinaman dreamed that he was a butterfly or was he really a butterfly who had dreamed that he was a Chinaman? It didn't make much sense, but somehow it made her feel good -- and safe enough to fall asleep. Maybe when she woke up again she would know all of the real answers to the wheel of fortune.

THE RUNAWAY COMPUTER

It was running away from her again, out of her control. Ethel tried to focus on the lecture she was trying to prepare, but her computer wouldn't respond. Her word processor displayed entire paragraphs that she knew she hadn't written -- weird snatches of some strange puzzle that had no beginning, no end. "Find the three great truths and you will find the way. All are one, but the sum is always greater than its parts." When she deleted them, new paragraphs appeared, different from before, but connected in an integral way. She read from the screen:

The Himalayas spread before her -- massive heights, snow and haze enveloped, but awe inspiring. Her flight from Kathmandu had skimmed their icy peaks in a sky of pure azure until it had descended through the clouds to its Tibetan destination. The five intrepid travelers trudged to the hotel where they had been advised to rest that afternoon. Tomorrow they would embark on their temple tours.

Ethel, rather blithely, had left Roscoe back in Bombay where he still had meetings to attend. She had planned to visit both Nepal and Tibet on her own, but when the friendly English couple at their hotel invited her to join them and another two friends, she had accepted enthusiastically. Roscoe agreed to join them in Lhasa.

Previous paragraphs had been less lucid, Ethel noted, so this time she decided to save the material. What was going on? She turned off the computer completely and rebooted. Now, as she began to type, her lecture emerged without further detours. A professor of international relations, Ethel had developed a new course on transnational problems -- international terrorism, development, environmental degradation -- and was now writing the lectures. She had recently attended an international world health conference in Bombay, and wanted to incorporate the presentations into her lectures.

She couldn't budge her mind away from the enigma of her errant computer: How could that inanimate machine write something she didn't type? How could whole paragraphs suddenly appear on her monitor without her input? Had she dozed off, perhaps, and in a semi-conscious state written about Nepal and Tibet? Admittedly, while in Bombay she had wanted to fly up to the Himalayas -- particularly to Tibet. But Roscoe hadn't wanted her to go on her own, and there had been no "friendly English couple" who invited her to join them. She and Roscoe had returned home as planned.

She was wandering through the Potala Palace in Lhasa when she saw Willy. He was nonchalantly turning one of the prayer wheels on an open verandah while watching the saffron-robed monks file past on their way to prayers. "Willy," Ethel exclaimed, in as loud a whisper as she could manage. "What on earth are you doing here in Tibet?"

"Hello, Ethel. You know I like exotic places. Why not Tibet? Besides," Willy grinned with a wink, "I couldn't be here without you, you know. Roscoe says that I'm 'a figment of your imagination' -- or

of your dreams, if you prefer. And I wouldn't have missed this one for anything!" He sat down on one of the woven mats and motioned Ethel to join him. "It's an unbelievable sort of place, isn't it? The Dalai Lama's been off in India for over ten years, and still all these people -- his people -- are waiting for his return." Willy shook his head in wonder. "Absolutely unbelievable."

"No more so than you always showing up in strange places." Ethel leaned against one of the huge crimson pillars that lined the room. "What's this all about, Willy? My computer has gone completely off its rocker -- typing weird stories about the Himalayas. Now here I am at the Potala Palace. Are you sure I'm just dreaming?" But Willy was gone again. He always disappeared when she asked him hard questions.

When she awoke, Ethel jumped from her bed and rushed down to her computer. There it was -- three paragraphs about her journey to Tibet. She printed it, then tore it up, but finally saved the material on a disc before deleting. She didn't want Roscoe to see this until she made some sense of it herself. Ethel wished she had kept the earlier piece that her computer had written -- about the Dalai Lama and the "three great truths" of human existence. What great fun Willy would have had with that one!

It had taken some time for Ethel to come to terms with Willy. She first "met" him years earlier when floating in an isolation tank. The tank had created a climate of almost complete sensory deprivation in which she reached an extremely deep level of meditation within minutes. Willy visited her several times since. At first, she had simply dismissed him as a "figment of her imagination." After a few years, though, she looked forward to his visits and the fascinating conversations they always had. She knew he would be amused by the "three great truths" puzzle, to say nothing of the fact that her computer had written it.

Ethel began to type: "Three Great Truths." Perhaps she could cajole the computer into returning to its earlier theme. She had met the Dalai Lama several years ago in Dharamsala, India, where he had located after fleeing from Tibet. He had impressed her with his simplicity, his warm smile, and the boyish giggle he used to fend off embarrassing questions. But most of all, she now remembered how he had dealt with the seeming dichotomy between Western scientific *knowledge* and Eastern mystical *beliefs*.

"The Dalai Lama," she wrote, "believes that there is a growing convergence between Western science and Eastern mysticism. Just as the East has learned to respect the progress of science, the West has come to recognize the inability of man to *prove* everything scientifically and his need, therefore, to accept some things on faith." Ethel paused, but her word processor continued: *"This, then, is the first great truth. Belief needs science to prove its underlying reality, but science must ultimately rely on belief. The two, in fact, are one."*

Ethel returned to the Potala Palace the next day, hoping to engage Willy in her new quest. At first she didn't recognize him, dressed as he was in a saffron robe, but then his presence became clear: His shock of white hair spilled out from under his hood and he stood a foot taller than the monks with whom he mingled. "My word, Willy," Ethel said as he approached. "What in the world are you doing wearing that robe?"

"Well, maybe it will help me to acquire some Eastern insights. I figured you'd want to pursue your question about dreaming versus reality -- especially now that you're seeking the three great truths." Ethel knew better than to ask how he had learned that.

"I suspect," Willy continued, "that if we can solve this dilemma over what is a dream and what isn't, we'll have the answer to the second of those truths. What do you think?"

Just like Willy, Ethel thought. Throw the question right back to her. "Oh, Willy, I don't know. Right now I feel as if nothing is more real than standing here with you in the middle of this Tibetan temple in the Himalayas. But I also know that the real me is back in bed somewhere in dreamland, facing an awakening to a malfunctioning computer and a new course I've never taught before. So, which is real?"

Willy again smiled that infuriatingly condescending smile of his as he shrugged, "I think you know the answer to that yourself, Ethel. It's just like science and belief, isn't it? Two sides of the same coin. Ultimately, we are the sum total of all our thinking, and feeling, and dreaming. 'Reality' exists as much in the essence of our thoughts and dreams, as in our physical presence or actions. The truth, I think, is that we are both dream and consciousness, spirit and body. What do you think?" But, in Willy's usual fashion, he didn't stay to hear her answer.

Roscoe looked up at her over the top of his paper. "What's wrong, Ethel? You've not been yourself since we came back from India. I know you wanted to visit Tibet, but it simply didn't work out. It's not like you to fuss about things like that."

Ethel nodded absently. "No, I'm not fussing about that. I've just been thinking about a lot of things lately that I never really thought about before. You know, deep stuff -- like I do when I've had three glasses of strong Scotch."

"Oh, the meaning of life question?" Roscoe shook his head and returned to his paper. He wasn't about to be drawn into that again. "Did you get your computer fixed?"

"Well, sort of. At least I've come to terms with it." Ethel debated whether she should say anything more, but decided against it. "I think I'll work on another lecture before I turn in." But when she sat down at her computer, Ethel saw the final entry on her mind's journey to Tibet:

Ethel was invited to a special introspection group that Willy had organized. It consisted of the English couple, Willy and Ethel, and four of the monks. They were talking about the beginning and ending of life, creation and death, the alpha and omega of existence. Ethel knew that this was the third of the great truths she was destined to learn. The head monk distributed two small crystals to each of the eight participants and told them to hold one in each hand.

"Now, as you look into the crystal in your left hand, I want you to think of the earliest memory you have -- the very first feelings or thoughts or dreams you can remember." All of them concentrated on their crystals and reached back into the furthest depths of their memories. Ethel couldn't focus on anything at first; the crystal lay lifeless in her hand. But gradually she saw the sea merging with the sky in a brilliant blue, broken only by a myriad of stars. An intense feeling of love enveloped her. Was it the waters of her mother's womb? Or something that preexisted even before the womb? She didn't know -- she could only feel the comfort and warmth of that love.

"And now I want you to concentrate on the crystal in your right hand. It is the last thought you will have, the last feeling you will experience when you die. You cannot predict what it will be -- give yourselves freely to the power of the crystal and you will know what the end will bring." Ethel forced her mind and body to relax to the soothing sing-song rhythm of the monk's voice. Gradually again, the blue sea-sky of darkness was illuminated by the stars of her inner crystal. A warmth suffused her body and the presence of love surrounded her spirit.

The same, she thought -- it's all the same. That's the answer to all three truths: belief uses science to prove itself, but science must rely on faith when it ventures beyond the realm of proof; the reality of our essence is found not only in our consciousness, but also in our dreams, in both our body and our spirit; and the beginning and the end are also the same -- the presence of an everlasting love that was there at our beginning and will prevail beyond our end.

Ethel saved the entry, but erased it from her monitor when Roscoe entered. She smiled up at him as he leaned down to kiss her cheek. "Just came in to say goodnight." He moved toward the door and added, "You about ready to come to dreamland?"

"Yes, I'm on my way." Or perhaps, she thought, I'm already there. She put the computer into its sleep mode and turned out the light.

FOOTSTEPS

"Roscoe! Wake up! There they go again."

He groaned, but turned reluctantly on his side and peered over at her with one eye, the other still covered by the blanket. Ethel was sitting up in bed, shivering, the pillow scrunched behind her back, as she stared up at the ceiling. The decorative lamp on the nightstand gave forth only a pale glow in the pre-dawn darkness.

"Listen! Now they're right overhead." The slow steady thumping sounds echoed ominously through the empty attic above them -- back and forth, back and forth. "Now, you can't tell me that those aren't footsteps!"

"Ethel, haven't we gone over this often enough? There's nothing there. Not even the sign of any animals. I've examined that attic more than a dozen times -- when we hear the sound, like now, and during the day as well. Do you want me to go again?"

"Yes, but I'm going along." She slipped into her scuffs at the side of the bed and grabbed a robe from the chair in the corner.

"What's with the robe?" Roscoe laughed. "Who's going to see you -- a ghost?"

Ethel shivered in reply. "I'm just damned cold. If you didn't keep it so frigid in here at night, I wouldn't need it." She looked closely at the thermostat and pushed the control button up to 68 degrees. "There, that's better."

Shaking his head, Roscoe stepped out into the hall and flipped on the overhead light. "C'mon then, let's go up." Opening the door next to their bedroom, he started to climb the attic stairway. Ethel pulled his pajama sleeve and whispered, "Just listen, first. Can you still hear them?" They both stood still and held their breath as they listened. Nothing. The sound had stopped. When they reached the top, they methodically searched every nook and cranny -- again, nothing. Whatever it was, whoever it was, was gone.

"So, tell me again when these noises began, Ethel. And what you've done to find out where they're coming from." Willy had joined Ethel as she walked with Eskimo in the park near their home. He always seemed to materialize from nowhere and often appeared when she was about to embark on one of her strange adventures. Eskimo, their Malamute dog, loved Willy, but the same couldn't be said for Roscoe who wouldn't even admit that he existed. "Maybe there's some bird or animal that somehow got into your attic -- or maybe just branches from those huge elms next to your house?"

Ethel shook her head firmly. "No. That's what we thought at first, too, but Roscoe had some exterminators check out the attic and there's no opening anywhere -- not even space beneath the eaves. They also looked for any droppings, but I could have told them there was nothing there since I had already scrubbed that floor from one end to the other." She shook her head again. "No, Willy, it wasn't any animal, and it wasn't any tree either. Roscoe climbed up on the roof himself and none of those branches are closer than six or seven feet to the roof. Besides," she frowned, "the sounds aren't sporadic, like branches might make -- they're steady and regular, like footsteps."

"So, what do you think, then?" Willy grinned up at her as he bent to scratch behind Eskimo's ears. "You don't believe in ghosts, do you? Not you, Ethel."

Ethel just smiled back as she murmured, "I don't know, Willy. I don't know. Let me tell you a little more about our house -- and then you answer your own question." She pointed to a bench by the little brook that wended through the park. "Let's sit here."

"We bought the house in early April, a little over a month ago, directly from the owner, a Mrs. Marden. We had been looking for a larger place near the park and often drove around the area in hope of maybe stumbling across something we'd like. When we saw the real estate sign, we both felt that house was it. If you've seen it ---" (Willy nodded) "well, then you know. We liked the brick exterior, the leaded glass windows, and the location. Then later, when we saw the inside, we were sold on it."

"We acted on impulse -- parked, went up to the front door, and knocked. As soon as we explained our interest, Mrs. Marden invited us in and showed us the whole house. She couldn't have been more gracious. She said that her husband had died recently and the place was too big for her alone. She had listed the house with a real estate company, but the agreement ran out and they forgot to remove the sign. 'Too bad,' she shrugged, but she now planned to sell the house by herself. 'If you kids are interested,' she said, 'I'll send along some information on room sizes and what's included with it, and you can read it all over at home. But before you leave, take another look around by yourselves.'"

"We took her up on it. The place is older, maybe built in the twenties or thirties, but well constructed, and we liked the layout of the rooms. The living room has wooden beams on the ceiling, there's a nice separate dining room, the kitchen needs redoing but that's okay, and there are four good-sized bedrooms. The kids are gone now, but often come for long weekends, so the extra rooms are nice to have. We're using the fourth bedroom as an office, with a pull-out couch for company."

Ethel paused, and then frowned as she went on. "The only weird thing we noticed was the huge padlock that was attached to the upstairs hall door which leads to the attic. We asked Mrs. Marden if we could see it, and she immediately gave us the key, but didn't go up with us. She said that her husband had been in his attic office when he passed away one night from an apparent overdose of his medications. 'He was an inventor, you know. Always fussing around up there with one thing or another -- never any time to go out or even socialize with the neighbors.' She said that she just couldn't fathom his sitting all alone in that attic all the time."

"She didn't elaborate much on anything and even seemed kind of disconnected from it all -- as if she were talking about the weather or a total stranger. As she turned to go back downstairs, she only added that the attic had always been kind of damp and drafty and repeated that she never knew how he could spend all that time in that cold office. Now, with these awful memories, she said, she simply didn't go up there anymore. Roscoe agrees that Mrs. Marden said absolutely nothing about the lock, even when we opened it. At the time, we didn't think much about it, but now ...."

"Anyhow, we took a whole packet of information with us -- I think it was probably put together by the real estate people -- and looked it over the next day. It even included an asking price which we thought was pretty reasonable. We were going to call Mrs. Marden that night to make an offer when at about seven o'clock our doorbell rang and there she stood -- fur coat and gloves and all."

"Before we could invite her in, she swept into the room, plunked herself down on our sofa and said: 'I like you kids, and if you want it, I'm going to sell you my home at $10,000 below the asking price those real estate people listed. Now that I'm selling it directly by myself, I won't have any commission to pay; but even more important, I know you'll love it there and take good care of it. Do we have a deal?' And that's how we bought the house."

Ethel paused again to catch her breath, but soon continued, *"Now, let me tell you about those footsteps."* She vividly remembered the first time she and Roscoe heard the noises. It was only a few days after they had moved in and they were in bed, drifting off to sleep. At first they dismissed them as the natural creaks and groans of an old house. But as the sounds continued in their steady pacing, they decided to investigate.

"It was just the first of several times when we climbed those steps and searched the entire attic -- only to find nothing. And Willy, no one else has found anything, either. But ---"

"But ---?" Willy grinned at her with that superior look of his that had always infuriated her. *"But now tell me the rest of the story."*

29

Ethel sighed and then relented. "Well, there was this one time when I saw -- or I thought I saw -- the presence of someone there. I was alone in the house and had decided to get a little writing done in the office when I heard some noises down the hall. I rushed to our bedroom, but when I got there, I could tell that they were again coming from the attic. This time I didn't turn on the attic light, but grabbed a flashlight instead; I kept the beam low and pointed down on the steps."

"When I reached the top of the stairs, I could feel a cool, damp draft surround me and I saw – or I thought I saw -- a pale face staring at me. I'll never forget that look -- sad, but somehow angry at the same time. Then he -- it -- moved quickly away to the far corner of the attic. He didn't float. He walked, and I could hear his footsteps. I was petrified, Willy -- as if I had suddenly found myself in one of those TV horror films. But then I aimed the flashlight beam in the direction of whatever it was and followed it. When I got to the corner, it was gone. Willy, I really do think it was Mr. Marden's ghost."

"His ghost?" Willy interjected, with a tinge of humor in his voice.

Ethel was too absorbed in her own recollection to become angry. She stared at the flowing waters of the brook as if mesmerized. Only a tug from Eskimo on his leash finally brought her out of her trance. "Yes," she nodded, as if to herself, "his ghost."

"But why would his ghost return?" Willy asked thoughtfully. "In all the literature on this kind of para-normal phenomena, the ghost returns for a specific purpose, for some reason. What could have motivated Marden's ghost to return to his attic haunt?"

It was Willy's remark which led Ethel to begin what became a lengthy research investigation into the death of Morris Marden. Marden, she learned, had been an eccentric inventor who had several off-beat and unrelated inventions attributed to his name. He had invented the swing-back drapery rod, which once adorned many stylish homes, the tilt mechanism used for Venetian blinds, and the "cow catcher" device which was attached to trolley cars in the days when cattle still roamed the streets of small towns and semi-rural suburban areas. Mr. Marden lived in virtual isolation in his attic office, the obituary stated, where he had been found dead from an overdose of his prescription sleeping pills. It was widely assumed that he had committed suicide, although the official coroner's description was "accidental death."

"You know what I think, Roscoe?" Ethel asked one morning after she had jotted down the little information she had gleaned from the Marden's neighbor, an elderly lady who lived next door. She waited until he looked up from his paper. "I think that Mr.

Marden was a lonely old man who had no one to talk to about his work (I don't think

Mrs. Marden was too interested in cow catchers) -- and not much more to live for. I think those newspaper speculations were right on target. He did commit suicide."

"That may well be, Ethel. But it still doesn't shed any light on why we hear those strange noises from the attic -- footsteps, if you insist. Even if one accepts your belief in some sort of supernatural apparition, that in itself doesn't explain why it -- or he -- insists on coming back to haunt that attic. Why has he returned?"

"I don't know." It was the same question Willy had asked. Ethel wondered if maybe he had the answer.

Ethel was once again climbing the stairs to the attic. Autumn had blustered in with a vengeance, she thought, as she pulled her robe tightly around her. The Halloween parade of neighborhood kids had dribbled off to only a few laggards by nine-thirty and she and Roscoe had gone to bed shortly after ten. The phosphorescent arms of her bedside clock now pointed to midnight. The howling wind which awakened her had drowned out the muffled voices which gradually became clearer as she neared the top. "Willy?" she whispered. "Willy, is that you?"

"Stay there, Ethel. Don't move." Willy held up his hand in warning, while the hazy figure next to him crouched back against the attic wall. "This is Mr. Marden, Ethel. He has just been telling me an interesting story about his life -- and death." Willy turned to the specter and

31

nodded. "Go on, Mr. Marden. You were saying that your wife brought you the pills as she always did, just before she retired for the evening? And then?"

The spirit's voice was low and guttural. If there ever were a voice from the grave, Ethel thought, his was it. "And then I swallowed them -- with my coffee. I often slept up here. It's quiet -- except for the wind." He glanced at Ethel's robe with what she supposed was a smile. "My wife was not a quiet woman, you see. She doted on company -- and talking. I wasn't much of a companion, I fear." He frowned as he shook his head. "But I never thought she was desperate enough to poison me -- to kill me."

He was silent until Willy nodded. "Is that what you believe? That she poisoned you?" Ethel could feel her stomach muscles tighten as she waited for the answer.

The spirit raised his eyebrows in surprise and then again curled his lips into a humorless smile. "Of course she poisoned me. I'm dead, aren't I?" He rose and walked slowly toward the corner of the attic where he had disappeared when Ethel last saw him.

"Oh, don't go!" she cried. "Please." He paused. "Don't go until you tell us why you've come back -- why you've been pacing back and forth in this attic for all this time."

"Surely you must know the answer to that, Ethel. First, I wanted to scare Isabelle -- to let her know that I knew what she had done. And then when you and your husband moved in, I wanted to let you know, too." The specter shrugged and shook its head. "I can't rest, you see. Not until she gets her proper reward." With one last grimace of his eerie smile, he added, "Yet, that too may come. Perhaps sooner than one might think." Turning his back, he slowly faded away.

"So," Willy looked up at her, "it wasn't suicide after all, was it?"

"No. It was murder. But how could we ever prove it, Willy? Mrs. Marden will never confess, and what other evidence do we have -- the testimony of a ghost -- a dead man?" There was no answer. Willy was also gone.

Mysteriously, the footsteps stopped the very next night. And the following day Ethel believed she had found the reason why. Roscoe was sitting at the kitchen table quietly reading the morning paper when he suddenly erupted.

"For Pete's sake, Ethel, listen to this!" and he read the brief obituary aloud: "Mrs. Isabelle Marden, the wife of the eccentric inventor, Morris Marden, was found dead yesterday morning inside the entrance to her apartment in downtown Madison. A neighbor, noticing that her door was partially open, looked inside and found Mrs. Marden lying on the floor next to a spilled dish of Halloween candy treats. She called 911 and the attending physician diagnosed the cause of death as a heart attack. It is assumed that Mrs. Marden was inordinately frightened by some late night revelers who had come to 'trick or treat' in the early morning hours. Mr. Marden passed away last year and there are no other known relatives. Funeral arrangements are yet to be made."

"Well, that's one mystery you won't be able to solve, Ethel. I know you had it in your head to try to talk to Mrs. Marden again about her husband's death -- but now she's gone too. The paper says she died two nights ago." He looked at her quizzically. "Wasn't that the night you thought you saw Marden's ghost up in the attic?"

Ethel nodded. "Yes, that's when I last saw him -- and," she added with a smile,

"it was the last time we heard the footsteps. I think that Mr. Marden finally found his rest." She paused for a moment. "And perhaps Mrs. Marden found her final reward."

BIG BUCK

The sled swerved up to the snowy embankment, perched precariously on the edge for a moment and then plummeted over the side into the chasm below. All of the dogs were pulled along after it into the swirling waters of the icy river which cascaded along the bottom. But Big Buck once again saved the day. Struggling toward the nearest shore, he guided the team to a bank sheltered by two pines whose trunks caught and anchored the sled; safe for a moment, the Inuit driver was able to climb out of the water and cut the harnesses of the team. One by one, the dogs clambered up the bank to the shelter of the evergreen forest. A fire was lit as darkness descended, and the background music thundered to pronounce the victory of Big Buck, prince of the Alaskan trail!

Ethel turned off the TV, let Eskimo out, and moved quietly into the bedroom where Roscoe was already sleeping. She had stayed up for the end of the late movie, though she now wondered why. The Alaskan scenery had compensated somewhat for the lack of any plot worth watching, although Eskimo had been transfixed by the handsome Husky who played "Big Buck." Sporting the colors of a German Shepherd, Eskimo had the curled tail of a Malamute and the floppy ears of a border collie. Mutt though he was, he had become Ethel's constant companion for almost five years. He accompanied her on her walks in the countryside, occasional trips into town, and summer days at the beach. The only place he wasn't allowed was in the classroom when she taught her seminars. As she crawled into bed, Eskimo jumped up next to her and circled about once or twice before settling down at her feet.

Interesting, Ethel thought, how Eskimo always reacted to the Big Buck shows. He usually hated other dogs on TV and would bark at them continuously until they disappeared from the screen or Roscoe muted the sound. But Big Buck was the exception -- Eskimo adored Big Buck. He had followed this last episode from beginning to end, almost as if he understood the entire plot (such as it was). When Big Buck had been swept into the raging waters, Eskimo had panted anxiously as he watched. Then, as the sled team emerged from the river and made its way to the safety of the woods and the warmth of the fire, Eskimo's eyes blinked once or twice as if to stifle some errant tears. Ethel knew, of course, that the dog wasn't really crying, but she was intrigued by his curious behavior. What was it about Big Buck that so fascinated him?

"So -- what happened to Big Buck?" Roscoe asked during breakfast the next morning. "Did he again save the Alaskan countryside from the perils of pollution?"

"Not exactly, but he did save his driver and the rest of the team from a watery grave when their sled veered over an embankment into the river," Ethel smiled in return.

"And Eskimo?" Roscoe glanced in the next room where the dog was busily engaged in growling at some squirrels who had dared to invade his domain. "Did he watch his hero to the end or come up to bed before it was over?"

"Oh, he'd never miss a second of Big Buck's adventures," Ethel laughed. "I really wonder what it is about that dog that so fascinates him." Eskimo had trotted into the breakfast nook when he heard the words, "Big Buck," and sat listening as they spoke. "He hates other dogs on TV, but he almost worships Big Buck as his canine hero. I'm going to ask Ilse to talk to him about it." Roscoe rolled his eyes as he always did when Ethel even mentioned Ilse, her "animal communicator" friend.

35

"You don't really believe that that woman can talk to animals, do you? I mean, *really?*" He put the paper down and waited for her answer.

Ethel didn't even want to start on this right now -- she had a class at 10:30 and had to look up a few dates before her lecture -- but Roscoe wasn't going to be satisfied with a mere shrug. "I don't *really* believe it or disbelieve it, Roscoe. I don't know. All I know is that Ilse is not a weirdo or kook or whatever else you might want to call her, and she believes she can talk to animals. And there are others, too," Ethel continued as Roscoe got up and started to leave. "Why do you always do that?" she demanded.

"Do what?"

"You know -- start on something like this and then when I begin to discuss it seriously, you walk away!"

"Well, I've heard it all already, haven't I? I know what Ilse thinks. What I asked was what *you* think. Do you really believe that people can talk to animals?" He had stopped in the hallway and waited for her reply.

"I don't know." Ethel fumbled in her purse for her car keys. "I have to get to class," she said as she left through the kitchen door. "Bye. Bye, Eskimo."

It seemed more like a TV drama than a dream. She was lost in a white desert of snow. A blizzard was raging all around her, but she didn't feel the cold. Her fear warmed the pit of her stomach and forced her heart to pump the blood to her waxen finger tips. Ethel couldn't see beyond the length of her arm and her tears froze on her checks before they could fall to the ground. She didn't know where she was, nor how she had gotten there. All she knew was that she would die unless someone saved her. She forced her feet to move on, one step at a time, but they too became as heavy as her arms which had long since dropped the knapsack she had carried. She fell, and finally surrendered to the soft welcoming embrace of the snow. As she closed her eyes, she thought she heard the bark of a dog in the distance.

"Ethel, wake up! You have to move; we have to get you out of that snowbank." It was Willy! The words were accompanied by a slurping wetness on her cheek. As she opened her eyes she stared into the laughing mouth of a huge Husky. "Oh, for God's sake, it's Big Buck!" She turned to Willy: "What are you doing here, Willy?"

Big Buck led them to a forest ranger's cabin no more than a hundred yards from where Ethel had fallen. Willy built a fire and handed Ethel the flask he carried in his own knapsack. "Always well prepared -- right, Willy?" Ethel flashed an appreciative grin as she swallowed a healthy sampling of the Glenfiddich Scotch. "And always the best. So, how did you find me?"

Willy shook his head and shrugged. "I didn't find you. It was Big Buck. We were out scouting for deer when the storm hit us and I was hightailing it back to the cabin when suddenly Big Buck darted off at a tangent to the trail. Knowing his reputation, I just followed him -- and there you were." Ethel hugged the big Husky as he sidled over beside her. "So you're the hero once again," she murmured into the thick fur around his neck. And she seemed to sense his reply: "I'm only doing my job."

When she awoke, Ethel found that she had been napping at her desk, something she had never done before. It was already getting dark and she flicked on the office light to glance at her watch; it was almost six o'clock. All she could see from her window was the blowing snow. The last she remembered was her morning class. No, after class she had returned to her office and had been watching the few flakes of snow that drifted past her window as an early warning of the weather to come. While she had been sleeping, the storm had evidently descended upon them in full force. She phoned Roscoe and told him that she had lost track of the time while correcting papers, but would soon be home. Frowning to herself over her "little white lie," Ethel hurried to stuff the unmarked bluebooks into her briefcase, along with a couple of books. The way it looked, she thought, she might not be able to get into the university the next day.

Eskimo greeted her anxiously as she shut the door against the wind and snow. "Hi, Roscoe," she called into the den. "I'm back!"

"Looks bad out there," he said as she joined him. He poured some Scotch for her and began to mix a martini for himself. "I put the casserole in the oven right after you called; it should be hot in about another half hour. How was the driving?"

"Okay, but getting slippery -- you know how I hate that. No control." She sipped the Scotch and settled into the large wingback by the fire. "Nice fire." He had already flicked on the evening news and they watched the weatherman's prognosis of up to eight inches of snow, icy roads, and several school cancellations. "That's just what I thought might happen," Ethel nodded toward the TV. "I brought my exams home to correct -- to finish correcting," she amended, "and a couple books I've been wanting to read. Probably no classes tomorrow." Roscoe nodded as they both watched the television snow scenes of nearby traffic accidents and busy plows. "Nice night to be at home," Ethel commented as she went into the kitchen to get out the casserole.

"So what's so strange about Big Buck talking to you?" Willy was well oiled by this time and Ethel had abandoned the idea of asking him what he was doing in Alaska -- particularly with Big Buck. Willy always appeared at the oddest moments and in the strangest places. When awake, Ethel thought of him as a figment of her imagination, but when he joined her in dreamland, Willy was her guide and mentor, her friend and traveling companion. He persisted, "You talk to Eskimo, don't you?"

"Well, yes -- but he doesn't answer me," she countered. "Besides, it's more like just knowing that he's hungry or has to pee. We don't have a big discussion about it."

"But, you see, you are communicating -- back and forth. And if you'd just relax and open up a bit, you'd probably be able to talk a lot more." Willy passed her the flask and she had another swig. "The problem with you, Ethel, is that you're snarled up in your own belief

system -- the one you were brought up in, the one you're comfortable with. At the same time, you have a relatively open mind -- or spirit. More open than most. What's happening now is a kind of struggle for that spirit -- between your traditional ways of thinking about things and the new realities that are being revealed to you. Get it?"

Ethel nodded wearily. "Yes, I guess so. Like when I was in the isolation tank or when we were in Tibet?"

"Exactly." Willy turned to Big Buck. "Well, what now?"

"Now Ethel has to internalize all this somehow. She understands the dichotomy you explained while she's here in her dreamworld. Intellectually, she understands it. Buts it's not really a part of her inner belief system yet. Look at her -- she 'hears' me (that is, she senses my message), but she's still looking to see if my mouth is moving. She doesn't quite get it, Willy. Maybe Eskimo can help her when she goes back."

Ethel stared at Big Buck as she comprehended his words. Was she absolutely out of her mind, she wondered. Willy sat there, flashing his infuriating grin, and Big Buck flopped down by the fire, turning his back in indifference. If she wasn't going to give credence to all this, he seemed to be saying, so be it. Ethel sat now in silence, partially mesmerized by the fire, periodically glancing at her two strange companions. How did a rational, middle-aged professor ever get involved in something as bizarre as this?"

"I'm going to drive over to see Ilse, Roscoe. Want to come along?" Ethel stood in the hall putting on her coat. "And what about you? Want to come along with Mom, Eskimo?" she asked, and the dog ran eagerly to the door. "Roscoe, did you hear?"

"Yes, I heard," he replied as he emerged from the den. "No -- thanks for asking, but I think I'll skip the pleasure of an afternoon with Ilse." He smiled as Ethel shook her head. "Just be careful on those roads. They're still likely to be slippery."

"Okay, I should have known you wouldn't be coming. I won't be late and I'll watch the ice. Bye."

Ilse Eccleton lived the country some twenty miles from Ethel and Roscoe. Ethel had met her four years ago at a university lecture on telepathy and they had become close friends. Ethel had never quite "bought in" to some of Ilse's more extreme beliefs, but she was fascinated nonetheless and enjoyed discussing them. Eskimo loved to go along to Ilse's big rambling farm house where in summer he could run freely in the nearby fields and woods.

"So, what do you make of it all?" Ethel waited as Ilse sipped her tea.

"What do *you* make of it?" Like Willy, Ilse frequently answered her questions by repeating them. Ilse peered at Ethel inquisitively, while petting Eskimo.

"Well, I'm getting used to seeing Willy in my dreams, and even talking to him," she paused. "But talking to a dog character from a TV serial? I just can't buy that."

Eskimo was resting by the fireplace. "Let me see if I can reach him," Ilse offered. She faced the window and stared out at the snow. Ethel had never been present when Ilse "communicated" with the animals – her friend previously had just related whatever conversation she had. Ethel felt uncomfortable now as if she were somehow intruding on a private discussion. But she listened.

"So, Eskimo, what message do you want me to give to Ethel?"

"Tell her that Big Buck is my 'dog spirit' -- that's why I love to watch him on TV. Don't let her get the wrong idea. I love my life with Mom and Roscoe, but it is kind of quiet and uneventful. When I watch Big Buck, I can experience the thrill and excitement of his adventures, even though I'm doing it vicariously." He seemed proud of his vocabulary.

"But you know that it's just TV, don't you?" Ilse asked. *"I mean, those stories aren't real."*

"What's real?" Eskimo replied. *"I used to be a police dog, you know -- in my former life. That was as real to me as my life now. Big Buck is real, too -- in that sense."*

40

"Well, Ethel is confused. She doesn't know what to believe about Big Buck. She says that he talked to her, but that you don't talk to her in the same way. Why?"

Eskimo paused and glanced at Ethel. "Tell her that I do talk to her -- all the time. But she doesn't listen. She's just too busy with her work, her classes and lectures. Mom has the capability to talk to me and to hear me -- she just doesn't listen."

But this time Ethel heard it all.

The snow was actually worse now than when she had left home; four or five inches covered the road enough to hide the icy spots and blur the shoulders. Though Ethel had her defroster turned on to full blast, the windows were still steamy with moisture. She drove slowly and carefully, but knew that she had no real control -- especially if she went into a spin. Luckily, she thought, there wasn't much traffic. An occasional truck flew past, sending up sprays of slush and ice over her windshield, and a few large suburbans also surged by, their horns blaring. Otherwise, the road was deserted.

"Damn," she murmured to herself as she turned the wipers to high and tried to wipe off the haze from the front window. Eskimo sat nervously beside her on the passenger side. She had only driven some ten miles since she left Ilse's house, and it had taken over a half hour. She fretted aloud, "Roscoe will be worried -- I told him I wouldn't be late, and with these roads it'll be another half hour or so before we get back." She sensed that Eskimo was looking at her, but she heard nothing.

Then it happened. She was going around a bend and the car began to slide. Ethel knew that she shouldn't ram on the brakes, but her reactions were stronger than her intellect. The car went into a full spin and a bank of snow loomed in front of her as she skidded off the road into the ditch on the other side. She tried to hold onto Eskimo's collar, but she heard him whine as banged his head on the dash. Then she lost consciousness.

"Wake up, Mom - wake up!" Eskimo was licking her face and talking to her at the same time. "Are you okay?"

Ethel opened her eyes, but couldn't see anything. The car was resting on its back wheels, the front end rearing in the air and the windshield covered with snow. Her head hurt and her chest ached from where the seatbelt had held her back from further injury.

"Eskimo, are you all right?" she asked as she moved her right hand over his body. The side of his head felt wet and her stomach turned as she realized that he was hurt.

"I'm really okay -- only a cut above my one eye. Head wounds just bleed a lot.

Despite the danger of her situation, Ethel couldn't help but smile. She hadn't hit her head that hard, she knew -- but she could hear her dog talking. All she needed now was for Big Buck to appear on the scene and rescue them both.

"Don't worry. Big Buck will come -- if only in spirit." Eskimo said, as if reading her thoughts. "If you can get your door open, I can squeeze out and go for help." Was she just imagining all this? All of the doubts born of her rational mind crowded in on her as she tried to look at the dog beside her. "Don't waste time, Mom. It's cold out there and the snow is piling up. If it covers the car, we'll really be in a mess. Let me out of here -- I'll get help."

Ethel was fading away again, but she managed to unlock her door and force it partially open. Eskimo jumped out and ran toward the road. "I'll be back -- don't worry," she heard him say before she blacked out.

"You're one lucky lady," the trucker grunted as he lifted her through the open door. "And your dog is, too. I damned near ran him down as he was jumping around on the road over there. When I stopped, I saw that he was bleeding and followed him over here where I saw your one headlight. We had to dig down to get you out."

"Where is he? Where's Eskimo?" Ethel asked, still in shock. Then she felt his wet tongue on her cheek, licking away her tears. As they drove on toward home in the front cab of the truck, Ethel hugged Eskimo close against her and tried to see where he was cut. But the dog was too busy peering through the window at the road ahead.

"He almost seems to want to drive this rig," the trucker laughed. Then, more seriously, he added, "You know, it's funny, but I was almost certain that I saw two dogs out there in the road." When Ethel turned to look at him, he continued, "Well, I wouldn't swear it -- but I thought there was a Husky out there too -- jumping and prancing around right next to your dog. But when I stopped and got out, he was gone."

When Eskimo looked up at Ethel, she could swear that he winked his eye. "I told you that Big Buck was my 'dog spirit.' When I really need some help, I can count on him -- he's always there."

That night when Ethel and Roscoe turned on the Big Buck program, Ethel held Eskimo on her lap while they watched it all together. Somehow, she thought, it didn't seem so corny any more -- not corny at all.

BLACKJACK

There was simply no question about it -- Las Vegas was glitzy! As their cab sped down the main drag on its way to the Excalibur Hotel, even Ethel was impressed by the onslaught of visual effects. Lights turned the night into day, mammoth hotels lined the street, and casinos everywhere invited gamblers to part with their money. Many of the hotels looked like the stage sets where strange and exotic pictures would be filmed.

"I hardly recognize the place," Ethel exclaimed. "When were we here last? Why, it must have been sometime in the '70s -- over thirty years ago."

Roscoe nodded his head in agreement. "Yeah, I think the Sands was one of the showcases then -- now it's gone." He leaned forward to ask the driver, "How much further to the Excalibur?"

"Not far. Just up beyond the next intersection. Why? Can't wait to bet?" The cabby smiled back at them over his shoulder. "Had a real winner last week. He dropped a couple hundred at craps, but then went over to the $100 blackjack table and won over $30,000. They kept changing dealers, but the guy couldn't lose. Gave me a $50 tip!" He eyed Ethel and Roscoe through the rearview mirror, figuring that these two weren't likely to come anywhere near that.

A few minutes later they were in their room, unpacking the few clothes they had brought along. Ethel had won their three-night "all included" package at a charity raffle and had been looking forward to a break-away from the wintry winds of Wisconsin. "It seems mild enough to go out without our coats, don't you think?" she pondered aloud while hanging them in the closet. "But right now I could go for a Scotch before dinner."

Roscoe had already scouted the hall for some ice and doused the cubes with a generous half glass of the Glenfiddich they had brought along. "Well, here's to luck," he smiled. "Are you going to start with the slots or go for the big time?"

"First, let's just relax and enjoy the view. I'm surprised they gave us such a good room." Their window overlooked the front entrance out onto the main street where the passing traffic embroidered the highway with a moving display of flashing lights. "Then, I think, we might want to have dinner before it gets real late, and then ---," Ethel grinned back, "then we might want to try our luck."

The din from the clanging slot machines assaulted her ears and the smoke from the cigarette puffer next to her stung her eyes. There was a "no smoking" sign at the blackjack table, but no one paid any attention to it. The air was heavy. Ethel didn't remember coming to the table or buying the stack of chips that stood in front of her. She looked curiously at the six other players. There was the smoker to her left -- a seedy type perhaps in his sixties. His fingers, stained from the nicotine, tapped restlessly on the green felt table cover except when he was signaling a hit or a stand. To Ethel's right was a flabby woman with a jolly laugh, which exploded whenever the dealer tossed her a card; it didn't seem to matter whether she won or lost. The next two players were well-tailored, but strangely sinister looking. They said little, and watched with intense concentration as the cards were dealt. To the far right was a young couple, probably on their honeymoon and much more interested in each other than in the game.

"Well, lady?" the dealer asked. "What will it be?" Ethel realized that he had dealt her two cards -- a ten and a queen. He was waiting, somewhat impatiently.

"Oh, I'm sorry. I'll stand," she said. He had a king, but unless he drew an ace, she had a good chance to win. He turned over his card and it was a ten. "Push," he said, and left her five dollar chip on the table in front of her. Push, she knew from previous games, simply meant that she and the dealer were tied at twenty points each.

Just then Willy joined the group. Willy always showed up at the most unexpected times and places, so Ethel was not terribly surprised to see him. Besides, she thought, this was probably just one of those surrealistic dreams she had been having lately.

"Hello, Ethel," he winked at her as he scrounged in between her and the smokestack. "How're you doing?" He threw down two fifties for the dealer to change into ten dollar chips. "I feel lucky."

"Hello, Willy," she smiled back. "I'm not sure how I'm doing. Roscoe is still playing the slot machines, but I came over here about an hour ago, I guess, and seem to be holding my own." She glanced at the stack of chips in front of her. "Although I'm not quite sure how many chips I bought in the first place." She gave the dealer a quizzical look, but he chose to ignore her. "Probably not more than fifty dollars worth." "Well, maybe I'll bring you some real luck." Willy motioned her to double her bet, as he threw down four chips in front of himself. Ethel carefully put down a second chip. She usually limited her bets to five dollars a game.

The dealer dealt the first round. The honeymooners were playing together and drew a five. They asked for a hit and drew a seven. The dealer had a ten showing. The lovers asked for another card and were handed a jack. A bust -- too bad. The two nervous types each drew a face card and asked for hits; one got a seven and stood pat, while the other drew a nine and also stopped at that. The jolly lady next to Ethel had an eight, then a five, and then a nine -- a bust. But she guffawed loudly just the same.

It was Ethel's turn. She had a king and drew an ace -- blackjack! Willy had an ace and drew a queen -- another blackjack. The dealer drew another ten and took the chips from everyone except Willy and Ethel who had both doubled their money and then some. Ethel was ecstatic. "Willy, you did bring me luck. That's the first blackjack

I've had all evening long!" She piled up her winnings into another neat stack in front of her.

When she awoke late the next morning she was still smiling. "Well, how'd you do? You were hard at it early this morning when I left you at the blackjack table. It must have been after two." Roscoe was already dressed and had brewed some coffee in the small courtesy pot in their room.

Ethel sipped from the styrofoam cup before she tentatively answered. "Well, I don't really know how I did, Roscoe. I dreamed about blackjack last night, as well as playing it, and I'm not so sure what was real and what was in my dream." She reached for her purse and poured the chips out on the bed. "My Lord!" she exclaimed. "There must be a couple hundred of these -- and they're all ten dollar chips!" Roscoe began stacking them up and counting aloud.

"Ethel, there's two thousand, three hundred and twenty dollars here! Now don't tell me you can't remember winning that amount of money." He stared at her quizzically as she moved toward the shower.

"Well, I can't. Don't you think I would have woken you up if I'd known how much I had? I suppose I just kept on winning a little at a time." She smiled as she shrugged and disappeared behind the shower curtain.

They had signed up in advance for a matinee performance of "Cats" which Ethel had already seen in London and wanted Roscoe to see. It was all done in the round, and they both enjoyed the music. But Ethel was preoccupied over dinner that night and Roscoe knew that she was trying to remember more about the previous evening. He had grown accustomed to some of her strange "adventures" as she liked to call them, but this one was a real doozy!

At the blackjack table that night the fat jolly lady who had been in her dream welcomed her with her irrepressible laugh. "Well, well, the winner returns!" she snorted. "I never learned to keep it either," she added. "You win one night and lose it all the next. Just another round in the great game of life. Well, good luck!"

Ethel wasn't inclined to respond to this philosophical analogy. She smiled uncomfortably and looked around at the other players. The smoker was not there, thank goodness, but the two professional gamblers (at least, that's what she thought they probably were) sat in their former places down at the end.

The young honeymooners walked up as she settled in. "Hey, the new groom said,

"you really did okay last night. Where's your partner in crime?" Ethel smiled, but ignored the question. She hadn't told Roscoe that Willy had made another appearance.

"Well, I guess I'll try my luck here again tonight," she said to Roscoe who was looking at her strangely. Do you want to play, too?" He shook his head and just stood there with his hands in his pockets. "Going to watch a while? Or are you going to try the slots?" She hoped he would; she never had any luck while Roscoe was with her.

"No, but I may play some bingo though. I'll be back later." Roscoe didn't really like to gamble, but he tolerated Ethel's penchant for it every now and then. She felt a little guilty as he walked off alone toward the bingo salon. But then she shrugged as she thought, "Never mind. As long as I won this trip, I might as well enjoy it."

Just then Willy sauntered up. "Hi, Ethel." He slid onto the seat beside her.

Ethel bought a hundred dollar's worth of the five dollar chips, while Willy bought twenty ten dollar chips. He answered her unspoken query, "Well, I did pretty well last night, too. Remember?" No, she didn't remember. That was the problem.

"Willy, after we play a while, could we have a drink and maybe chat a bit?" she asked. He nodded agreeably as the new dealer replaced the six old decks with those that had been shuffled by the automatic shuffler. The smoker now made his appearance, but he sat over by the

honeymooners, much to Ethel's relief. When she got up this morning she could still smell smoke on the clothes she had hung in the closet the night before.

She now turned her attention to the game.

Her luck had not left her. The face cards abounded, and her scores of nineteen or twenty on four games in a row were followed by two blackjacks. She had doubled her bets after the first win and the chips were piling up in front of her. Willy was doing even better with his ten dollar bets. The fat lady finally won a couple of times, as did the young couple on the other side. Only the two dour "professionals" were losing to the dealer, who wasn't happy with his own run of bad luck. A new dealer came up to take his place.

Ethel turned to Willy. "Let's take a break. We can take our chips along and cash them in later on if we don't want to play any more." They slid off their stools and went to the bar. Willy ordered her Glenfiddich and had a bourbon and soda for himself. "So," he eyed her with his wry smile, "what's up? What's this 'chat' we have to have?"

"Willy, it's simply getting too confusing." She took a healthy swallow of the Scotch. "I keep having these strange experiences -- some that seem 'real,' some that seem to be dreams, and some that seem to appear out of nowhere when my mind wanders or while I'm meditating. And then, when I 'come to' or 'wake up' I'm not sure what really happened. Like last night." Willy glanced at her with a questioning frown.

"Well," Ethel continued, "I didn't know that I had actually won all that money until I emptied my purse and poured out the chips on the bed this morning. I remember being at the blackjack table after Roscoe left for the slots, but from that point on it all seemed more like a dream. Then you appeared from nowhere -- like you so often do. And then ..." She let the sentence end in silence.

"And then -- what?" Willy prodded. "and then you won a couple thousand dollars -- right? So what's so confusing about that? It's a lot like life, Ethel; you win a few and lose a few. It all depends on who's dealing the cards. But we don't always know that, do we? Eventually, it all comes down to the bottom line: if you end up with the chips, you must have won. It doesn't really matter how or when it happened, does it?"

Ethel shook her head in exasperation. "Yes, Willy, it does matter. At least to me, it does. There's something out there called 'reality,' and there are other things that aren't real. Life isn't a glorified card game that you can choose to play or ignore. Some things really happen; others you imagine. There's a big difference between the two, and I can't go on jumping back and forth between them as if it didn't matter."

"But why not?" Willy whispered. And then he was gone. But he left behind the

Chicago Tribune with a picture of two bank robbers on the front page. Their faces stared at Ethel with eerie familiarity. By the time Roscoe joined her, she had recognized them.

"Drinking alone?" he asked. "You must be losing."

It was the afternoon of their last day at Vegas. Ethel had won over six thousand dollars, most of it all at blackjack. She occasionally liked to play draw poker on the slot machines, and she had won a five hundred dollar pot there as well. At first, Roscoe was annoyed with her lapses of memory, but his irritation left him as the winnings piled up.

They were going to a stage variety show in the evening, so Ethel insisted that she take one more fling at the blackjack table that afternoon.

Ethel had told Roscoe that she was convinced that the two professional gamblers who had played at her table the two previous nights were in fact the bank robbers pictured in the paper, so he accompanied her to the blackjack table. They both were disappointed that the suspects weren't among the players already there. When she looked up at the dealer, however, she was shocked to recognize him as one of them. She shivered at the strange feeling of evil that emanated from his presence.

"That's him," she whispered to Roscoe as she nodded her head toward the dealer.

"But I don't see his partner anywhere."

"Should I notify one of the security guards?" Roscoe whispered back.

"Are you betting or not, lady?" the dealer interrupted impatiently. Ethel obediently placed a five dollar chip in front of her. Unfortunately, Roscoe stood solidly next to her as she placed her bets -- and lost. Although she limited them to five dollars each, eight of the ten chips she bought were soon gone.

She wanted to leave the table and talk to Roscoe away from the scrutinizing eyes and listening ears of the dealer. "Roscoe, I'm going to take a break," she said aloud.

"Maybe I'll play the poker slots for a while. I'm just not getting anywhere here." She picked up the two remaining chips and left the table, nodding at the honeymooners and the fat lady who was still playing.

"Okay," Roscoe agreed. They walked together toward the slot machine area and

Roscoe again asked, "If you're right, Ethel, we should contact the security people. You'd better come along since you're the one who recognized them. Did you bring the newspaper clipping?" Nodding, Ethel accompanied him to the upstairs security office which looked down onto the casino floor though a one-way window. She couldn't fathom how that gambler could now be a dealer. Or had she only imagined what they looked alike? She wished Willy were there. He'd know what to do. But Willy was nowhere in sight.

The security man listened tolerantly, glancing only briefly at the clipping. When he noted the table Ethel pointed at and saw the dealer she identified, however, his interest perked up. "Well, he's not one of our regulars. That's for sure. But we do hire several part-time dealers during the busy season. I'll look into it. Thanks for letting us know, ma'am. If you're right, there may even be a reward in it for you."

He escorted them to the door. Ethel made her way back to the table as Roscoe went up to their room. "I'll wait for you there. But remember that we have that other show tonight."

Ethel was again down to two chips. Her cards had been miserable; even when she once managed to draw two face cards, the gambler/ dealer had countered with a blackjack. When it was time to change dealers, Ethel stared in disbelief as Willy appeared behind the table. He looked kind of silly wearing the garb of an old-time professional dealer with a green shade pulled down low over his forehead, but he handled the cards with poise and finesse. She couldn't help but smile when he asked her if she wanted a hit. (After all, she had drawn a queen and a ten!) Ethel stood pat and won the hand with her twenty to Willy's nineteen. Maybe Willy was right: it did matter who was dealing the cards.

That started her third winning streak of the trip. She now began to bet twenty dollars at a time, knowing that she couldn't lose. The two professional gamblers had returned to the players' side of the table and Ethel could hardly mask her pleasure at their persistent losses. She was even more pleased when two uniformed policemen approached them from behind and led them handcuffed from the casino. With Willy dealing, not only did Ethel continue to win, but so did her jolly companion with the hearty laugh, the honeymooners, and even the smoker, who had temporarily run out of cigarettes. It was a glorious afternoon and a proper finale to her Las Vegas adventure.

"Ethel," Roscoe nudged her. "Wake up. We're about to land." The lights at

Milwaukee's Mitchell Field glinted on the few patches of snow that had been pushed to the sides of the runway. She shivered in grudging acceptance of her return to a

Midwestern winter.

"Well, what did you enjoy most?" Roscoe smiled. "the Las Vegas stage shows, the arrest of the bank robbers and your reward -- or blackjack?"

Ethel nudged his arm, patted her purse, and winked. "As if you didn't know."

She couldn't quite accept Willy's contention that life consisted of no more than a series of gambling choices, but she also wasn't worried about what was "real" anymore. After all, when she boarded the plane, she had seen Willy in the cockpit.

CHANCE ENCOUNTER

Taking the aisle seat, the short, middle-aged lady glanced sideways at the man seated by the window reading *The New York Times*. She pursed her lips and frowned slightly as she tried to remember who he looked like. He was perhaps in his mid-forties, dark complexion, black hair combed straight back above a high forehead, and even features. His eyes narrowed as he turned to her. "Should be a pleasant flight," he commented. "And a relatively short one, I think."

"Yes," Ethel replied. "It's less than an hour from LaGuardia to National." Still trying to recall where she might have seen him before, she simply could not think of whom he reminded her. "You look so familiar," Ethel ventured. "Have we met -- or should I know you from somewhere?"

"I doubt it," the man said, and shaking his head, he smiled briefly and returned to his paper. Ethel opened her book to her bookmark and turned her attention to the latest Stephen King mystery she was reading. The plane banked over Manhattan, leaving the New York skyline below as it climbed to cruising altitude.

When he came into her hospital room, he walked hesitantly with his shoulders slightly drooped, as if exhausted by a long day of life and death decisions. He looked like a younger version of the 1960's TV hero, Dr.

Ben Casey, and flashed the same rugged smile. "And how are we today, Dr. Matson?" he asked, not really expecting an answer.

"I don't know how we are," Ethel answered, "but I feel like I've just been hugged by an American Godzilla. What happened? How did I get here?"

"You don't remember the bombing?" He noted something in his record book as she shook her head. "You may have a concussion -- in addition to the bruises and abrasions caused by the flying debris. You were unfortunately in the wrong place at the wrong time -- as the saying goes.

Ethel tried to recall the events leading up to that careening ride in the siren-screeching ambulance which had brought her to the hospital -- GW, someone had told her. One moment she had been seated with the other academic and government experts in the spacious committee room of the Old Executive Office Building, and the next she was sprawled out in the ambulance, speeding through the streets of downtown Washington.

Dr. Casey (or so Ethel now thought of him) aimed the piercing light at her pupils and again noted something in his book. He removed the light cotton sheet that covered her and began to check her bruised and bandaged arms and legs. She groaned as he rolled her on her side and pressed his hand along her spine. He checked some x-rays clipped to the foot of her bed and then sat down in the nearby chair.

"You're one lucky lady," Casey said with his charming smile. "A car bomb exploded right next to the building on the floor below your meeting. Those seated near the windows were killed almost instantly. Those of you on the other side of the table escaped with some bad cuts and bruises." He paused. "You don't remember?"

The plane had begun its descent toward National Airport when Ethel's seat companion excused himself to recover his carry-on from the compartment overhead. "I'm on a tight schedule," he explained. Ethel moved to the window seat so he could leave more quickly when the plane landed. As he sat back down, Ethel again had the nagging feeling that she somehow knew him.

Her mind turned the pages of her memory back to the Anti-Terrorism Seminar she had attended in London some five years ago. She and the other experts assembled by the European Union had discussed the "new" techniques of nuclear and biological terrorism which might emerge on the global scene. But after all their discussion, a consensus had been reached that for the foreseeable future at least, plain old-fashioned bombings would continue to prevail.

On the second day of the seminar they had viewed pictures of some of the most notorious terrorists still in circulation. In addition to the usual ultra-nationalists, religious fanatics, and ethnic extremists, there had been a few who were in the game purely for the money. Their services could be bought by the highest bidder for any job -- bombings, assassinations, hijackings, kidnappings, and embassy takeovers. You name it.

Geraldo had been one of those. "Geraldo" was the popular code name for a former member of the Shining Path in Peru. He had left Peru to seek international fame and fortune when the Shining Path had come under increasing pressure by the military. Over time, Geraldo had put together a global network of resources -- money, safeplaces, training camps, supply depots, and escape routes. His most publicized exploits had been featured at the London seminar, and as Ethel could now recall, his photograph eerily resembled her friendly traveling companion.

Dr. Somerville (Ben Casey's real name) had reviewed Ethel's case with her and told her that if they found no evidence of concussion she could be released the next day. "I'm going to give you a mild sedative, Ethel. Try to rest as much as you can." She closed her eyes for a moment, determined not to stay in that hospital overnight. When she opened them, the doctor was gone, and the well-dressed FBI agent was sitting in his place. The sequence of events was still blurry to her and she didn't know when he had come in.

"Agent Sikorski," he had said when he flashed his ID badge. He now asked, "Are you up to answering some questions?" Ethel nodded. "First,

are you clear about all the facts?" She shook her head hesitantly. *"Well, in brief, you were attending that State Department Terrorism Briefing at the OEOB when the bomb exploded; unfortunately, most of your colleagues were not as lucky as you. We have been trying to interview those survivors who are well enough to talk to us."*

When he paused, Ethel jumped in, *"Agent Sikorski, I think I saw the Peruvian terrorist 'Geraldo' on the plane I arrived on. In fact, I believe he was sitting right next to me. He left the plane the moment we landed and when I recollected who he reminded me of, I tried to follow him."* She shrugged her shoulders impatiently. *"But he had already disappeared by the time I came out of the baggage terminal. He was carrying his bag."*

"Well, frankly, that's why I'm here. You were ranting about 'Geraldo' when they brought you in, but there's absolutely no evidence that he was on board that plane. There was a Peruvian diplomat who was seated next to you, but we've examined his credentials and they all check out -- Senor Arturo Ramirez Rosas. An embassy car evidently met him at the airport and drove him to the embassy for a briefing. We were able to interview him there. He's in town to attend a meeting of the Inter-American Development Bank."

Ethel was sitting in her hotel room, sipping some Scotch and watching the news account of the bombing when her phone rang. It was Ray Bainbright from the Bureau of Intelligence and Research at the State Department with whom she had worked when serving at State. "Ethel, I checked with the Agency on this Arturo Ramirez Rosas from Peru and he's legit as far as their records show. Ramirez joined the Peruvian Foreign Service some eight years ago and was on his way to a meeting at the IDB. Interestingly, he's staying right in your hotel."

Putting down the phone, she shivered, took a healthy swallow of her Scotch, and tuned back in to the news account. The wreckage of the Old Executive Office Building flashed across the screen and Peter Jennings repeated that among the casualties were several antiterrorist specialists attending a high-level briefing sponsored by the State Department. No group had claimed "credit" for the bombing, although the FBI was checking into a number of radical groups with cell members known to be in the DC area.

Ethel's buzzer rang before she could hear the end of Jennings' report. As she opened the door, the face of Arturo Ramirez appeared before her. "Dr. Matson," he inquired politely, "may I come in?" But before Ethel could slam the door, he pushed his way into the room, followed by "Ben Casey" and agent "Sikorski." The blow to her head stifled the scream just beginning to form in her throat and she sank to her knees as her legs gave way beneath her.

Dr. Somerville -- or was it really Ben Casey? -- was peering down at her with his full lips pressed tightly together as he removed the needle from her arm. "I had hoped my last injection would settle you down, Ethel, but you insisted on leaving the hospital last night and now look at the trouble you're in." She could see "the Peruvian diplomat" peering out of her hotel room window, while agent Sikorski talked quietly on her phone.

"No," Sikorski said, "she doesn't know anything yet. As soon as Somerville heard her ranting about 'Geraldo,' he gave her an injection and called me. I tried to play down her suspicions, but wasn't too successful. Somehow she managed to leave the hospital. Luckily, the good 'doctor' had found her hotel reservation in her purse; when we learned that she was in the same hotel as Arturo, we decided to handle it here." He nodded as he listened to the response. "I think we can manage to make it look like an overdose -- I brought along some fake sleeping pills." He nodded again and hung up.

Ethel kept her eyes on Somerville, while listening to Sikorski's entire conversation. So much was still unclear, but she now saw the broad outlines of the picture. "So you're not a real doctor," she said to Somerville and, nodding at Sikorski, she added, "and you're not really FBI."

The Peruvian then turned to her from the window and smiled, "But I really am Arturo Ramirez, Dr. Matson -- not the infamous 'Geraldo,'

*as you thought. Unfortunately for you, though, I do work for Geraldo."
He shrugged, "Since he is my cousin, I suppose we do look alike."
Ramirez continued. "We couldn't take the chance of anyone taking
you seriously. When I suspected that you might think I was 'Geraldo,' I
knew that you would draw the obvious connection between him and our
planned bombing of the DOS briefing. We couldn't count on your being
killed in the explosion, so we proceeded with the plan but made sure that our
good 'Dr. Somerville' would be on hand to sedate you as soon as you gained
consciousness. GW Hospital is the closest medical facility to the OEOB, so
we planted him here. For added insurance, we also sent 'Sikorski' here," he
nodded toward the would-be agent, "to try to get you off that track. But,
---" Ramirez again shrugged, as if the subject were now closed.*

*The injection Somerville had given Ethel was beginning to have
an effect. When the phone rang, she could hardly pick it up. As
Ramirez handed it to her, he covered the mouthpiece with his hand.
He whispered, "If you value your life, don't try anything." He listened
as she put the phone to her ear. It was Ray. "Ethel, lock your door and
don't let anyone in. Police are already on their way -- I'll explain when
I see you." She slowly let her arm drop as she lost consciousness -- but
she could hear the sirens at a distance.*

Ethel held a cold washcloth pressed against the back of her head
as she lay propped up on one of the twin beds in the hotel room. Ray
Bainbright was seated across from her on the other bed and someone
who looked like Doctor Kildare was checking her pulse. "Thank
God you're not Ben Casey," Ethel smiled, and then just shook her
head when he and Ray looked at her quizzically. "Never mind," she
said, "It's an inside joke."

"After we talked the first time," Ray said, "I watched the news
account of the bombing and thought again about your belief that
your Peruvian friend was really Geraldo. I then called my buddy at
the Agency to check further on his background. It turned out that
a Rosas family had been actively involved in the earliest years of the
Shining Path. One of them, Julio Rosas, was the father of 'Geraldo'

who operated under his mother's name, and another, Julio's sister, married a Ramirez and was the mother of our Peruvian 'diplomat,' Arturo Ramirez."

Ethel had never been very good with Latino patronymics, but she followed Ray's explanation closely. "As soon as my CIA friend saw the connection, he contacted the police and called me. Evidently, we arrived just in time." All three of the terrorists had sped out of the room and down the hall when they heard the sirens, but not in time to avoid the police who had surrounded the hotel and sent a special squad directly to Ethel's room. Ramirez pleaded diplomatic immunity and was temporarily handed over to the Peruvian Embassy.

"And what about the real Geraldo?" Ethel asked after Ray had finished.

"Well," he frowned, "it's pretty clear that he master-minded the bombing, but for whom, we just don't know. His intelligence sources were well aware that a number of anti-terrorism experts were going to be at that meeting at the OEOB and Geraldo figured that this was an opportune time both to get rid of some of them and to make a publicity splash." Ray smiled at her sadly, "He managed to do both."

The doctor had finished examining her and said he'd be back to check on her the next morning. Ethel invited Ray to stay a bit, and they reminisced about the good old days when Ethel had worked in INR. "You know, Ray," she thought aloud, "if I had never attended that seminar in London five years ago, I never would have thought that Ramirez looked like Geraldo, and all three of them would probably be free right now. But it still didn't stop the bombing, did it? And all of those friends of ours are still dead." Ray nodded, "No, it didn't stop the bombing. But we caught a few of the bastards, Ethel. That's some consolation, isn't it?"

"Yes, I guess so," she said softly as he left the room. "I guess so." And as Ethel drifted asleep, she hoped that she would dream of "the real" Dr. Casey in those early days of television when -- somehow -- the good guys always won.

THE TUSCAN TURRET

Ethel breathed deeply of the chilly morning air as she stepped out onto the villa's flagstone verandah. The sun gilded the hills on the other side of the valley, but the lowlands between were still sheathed in a soft white mist. Ethel shivered at the thought of her daughter's dip in the unheated pool just moments before. Settling down with her half-read paperback, she warmed herself with a healthy swallow of hot *cafe latte*.

Her vacation had hardly begun, but Ethel knew it was going to be one of the best she had ever taken. Villa Montalcino was located in the heart of Tuscany's chianti district, and yesterday, on their way up the winding, bumpy roads, she had noticed that the vineyards were laden with ripened grapes, clearly ready to be harvested. It was not until this morning, however, that she realized how high they had climbed and how beautiful the surrounding scenery was. Interspersed between the vineyards were groves of olive trees whose undulating rows climbed up and down the gentle hills.

Ethel no sooner opened her book when Kathy emerged from the arched entrance, drying her hair with a towel in one hand and carrying her coffee cup and a pile of doughnuts carefully balanced on a plate in the other. "Isn't it gorgeous, Mom? Emery sure knew what he was doing when he picked this place. How did he ever find it?"

"They got it last year through a rental agency and liked it so much they decided to come back for another two weeks this year, but in the fall rather than the spring. That's when they asked us to go along." Ethel and Roscoe Matson knew Emery Laine through their support of the repertory theater which he managed. When two of his other friends were unable to go at the last minute, Ethel suggested taking along their two daughters. Recently divorced, Kathy had jumped at the offer, as did Chris, once her Russell assured her that he could handle their four-year-old daughter and three dogs. So it had become a Matson family vacation, along with Meg and Emery Laine.

"The villa is just so neat -- those tall ceilings, that huge old fireplace, the funky windows -- everything. And the countryside around here -- isn't it lovely?" Kathy was nothing if she wasn't enthusiastic. Outgoing, optimistic, caring, hard-working, and full of energy, she had persevered in her failing marriage to her Latino college beau far too long (in Ethel's opinion). Finally recognizing the incompatibility of her independent and career-minded upbringing with his more traditional (if not chauvinistic) views of family life, she had divorced him earlier that year. The scars were still there.

They munched on the doughnuts and sipped the coffee in comfortable silence as they absorbed the constantly changing effects of the evaporating mists, slowly giving way to the penetrating rays of the Tuscan sun. "Hey, where'd you get the doughnuts?" Chris called down from her small, thin window on the third story.

"Come on down -- we got these on the way yesterday afternoon -- at that funny little shop. Remember?"

But Chris had already gone and soon appeared on the verandah with some coffee and a handful of grapes. Taking one of the doughnuts, she settled next to them at the table. "Yeah, I remember now. But I thought they were for breakfast."

"Well, this is a pre-breakfast snack," said Ethel, inwardly enjoying this quiet family banter.

"Isn't this great, Mom?" Chris echoed her sister's enthusiasm. More quiet and contemplative by nature, introspective, but ultrasensitive to the feelings and moods of others, she found an outlet for her perceptivity in her writing. She had published several short stories and had won two statewide creative awards in Colorado. Russell taught at the university in Boulder and their marriage was cemented by mutual respect and a lot of love. Ethel loved Russell too and felt a little guilty that he had been left behind. But both she and Roscoe thought that little Amy was too young to go along, and neither Russell nor Chris would leave her with a sitter. Ergo........

As Ethel gazed at the hills across the valley, she became aware of a tingling at the nape of her neck -- as if someone were watching her. Turning her head back toward the villa, she glimpsed a flash of movement in the turret window. The turret room was on the same floor as the girls, but at the end of the hallway; it was a tiny circular cubicle with a very narrow window, probably designed for the days of bows and arrows -- sufficient space to shoot out, but not wide enough to provide an easy target. Ethel had seen other turrets like this one, both in Spain and Portugal as well as in the north of Europe. But none of them had given her the skin-crawling feeling that she now remembered she had felt upon seeing this room when they first arrived. She squinted at the turret now, but there was no movement. Well, maybe she had imagined it.

They had locked her in the turret again. The door had been bolted shut and they had taken the candle away. The narrow window let in only a pale, dying reflection of what might have been a moon on the other side of the villa. She sat in the thin black gown that she had worn to bed that night. Why had they put her in the turret room again? They knew that she was frightened of it -- no, she hated it! She hated the spiders that she knew were watching her from the tall ceiling above. But most of all she hated them, and she feared what they were going to do to her.

Angelina Corregio was the only daughter of Count Enrico Corregio, the owner of Villa Montalcino. He was a proud man who had sought and earned the respect of nobility and commoners alike. He doted upon Angelina, whose beauty and gentle manners had already begun to attract the attention of the region's eligible suitors. Though Enrico was determined to grant her hand to only the most deserving of them, it was on this issue that he and Angelina had had their first argument. Ever since the death of her mother, Angelina had wanted to enter the nearby convent and become a nun. It was only after hours of futile pleas and bitter tears that she had ultimately agreed to wait until her father's return from the forthcoming battle to discuss the matter further and to make a final decision.

But over a year had passed since the Count had left to join the forces of the Guelfis who were again fighting the Ghibellinis outside Firenze -- he had not returned. With no male issue, the villa had been claimed by his brother, Alfredo, who had always resented the wealth of his widowed older brother and his only child, Angelina. With Enrico presumed dead and no one to champion the rights of his daughter, Alfredo moved into Villa Montalcino with his wife and two sons. The new landlords brought with them their own servants and dismissed the cook and fieldhands who had served Enrico. Angelina was first ignored by her aunt and uncle, but soon became the plaything of their demented sons. It was they who had locked her in the turret.

Knowing of her desire to enter the convent and fearing that she might attempt to leave, they had deprived her of all outside contacts and gradually isolated her even from their own servants. Angelina was not allowed to eat with the family, nor was she included in any of the activities at the villa. Alfredo proved to be a poor manager, however, and the vineyards and olive groves which had produced so abundantly for his brother, soon began to show the effects of consistent neglect. This only angered Alfredo even more and he used Angelina as the object of his hatred and rage. She longed for some news of her father and his whereabouts, though she was beginning to fear that he might not return. When sent to the turret, she spent most of her time gazing from the window -- praying and waiting.

Roscoe Matson had decided that he would not be intimidated by these Italian drivers; moreover, he was determined to match the speedy pace that Emery Laine had set that first afternoon. Not usually a fast driver, Roscoe swore to himself as Laine's car swerved around the truck in front of him and then around two other cars before slowing down so that Roscoe could catch up. He didn't know the way into Florence and was pretty sure that Emery was having a little fun at his expense. Ethel was prompting him with her usual backseat driving which he actually appreciated on this occasion. "Just go at your own pace," she said. "He'll slow down when he sees you're not right behind."

They somehow reached the central train station in Florence where Emery knew of a parking garage, and Roscoe dutifully followed him down the narrow, hairpin ramp. Back up on the street they agreed on the agenda: Emery and Meg were going to the Bargello Museum where they especially wanted to see the sculptures by Michelangelo and Cellini, as well as the Della Robbia panels on the second floor. Ethel decided to join them. But, needing to unwind after that nerve-stretching drive, Roscoe accompanied his two daughters on their shopping frenzy in the little stalls and shops that he remembered fondly from his previous visit to Florence. They would all meet in three hours at the David replica in the Piazza della Signoria.

On the way to the Bargello Ethel saw a small sign pointing to the house of Dante. Since it was on the way, she suggested stopping, but Emery had already been there and knew it was just an approximation of what *might have been* the *kind* of house that Dante *might have* lived in -- a tourist trap, in other words. But Ethel liked Dante and was fascinated by the fact that he had lived at the time of the fratricidal wars between the Guelfis and the Ghibellinis. Those wars had also figured somehow in the history of Montalcino which she had been reading at the villa, surprised at finding an English edition. Telling the others that she would meet them at the Bargello, Ethel paid the entrance fee at "the house of Dante" and mounted the stairs to the third floor.

After a half hour of glancing summarily at the pictures, books, and manuscripts, she was about to leave when she saw a lithograph that immediately caught her attention. It was the Villa Montalcino! Not exactly as it stood today, of course, but if one blocked out the various additions which had been made over the years and concentrated only on the main square edifice and tower, it was clearly recognizable. The lithograph had been copied from one of

Dante's books and it portrayed a faint figure in the turret window -- a woman dressed in black. Ethel jotted down the title of the book, determined to find it and to learn more about that mysterious tower and its occupant.

Time had no markers. Days turned to weeks, weeks to months, and as far as Angelina knew, months had turned to years. She was now imprisoned in the turret -- a commode had been added in one corner and a small table with a few plates and cups had been provided for her meals. When her uncle told her that her father had perished in the great battle at Lucca, she had no reason to doubt him. As she almost abandoned hope, her hair turned gray and a solemn and quiet despair replaced the peaceful joy she had once felt when looking out across the Tuscan hills. It was only her faith in God which sustained her as she forced herself to eat the meager meals Alfredo's wife provided.

When Angelina first developed a throaty cough and then a bronchial infection from the cold, damp condition of her turret cell, Alfredo feared to contact a doctor who might question his treatment of his ward. Though they had then attempted to nourish her with warm broth and gave her a few blankets to keep her warm, they were too late. Angelina did not fear death; but she longed to see her father one last time and most of all she regretted that she had never had the opportunity to serve her Lord as one of his blessed nuns. Angelina died at the window of the turret, but not before she vented her fevered curse on all of them: "Surely as I now die, my death will lie upon your heads. 'Vengeance is mine, saith the Lord,' and He will wreak it out on you!"

When they returned to the Villa Montalcino after their excursion in Florence, Ethel decided to take a quick shower while the others got a head start on the wine they had purchased at the neighboring winery. She wanted to use the girls' shower since in their own bathroom she and Roscoe only had one of those funny hand-held shower attachments that she hated. As she climbed to the third floor, she thought she heard the sound of footsteps at the end of the hallway -- coming from the turret room. Moving slowly in her slippers and robe, she approached the turret quietly. From within came the low sing-song murmur of a Latin prayer. Ethel opened the door with a shaky hand.

There was no one there.

"Mom, what are you doing over there?" It was Chris who had come upstairs to change before dinner. As Ethel turned to her daughter, Chris frowned with concern. "What's wrong, Mom? You're deathly pale!" Ethel composed herself and just answered that she had thought she heard something in the turret room. Chris nodded thoughtfully, "At night, before we fall asleep, we hear it, too. Sometimes it sounds like footsteps, other times it sounds like someone singing. But we didn't mention it because we thought you'd all think we had too much wine." She grinned. "It's probably just the wind sighing against the window. Or maybe," she shrugged, "we've got a real Tuscan ghost living with us."

On their next visit to Florence, Roscoe and their two daughters toured the Boboli Gardens while Ethel met with Professor Corsini at the university. He had found the volume she had been searching for. Last year, Emery had met Corsini, a Florentine history scholar who specialized in the early centuries of the second millennium. He had several volumes of Dante, one of which contained the lithograph of which Ethel had seen the copy in "the house of Dante." Professor Corsini was more than willing to translate for her from the Italian text:

"When Count Enrico Corregio returned to the Villa Montalcino after ten years of engaging in intermittent battles on behalf of the Guelfis and the tradesmen and artisans whom they represented, he found the vineyards barren, the villa abandoned, and his only daughter dead. His brother, Alfredo, had fled to Firenze, seeking the protection of the

Ghibellinis and the Emperor whom they served. Though no one could tell Enrico exactly how his beloved Angelina had died, he blamed both his brother and his two nephews whom he pursued to Firenze. When he finally found them on the hillside roadway to Fiesole, he slew them with no remorse, severing their heads from their bodies while they were still alive. Then, returning to the battlefield, he himself was killed two years later. His daughter was buried on a Tuscan hillside next to the Villa Montalcino."

"The villa and its properties passed to Enrico's next of kin, a cousin, who took up residence there and gradually restored the vineyards and olive groves to their earlier fruitfulness. But he and his family only lived there for five or six years, moving back to Volterra from whence they had come."

"The cousin, also a Carregio, alleged that there was a ghost in the villa's turret, often pacing back and forth at night and appearing at the window during the day. Several workmen who came to restore parts of the villa in need of repair as well as a score of laborers in the nearby vineyards have sworn that a young woman in a black gown was frequently seen by them in the villa's turret window."

The professor smiled, put down the well-worn volume, and looked up at Ethel. "Well, Mrs. Matson, even our friend Dante was given to superstition, wasn't he?"

"Yes, I suppose to." Ethel said thoughtfully. "But, I wonder."

The time had sped by and it was the last day of their vacation in Tuscany. They had all gotten along together splendidly, despite the differences in ages and occupations. The several bottles (each night) of the smooth, locally-produced Chianti Classico helped, of course, as did the enchanting sights of Tuscany -- Florence itself, the walled city of Lucca, Pisa and its famous tower, the mountain towns of San Gimignano and Assisi, and the seaside enclaves of Portofino and Comiglia (not really Tuscan, but in the nearby area). They had toured the towns, eaten the food, drunk the wine, bought the ceramics and gold jewelry, and absorbed the sights and sounds of this delightful region as much in depth as anyone could do in a short two-week visit. Soon they would have to leave.

On their last afternoon Ethel wandered down the lane leading from the villa to the gravel road beyond. She had not been obsessed by the tragic story of the Corregios, she didn't think, but it had certainly left a deep impression. As she turned back toward the villa, her eyes once again glanced up at its Tuscan turret and, once again, she thought she saw the wispy shadow of a fragile figure in black. Was it Angelina's spirit, still waiting for the father who didn't return until after her death? No -- Ethel had never believed in ghosts. But then, she had never ridiculed those who did. What was it that Hamlet had said? "There are more things in heaven and earth, Horatio, than are dreamed of in our philosophy." Perhaps this was one of them.

Chris and Kathy were at the villa door. "Hey, come on, Mom! Dad's pouring the wine and Emery got out some of that great biscotti. This is our last night -- we have to celebrate." And so they did. The mystery of the turret room would be left behind them for someone else to solve. Or perhaps it would remain just that -- a mystery.

THE GARNET RING

The ring beckoned to her as she surveyed the dusty display case tucked back in a dark corner of the antique shop. The large oval garnet in the center was set in gold and surrounded by several smaller garnets, all matching its deep blood-red color. It glowed, rather than sparkled, with a warm light that seemed to emanate from the stone itself.

Driving leisurely and making one of several detours on their autumn vacation trip in southern Germany and Austria -- from Frankfurt south, through Baden-Wurttemberg, toward the Black Forest and the Bodensee -- Ethel and Roscoe had stopped at the ancient spa town of Baden Baden. There, they meandered down its winding streets, peering into store and restaurant windows as they sauntered by.

"Let's go in here," Ethel said suddenly, when she spotted the quaint shop with its massive wooden door and its bay windows divided into small panes of wavy glass. Rolling his eyes, Roscoe nonetheless followed his wife into the dimly lit interior. Sitting behind a counter, the shopkeeper looked up at them over the top of his rimless half-glasses -- a middle-aged couple, he judged, the portly man obviously lacking interest, but the short professorial-looking woman keenly viewing the antiques. He smiled politely and nodded his head, but made no move to assist them. Only when Ethel stopped at the case which held the garnet ring did he rise hesitantly to his feet.

"Womit kann ich dienen?" he asked. As soon as he noticed their bewilderment, he switched to English. "My apology -- it is late in the season for tourists. May I help you?"

"The garnet ring," Ethel smiled. "May I see it?"

He switched on the small lamp on top of the case, reached inside, and carefully removed the black velvet box in which it lay. "It is not new, you know. In fact, it's very old, dating back to the Thirty Years' War in the early 17th Century." He looked up at Ethel and asked, "You are familiar with German history, mein Frau?"

Ethel rose to the challenge, and as she and the shopkeeper delved into the minutiae of the bitter religious struggles of the war and the politics of the Treaty of Westphalia which ended it in 1648, Roscoe frowned at this obvious dismissal of himself as decision-maker. He turned away and wandered through the labyrinth of tables and counters, cases and shelves that were scattered helter-skelter around the shop. He overheard the shopkeeper mention a "Baroness von Edelhaus" and "Bernice Kaufmann," but only when he heard Ethel ask the price of the ring, did he hurry back to the two of them, apparently now potential partners in a major purchase.

"You don't really need or want another ring, do you, Ethel?" he asked in the petulant tone that he knew would annoy her. The shopkeeper discreetly moved away, back to his chair.

"I can't believe that he's only asking $1,800!" She spoke softly, avoiding Roscoe's question. "It supposedly belonged to the wife of one of the Emperor's delegates to Munster and Osnabruck in 1645. In answer to his shrug, she continued, "They were large all-European conferences which aimed at ending the Thirty Years' War. He said he has papers to prove the provenance of the ring -- you know, who owned it when and where."

"How would you even know what they say, Ethel? Your German isn't that good. Besides, eighteen hundred bucks could buy some nice emeralds or sapphires -- garnets aren't that expensive, are they?"

"But emeralds and sapphires aren't my birth stones. And I think it almost perfectly matches that antique garnet bracelet I bought in Prague last year. Oh, I wish I had brought it along." She placed the ring on her finger and moved her hand back and forth under the lamp. "It's not the intrinsic value of the stones themselves, but the history of the ring that intrigues me. I felt drawn to it the moment I saw it." She forgot her initial annoyance with Roscoe's remarks, and her green eyes danced with excitement and anticipation. When she flashed the grin that had sealed his fate twenty-five years before, Roscoe knew that his cause was lost.

"So, okay," he surrendered grudgingly. "But let's see if he'll give us a better deal if we pay with travelers checks, rather than a credit card." As she grinned again, he added, "It'll have to be an early birthday present. Don't expect anything else next January."

They arrived late afternoon the next day in Bregenz, Austria, on the eastern shore of what Ethel insisted on calling the Bodensee, even though it was referred to as Lake Constance by most Americans. On their first European trip, a honeymoon taken two years after their marriage, Ethel and Roscoe had traveled through this same area of Germany and Austria, and had decided to celebrate their twenty-fifth wedding anniversary by revisiting some of their favorite spots.

They had made reservations at *The Post*, where they stayed in 1977. It was a large but somewhat nondescript hotel on a rise overlooking the town and the harbor. Further up the hill was the cable car which carried sightseers to the top of a mountain from which they could see not only Austria, but Germany and Switzerland as well.

"Let's just check in, leave our bags, and take the cable car up the mountain," Ethel suggested. "It's such a beautiful clear day, we'll be able to see for miles. And remember how the weather varied so constantly when we were here before?"

"Yeah, but that was twenty-three years ago. A lot can have changed since then."

"Well, weather patterns don't change, do they?"

Roscoe was tired from the drive and had missed his usual afternoon nap, but he knew better than to argue the point, even though he secretly hoped that the old cable car might not be running any more. But it was. At the top, they found that a cozy restaurant had been built next to the open observation platform that offered telescopic views for the tourists. After their obligatory scan of the horizons, Ethel proposed taking the two mile "scenic walk" that beckoned them with its rustic wooden sign, but Roscoe chose to wait for her in the restaurant.

"You go ahead, but I'm dying for a cup of coffee. Besides, I want to refresh my memories by reading this Fodor's guidebook I brought along." He smiled and checked his watch as he added, "According to our walking machine, you should be able to do those two miles in about an hour."

"It's called a treadmill," she corrected, shaking her head.

"Whatever."

Ethel set off at a sprightly pace, and soon found herself completely alone on the hardened dirt path that led her through thick evergreens and a verdant foliage of ferns and wild flowers. Evidently, most of the visitors were satisfied with a quick look at the bordering countries and maybe a bite to eat. What a shame, she thought. The sunny skies were dotted with fluffy clouds and the air was ozone-fresh, as if a rainstorm had recently passed. Absorbed in the quiet solitude of her rambles, she rounded a slight bend and was surprised to see a man sitting on a rock overlooking the valley below.

Unruly gray hair sprouted from under his visored cap and his rumpled jacket was open at the neck and thrown back over his shoulders. Something very familiar about him pricked at her mind, and as he turned toward her, she suddenly recognized him. "Willy!" she exclaimed. "I can't believe it! Willy, it's been over a year since I've seen you. What are you doing here in Bregenz?"

Willy rose, gave her a quick hug, and offered her the rock to sit on, while he dropped lightly to the ground next to it. "Take the weight off, Ethel. You still have over a mile to go to get back to the observation platform." He raised an eyebrow and added, "I suppose Roscoe's waiting for you there?"

They reminisced for almost an hour, Ethel bubbling on about her new possession. Then, glancing at her watch, she jumped hurriedly to her feet. "Oh, for Pete's sake! I should have been back half an hour ago. When I finally get there, Roscoe will be having a fit. But I have so much more to tell you, Willy. Are you staying in Bregenz?

As usual, Willie avoided the specifics, but agreed to meet her in the cemetery the next afternoon while Roscoe took his nap.

Ethel remembered the cemetery from her previous visit. Never having regarded them as particularly desirable places to visit, she had nonetheless been struck by its attractive layout, the fresh flowers adorning so many of the graves, and the serenity of its surroundings.

As she hurried off, Willy called after her, "And bring along that garnet ring you bought. I may be able to tell you something about it."

"Now, what does he know about that ring?" Ethel wondered. But then she shrugged it off. After all, that was just like Willy.

Elise had lingered too long in her lover's arms, ignoring the resounding gong of the grandfather clock which heralded the imminent arrival of her husband, Baron Klaus von Edelhaus. Von Edelhaus had served for three weeks as one of the Emperor's delegates to the Osnabruck conference, but that morning his advance horseman had announced his approaching return. The sound of the bugle in the distance now mobilized her into action. Finally realizing the danger to Wolfgang if her husband found him there, Elise tried to break away from his embrace, and urged him to leave.

"Go quickly, my love," she murmured, but his arms refused to release her.

"When will I see you again?" He held her tightly as his mouth sought hers for a last farewell kiss. "I must -- soon. When? Where?"

"In a fortnight's time I leave to visit my father back home in Baden Baden. You know where he lives -- in the same house where I grew up. You can meet me there. But be careful. Klaus will be visiting too, perhaps two weeks later." She pushed him gently toward the door. "Go, Wolfgang -- go." But he still hesitated.

Reaching in the leather purse attached to his belt, he pulled out a small packet which he shyly placed in her hand. Inside was a garnet ring. "I bought it in Prague," he said as he fit it on her finger. It had a matching bracelet, but --" he paused in momentary embarrassment, "I -- I couldn't afford them both." As they embraced once again, he added, "It will be our wedding ring." Then he turned abruptly and ran down the stairs and out the door to his waiting steed. Clutching the garnet ring, Elise moved quickly to her desk and placed it in the hidden compartment at the back.

Drawing near to his castle, Baron von Edelhaus saw the lone horseman ride away in the opposite direction. His dark brows drew together and the corners of his lips curled downward. He jabbed his spurs into the sides of his stallion and raced to the drawbridge which his servants had lowered for the departing horseman. A foolish quest to try to follow the rider now -- he would learn who it was from Elise.

A Catholic, Klaus von Edelhaus had served Ferdinand III, the Habsburg head of the Holy Roman Empire, first at Munster and now at Osnabruck. He had become one of the Emperor's most trusted advisors. An accomplished horseman and vicious fighter, Klaus was recognized by friend and foe as a force to be reckoned with.

His marriage to Elise Meier, the daughter of a Lutheran minister, had rocked the hierarchies of both religions, and when von Edelhaus's friends learned the details of his marriage, even they were shocked by his disdain for common decency. The Reverend Meier had challenged the Empire's restrictions on the Protestant right to worship freely, and had been imprisoned in Bavaria in the castle of a friend of von Edelhaus. On a visit, the Baron spied the lovely sixteen-year-old Elise who tended her father, and was immediately smitten by her virginal beauty. With her reluctant agreement, and ignoring the adamant opposition of her father, he arranged for the release of the Reverend in exchange for the hand of Elise. She only asked that her father be allowed to return to his home and parish in Baden Baden.

For Elise, her marriage to von Edelhaus destroyed all hopes of fulfilling the promises she had made to her youthful friend, Wolfgang Kaufmann. Though Wolfgang was four years older than she, the two of them had grown up together and neither ever doubted for a moment that their future would be as one. But with the dragging on of the Thirty Years' War, nothing was certain any longer. With the resurgence of Catholic power in the early sixteen hundreds, the Protestants had joined together in a defensive alliance, the Evangelical Union, while the Catholics formed the Catholic League to counter it. The battles began throughout Germany, soon to involve the entire Holy Roman Empire, as well as the kingdoms of Denmark and Norway, Sweden, and France.

Elise met her husband at the foot of the circular stairway she had that moment descended. "You returned early -- did the conference go well?"

Klaus ignored her question, as he removed his heavy cloak and the sword which hung from his belt. "Who was visiting?" he asked abruptly. To her questioning look, he added, "I saw a rider galloping off toward Heimstadt. Who was here?"

Elise had learned that dissimulation never worked with Klaus. She was a poor liar, at best, and blushed profusely at the smallest fib. So she phrased her response carefully. "It was Wolfgang Kaufmann, my childhood friend from Baden Baden. He studied in Prague, but has been living the past two years in Munchen, where he learned of our marriage and where we live. He heard of father's imprisonment through the church, and was seeking news of how he is."

"And?" Klaus raised his eyebrow slightly, as his lips formed a cruel smile. "Did you tell him that your dear Papa was released through my intercession on his behalf? In exchange, of course, for your lovely hand."

"Yes -- I told him," she replied tersely, bowing her head to hide her worried look. But Klaus had already seen it. Though he didn't pursue the matter, his mind made a mental note: And now this Wolfgang -- this 'childhood friend' -- was on his way to Baden Baden to see Papa and dig up all the gory details. He would have to keep that in mind when Elise visited her father in two weeks time.

Ethel and Willy wandered among the weathered gravestones, a few dating as far back as the early 1600s. "So the store-keeper gave me documents and a summary on all the owners of the ring since 1645 when it belonged to Baroness Elise von Edelhaus. Whoever gave it to her had her name and the date engraved in the gold band." Ethel took off the ring and showed it to Willy. "See, inside there -- *Elise - 1645*. But Elise was murdered, the store-keeper said, and the ring was lost until the end of the century. It reappeared in the possession of a Bernice Kaufmann, who also lived in Baden Baden. She was the sister of a Bavarian anti-Habsburg Protestant."

After examining the ring carefully, Willy returned it. "It's a rare garnet, Ethel. Very few are this deep a red, and the facets give off an exceptionally warm glow." Ethel was constantly surprised by how much Willy knew -- about everything -- but she had come to accept his pronouncements without question. This time she quickly agreed, as she too felt that the ring was special, unique unto itself.

Picking up on what Ethel had been telling him about the provenance of the ring, Willy asked to see the summary. They stopped to rest on a metal bench, invitingly situated in a copse of trees at the edge of the cemetery. His gray hair flopping in the breeze, Willy was silent as he read through the five pages of names and dates. "It's amazing that they can actually produce a record of ownership for that long a time," he said, apparently persuaded of the paper's validity. Looking around at the gravestones, he murmured, "You know, Ethel, if you and Roscoe could return to Baden Baden, it would be interesting to walk through the cemeteries there -- just to see if we could find the graves of either Elise or her husband -- or of Bernice Kaufmann. I'm heading up that way myself, and could join you there." Ethel was dubious, but promised to ask Roscoe.

"Drive all the way back to Baden Baden? What for? To try to find some graves from the mid-1600s?" Roscoe was both tired and frustrated. The previous day, when Ethel had failed to return after an hour and a half, he started to follow her, but soon deciding that it would be an exercise in futility, he went back to the restaurant and waited another half hour until she appeared. Now today, after her visit to that cemetery, she had embarked on this crazy idea of changing their whole itinerary. "And if we do find the graves, what will they prove? We already know they're all dead."

Roscoe had never been much of an adventurer, Ethel knew, and he hated last- minute changes or disruptions to long-standing plans. She decided not to risk spoiling what had been a wonderful anniversary vacation up until now. It wasn't worth it.

Speaking to Willy when he phoned her the next day, she tried to explain. "So I guess we'll just head up to Munich and our flight back home. But, if you're going to Baden Baden anyway, Willy, maybe you can see what you can find out? After all, you're the one who had the idea of embarking on this whole historical quest." They left it at that.

When the carriage neared Baden Baden, Elise could hardly contain herself. She hadn't seen her father since two years ago at the wedding he had so strongly opposed. They both had cried when he bade his farewell. That night, Klaus had provided her with little comfort, seeking only to satisfy his own carnal desires. Though she did not spurn him, Elise was repulsed by his sexual advances and only gasped in pain when he roughly entered her. But he appeared unaware -- or uncaring -- of her response, and never seemed to tire of her bed. Her only relief was in the many trips he took on behalf of the Emperor -- and the weeks he then spent away.

When Elise arrived at the parsonage, an elderly woman opened the door with a questioning frown, but her father rushed past her to clasp Elise in his arms. "It's my daughter, my daughter Elise," he murmured as he held her tightly against him. He nodded toward the servant, "This is Emmi, the new parsonage maid."

"Oh, father, it's so good to see you." But her words belied what her eyes saw and her heart felt. Her father had aged ten years in the two they had been separated. His bent back and slumped shoulders were a faded caricature of his once tall and proud stature. Wrinkled cheeks and deep pouches under his eyes bore evidence both to his age and to his sleepless nights. When she embraced him, Elise could feel the thin bones of his arms and shoulder blades through the sagging skin which covered them. "Oh, Papa, I missed you so. Did you get the letters I wrote?"

That evening, after Emmi left them, they bared their souls to each other and shared the deep pain and loneliness they both had suffered. Though Elise tried at first to hide the revulsion she felt toward her husband, her father's loving concern soon opened her heart, and her sorrow and despair poured out. "My only joy in two years was to see

Wolfgang again," she confessed, and her father could not bring himself to condemn the infidelity he knew she had committed. For himself, his return to his parish had been empty and unrewarding. The Emperor remained in control of the area, and although Pastor Heinrich Meier was nominally the minister for the Protestants in town, the Catholics had not permitted him either to preach or to conduct services. He was minister in name only, unable to answer the spiritual needs of his flock.

But before retiring for the night, Elise did tell her father of the one hope she still nurtured. "Wolfgang is coming to Baden Baden, Papa, and will visit us here at the parsonage within the week. Then he plans to go to France. He told me that the French Protestants have joined with the Swedes to fight against Emperor Ferdinand. He wants to join them. Maybe we can flee with him, Papa. Maybe all three of us can leave together and go to France." But they would have to decide and move quickly, she urged, because Klaus himself was going to join her in Baden Baden after another fortnight.

Elise did not have to wait long. The next morning, Emmi delivered the brief note that Wolfgang had sent by special messenger. He would see them in two days. When he arrived, her father greeted him as the son-in-law he longed to be. The two young lovers embraced with the blessing of the old minister, but in deference to his feelings, they held their passions in check. Wolfgang agreed with Elise's plan, and the three of them spent every moment in carefully preparing for their departure to France and their escape from the retribution of von Edelhaus. Elise knew that if they succeeded, he would be furious. Once he realized what had happened, Klaus would spare no effort and no money to retrieve what he regarded not so much as his wife, but as his property.

After almost a week of frantic preparations, Wolfgang reviewed their plan. "I will leave in the morning for Frankfurt. You two can follow in three days. Too many people here know all three of us and would immediately become suspicious if we left together. Though most are friendly, the Catholics are in control and we can't chance their stopping us or, equally bad, informing Klaus when he arrives as to where we went. We'll meet at Die Drei Turen Hotel on Schlussel Strasse where I will have rooms ready."

Sensing the need of the two lovers to be alone, Pastor Meier left "for a short evening's walk," he said, while Emmi busied herself in the kitchen. Wolfgang clasped Elise to his chest and kissed her long and passionately. She reached in her pocket and pulled out the garnet ring he had given her when he last saw her at von Edelhaus's castle. "Take it, my love. God forbid, but if Klaus should somehow catch us on the way, the ring would seal my fate. Keep it for when we meet again -- it can be our true wedding ring." He placed it on his little finger. When he kissed her goodbye the next morning, it was with hope in his heart and a smile on his lips.

Two days later, as Elise and her father packed the few clothes they were taking with them, Elise shuddered at the sharp knock on the door. She knew it was Klaus. He forced it open before either of them could respond. He glanced at the packed bags, not questioning why they were there, but verifying that they were. He obviously had been informed of their plans. But who? Elise could not believe that it was Emmi, but she would never know. To Klaus, the bags were clear evidence of his wife's infidelity to him and desertion of their marriage.

Glaring at Elise with burning eyes, he drew his sword and pressed its point against her father's neck. "Confess now, my dear Elise -- or kiss your father goodbye. Were you going to leave me?"

Elise couldn't speak, but nodded a silent "yes." The baron whipped his sword away from her father, and turned it instead toward Elise. Too late, her father sprang to stop him, but Klaus had already plunged it in her heart. She fell without a cry.

Pastor Meier buried his only daughter in the parish cemetery where he himself conducted the brief service for the dozen or so people who attended. Emmi's silent disappearance from the parsonage after von Edelhaus left them convinced Heinrich that she had indeed betrayed them. After the funeral he took his belongings, climbed into the carriage that had been readied for their departure, and drove alone to Frankfurt.

Wolfgang listened in silence to the old man as he told the story in broken words and sobs. Wolfgang persuaded him to return to Baden Baden where his younger sister, Bernice, still lived. "If Emmi doesn't return -- and from what you've said, I don't think she will -- then *contact Bernice. She has not married and lives with my parents; she can care for you as long as you need her. Give her the ring. Tell her it's from me -- and Elise...." He broke down then, as the tears cascaded from his eyes.*

"Where will you go, Wolfgang? What will you do?"

Wiping his eyes with the sleeve of his tunic, Wolfgang replied. "I'm going to follow our original plan. I'll go to France where I'll join the anti-Habsburg coalition. Maybe in some future battle, I'll meet von Edelhaus on the battlefield." He embraced his surrogate father-in-law warmly, and added, "But if not, don't despair. When it's all over, I'll seek him out wherever he is and avenge Elise's death -- on my solemn oath."

As soon as Ethel returned home, she searched in her jewelry box for the garnet bracelet she had bought in Prague the year before. Though the ring was over 350 years old, she had no idea of how old the bracelet was. The antique shop where she had bought it was more like a "junk shop," as Roscoe described it, and the owner seemed to have no idea of its value. If she remembered correctly, she had picked it up for less than $100. But now she could see that the ring and the bracelet matched perfectly!

When Willy called her the next weekend, Ethel was ecstatic. "You know that bracelet I told you about, Willy? Well, it *does* match the ring -- in color, in design, well, in everything! It's almost as if they were a set." She paused only a moment before asking, "But what did you find out in Baden Baden?" Knowing Willy, she was sure that he had stopped there to search the cemeteries for any evidence of the fate of Wolfgang or Bernice. As for von Edelhaus himself, they hadn't expected to find him buried there, but perhaps near the ruins of his castle at Heimstadt.

"I learned more than we had hoped for!" Willy, unlike his usual diffident self, was as excited as Ethel. "The Bernice Kaufmann whom the shopkeeper mentioned to you and whose name appears on the provenance papers as the first owner of the ring after Elise von

Edelhaus was the sister of a Wolfgang Kaufmann who fought at the end of the Thirty Years War as a volunteer with the French and Swedish forces. In the last phases of the war, they headed the Protestant coalition against the Holy Roman Empire. I found some hand-written records in the Lutheran church there which recorded the deaths of both Wolfgang and Bernice. Then, after some trudging around the cemetery, I found their graves. What's really interesting, Ethel, is that the Kaufmann plot is right next to the Meier plot which holds the grave of Pastor Heinrich Meier, the father of Elise von Edelhaus, who is buried right next to him. Wolfgang Kaufmann is on her other side!"

"But how did Bernice get the ring after it supposedly *disappeared*? Did Elise sell it to her? And what's the relationship of this Wolfgang Kaufmann to Elise von Edelhaus? And how...."

"Whoa!" Willy interrupted the stream of questions. "The murder of Elise was recorded in the church records as committed by her husband, Klaus von Edelhaus. By the time I learned that, I was intrigued enough to drive to Heimstadt to see if I could find his castle. The castle was in complete ruins, but in the adjacent churchyard I did find the grave of von Edelhaus. The inscription on the gravestone read: *Here lie the earthly remains of Klaus von Edelhaus, a loyal subject of Ferdinand, Emperor of the Holy Roman Empire, who was killed during the French and Swedish siege of Munchen in 1648 at the hand of Wolfgang Kaufmann, a Bavarian renegade in the employ of the anti-Habsburg coalition. May God have mercy on his soul.*"

It was too much to absorb at once. Ethel remained silent for a moment, as the myriad of facts and dates and people cascaded through her mind. Then she asked, "So this Wolfgang Kaufmann -- is he the same man who is buried next to Elise in Baden Baden?"

"Well, we can't prove it, but it seems highly likely. The dates are right. Von Edelhaus was killed in 1648, in the last major battle before the signing of the Treaty of Westphalia. Kaufmann's gravestone shows his birth as 1623 and his death as 1694; at the age of seventy-one, he probably died of natural causes. His sister lived on until 1704. My guess is that Wolfgang provides the missing link between

Elise's ownership of the ring and its later possession by Bernice, Wolfgang's sister."

Willy's natural tendency to dramatize took over. He continued as if narrating a mystery novel: "The church records show that Wolfgang purchased the Kaufmann plot in late 1648 after the death of von Edelhaus and the end of the war. Most of the plots sold at that time were at the eastern end of the cemetery, but Wolfgang chose to buy the last remaining plot at the northern end where the Meier's plot was located. Why? My guess is that Wolfgang and Elise were lovers and it was he who gave her the garnet ring. But then, sometime before she was murdered, she gave it back to him. Why? To signify the end of their illicit relationship -- or -- to keep it safely for her until they could be reunited? Again, my guess is the latter. If she had wished to stay with Klaus, why did he murder her? And, if Elise had the ring in her possession when he killed her, wouldn't he have taken it? But instead it ended up with Bernice, Wolfgang's sister."

There had been no comment from Ethel since Willy launched into what he regarded as a brilliant historical expose. "Well," he finally prodded her, "what do you think? Have I solved the mystery of the original provenance of your garnet ring?"

"Oh, yes, Willy -- with your usual flair. But...." He groaned as he realized what was coming. "But what about the bracelet? Where did it come from?"

"Ah, Ethel. That's another story." And with a smile in his voice, he said goodbye.

RED MOON OVER MOSCOW

Ethel had not been back to Moscow since her visit in June of 1988 when Ronald Reagan met with Mikhail Gorbachev for the strategic arms reduction talks which had marked the beginning of the end of the Cold War. That visit had been both amusing and insightful; she smiled to herself as she remembered it. A small group of Americans, professionals from different fields, had been invited to meet with their counterparts, along with a few government representatives, in Moscow and in Yerevan, capital of Armenia. Yerevan had been included because a pediatrician in the group, Dr. Phillip Matson, had wanted to visit the well-known children's hospital that was located there. When, at the last moment Dr. Matson had to cancel out, Ethel had been asked to take his place.

The fact that Dr. Ethel Matson (PhD) was not Dr. Phillip Matson (MD) and was a Political Science-type doctor, not a medical one, had not fully dawned on their Russian welcome committee members until they met the Americans at the Moscow airport and were introduced to a Dr. Matson who was a female. What followed after the initial confusion was an apt illustration of both the flexibility and the inflexibility of the Soviet system. The American delegation was driven to its hotel and rather unceremoniously dropped in the lobby, while the Russian government officials returned to their office to decide how to deal with this turn of events. A satisfactory solution was found: Yerevan would remain on the itinerary as planned, but the hospital would be dropped.

That night after dinner Ethel and two others from the group decided to visit the Kremlin and Red Square. The hotel desk receptionists were singularly unhelpful, but a Nigerian visitor overheard their request for directions and politely led them to the underground. There three elderly women, hearing them speak English, immediately offered their assistance. The Russian grandmas, with babushkas covering their heads, escorted the Americans into the subway and personally accompanied them all the way to the Red Square exit. When they emerged, they were amazed to see the Kremlin bathed in a rosy glow from a full red moon overhead. Ethel had never seen a red moon before and few of her friends believed her when she told them about it later. But there it was -- high in the sky over the Kremlin, large and full -- and red.

It was now eleven years later and as her plane landed Ethel wondered what changes she would see in this curious place called Russia. What Winston Churchill had referred to as "a riddle wrapped in a mystery inside an enigma" remained exactly that a half century later. For forty-five years the United States and the Soviet Union had fought the Cold War as the two global superpowers of East and West, the Soviets dominating the Eastern bloc's Warsaw Pact and the US serving as the leading power in NATO. It wasn't until the late 1980s when it gradually became evident that in fact the Soviet Union was basically only a developing country with nuclear weapons -- still dangerous because of those weapons, but no superpower in any other way. Now, in 1999, Ethel was part of an American academic team sent to Moscow by the US State Department to assess and to assist, if possible, the democratization efforts of the Russian government.

Despite the confusion over the substitution of Ethel Matson for Phillip Matson, their reception had been cordial and friendly and their luggage expedited. When they were dropped at their hotel, Ethel had been grateful that there were no formal meetings scheduled until the next afternoon; she was anxious to see a bit of the Red Square and then get back to her hotel for some real sleep.

She had another reason as well. The last time she had been in Moscow she had bumped into Willy at the Pushkin Museum and they had spent several hours together discussing the warming up of US-Soviet relations. Though she had seen him since then, they hadn't spoken much about Russia. Ethel felt that somehow Willy would appear in the morning. What would he say about her current mission, she wondered?

The women lined up outside the train station holding out their household wares to sell -- embroidered dresser scarves and hand towels, some homegrown vegetables, a box of dish soap, dishes, glassware, and anything else they could spare. Inflation and scarcity forced many Muscovites to sort through their personal possessions for whatever they might have of value that they could exchange for some desperately needed rubles. Ethel passed by with her eyes averted, knowing well that if she bought from one, the others would follow her with pleading cries: "Buy this, lady. Buy this nice shawl -- warm and hand knit. See how nice it will look on you, lady. Please, only ten rubles."

The policemen didn't bother the women. Only if they got in the way of the traffic or mobbed an unfortunate tourist would one of the officers stroll up and tell them, "Move along now, Mother. Don't pester our visitor. Step back there." The women obeyed as they had been taught to obey. No matter if it was the Communist agents of the old sullen Stalin or the laughing clown Khrushchev or, now, the somber and unpaid soldiers of the drunken "democrat," Yeltsin -- the women obeyed.

Clutching the shoulder strap of her purse and buttoning her raincoat against the cool Moscow breeze, Ethel forged ahead toward the subway next to the station. She vaguely remembered from her last visit that she should be able to connect there to the line that would take her to the Pushkin. But before she started to descend the littered steps, a firm hand grasped her arm and led her back toward the street. "What in heaven's name," she began to protest, but then she stopped. "Willy!" And there he was -- dressed in baggy peasant pants, a coarse smock hanging loosely over the top, and a visored gray cap upon his head. "What are you supposed to be? A Volga boatman?" He grinned his crooked grin as he led her to a small table in the station restaurant, "How are you, Ethel? What's up?"

Ethel had first met Willy when she was experimenting with sensory deprivation in an isolation tank that belonged to her daughter's boyfriend. Ethel had read some of the works of John Lilly, one of the gurus of the 1960s who had written about his experiences in isolation tanks. It was at that time, in a dream or in the tank, that Willy had appeared and announced himself as John's brother. Ethel had not been able to repress the fit of laughter that erupted from her when she repeated, "Willy Lilly! No, that's really just too much!" But Willy had taken the insult in stride and continued to appear at the strangest times and places. Ethel was delighted that he had come to Moscow.

An hour later she was still talking, "...and so you see, Willy, we're supposed to take a look at how they've set up the next Duma elections -- the rules for voting, counting the votes -- you know, the usual kind of monitoring. But then we're also supposed to make some recommendations and suggestions for other things to be done over time. Like strengthening the legal system, developing the judiciary, encouraging privatization. All of that kind of thing. We meet this afternoon with a group of business people, academics (economists, mainly), government representatives both from the national government and from the city of Moscow, and a few of the inevitable bureaucrats. "So," Ethel paused, "what do you think?"

"I think," Willy took a big sip of his vodka, "I think it probably won't make a damn bit of difference whatever you recommend. Unless old Boris can manage to stay off the bottle long enough to reassume some control and direction, the whole country will continue to disintegrate. Until some strongman comes along and takes hold, that is. You know how hard it is for any country, or any international agency for that matter, to actually influence or change another society. What makes you think that Russia is any different? Until the leaders themselves believe that reform is necessary and can actually be done without losing their own power, nothing really significant will happen." He shook his head at Ethel's pained expression. "You always were a bit of an optimist, Ethel. Not naive, perhaps, but an optimist. But things don't look very

*good here. I don't think so, anyway." He leaned back in his chair as if
waiting for her protest.*

*Ethel knew he was right. That was why she had accepted her
assignment -- the real reason she had come to Russia. While she pondered
whether she should tell Willy the whole story or not -- or whether he
already knew it -- he wandered off to the bar for his second vodka. Ethel
looked around the room to check whether anyone seemed particularly
interested in their intense conversation, but there were only a couple of
bus conductors on break, a group of women who had entered from the
line outside, and a drunk young man sleeping at the next table. When
Ethel turned back to wait for Willy's return, she realized that he had
left. A typical Willy ploy! She paid the bill and returned to her hotel to
get ready for the meeting.*

Sergey Smirnov listened to the discussion with a detached air of
boredom and indifference. These American advisors had been coming
to Moscow for seven or eight years now -- some of them experts on
Russian history and culture, but with little knowledge of practical
politics or how the system worked; others understood the fabric and
dynamics of democratic societies, but didn't have a clue as to how to
apply them to this vast Slavic empire of Russia. Sergey himself was
both skeptical and hopeful at the same time. He knew that Viktor
Arbatov, his superior in the Federal Security Service (the FSB, a
descendent of the KGB), believed that only a strong new leader could
save Russia from disintegration and chaos. Though Sergey shared
some of his doubts and was fully aware of the fragility of the Yeltsin
government, he was still hopeful that the promised reforms would be
carried out and would be effective. Besides, that was the judgment of
the FSB as an institution and Sergey wasn't going to alter or skew his
report of their honest assessment, not even for Arbatov.

Little known to most Americans, the secret agents of the former
KGB were alive and well in post-Cold War Russia, and they kept
their eyes open to the activities of all visitors -- especially those
involved in the efforts at reform. The Russian spymasters had

decided to support Yeltsin and his reform policies, at least for the short term. So they had formed an alliance of convenience with the CIA to help them assess the real progress being made, stripped of all political pretense. Over Arbatov's objections, Sergey had been assigned to contact Dr. Ethel Matson in order to pass on to her in some detail the current FSB assessment of the democratization process and its progress. Dr. Matson, he was told, was not a CIA agent, but because of her previous work in the State Department's Bureau of Intelligence and Research, she was frequently given ad hoc assignments of this kind.

He listened to her now, as she stressed the importance of developing the structures and practices -- "the societal context" -- necessary to make democracy work. Dressed conservatively in a navy blue suit and with her hair combed back from her face, Dr. Matson epitomized Sergey's image of a female academic. Still, her straightforward and earnest presentation attracted his analytical mind. "Sure, it's important to support the upcoming elections and to do whatever we can to assure that they are open to all and run honestly. But equally important over the longer run will be Russia's ability to develop a strong and unbiased legal system, an independent judiciary and media, and a working relationship between the President and the Duma."

She was right, of course, Sergey thought. But could the politicians rise above their personal ambitions and their petty suspicions of each other? Sergey shrugged as he reminded himself that his role was not that of policy maker, but analyst. He wondered how he could best approach Dr. Matson and deliver the FSB analysis to her.

The meeting broke up at 5:30 PM to allow adequate time for the guests to change before dinner and vodka (or vodka and dinner, Ethel thought). She had attended enough of these meetings to know that she would learn as much from the informal talk over drinks and dinner as from the formal exchanges. As she entered her hotel room, she was surprised to hear her phone ringing. Ethel had not kept up any contacts with the Russians who had been her hosts on her previous visit and she hadn't yet called Mike Ashmore, the only person she knew at the US Embassy. "Hello?" she said tentatively.

"Dr. Matson, this is Victor Arbatov. I am your FSB contact. When can we meet?" No subtlety there, she thought, but she liked his direct approach. "Perhaps later this evening?" she ventured. After dinner, Ethel took a short walk before her appointed meeting with Arbatov. She shivered slightly as she looked up to the darkening sky and saw that the moon was again red.

"So this Arbatov just called you on the phone, said that he wanted to meet with you, and you went? Just like that?" Willy's sarcasm caught Ethel off guard and she was more than a little irritated by it.

"Well, why not? We met right here in the hotel. After all, I knew that I'd be contacted by someone from the FSB, and Arbatov seemed to know all about my assignment. Besides, he showed me his ID card and a letter of instructions, Willy. Why should I have doubted him?"

"I don't know exactly. I don't like the feel of it somehow. That letter could have said anything. After all, you don't read Russian, do you?" Ethel shook her head, "No."

Willy had dutifully turned up at the Pushkin Museum when Ethel finally visited it on Sunday, her one free day. They wandered haphazardly from room to room, viewing the paintings, as Ethel told him about her meeting with Arbatov two nights before.

"So basically this guy is telling you that Yeltsin is on the way out and that the US ought to put its eggs in someone else's basket? And did he also say who that 'someone' might be?"

Ethel nodded, less confident than before. "Well, he suggested that Cherkov, the supposed hard-liner, isn't as bad as the Western press makes out. He also said that they, the FSB, feel that at least he can make things happen. They argue that it's essential that someone take charge, go after the crime syndicates -- the Russian Mafia -- and re-establish some kind of order. He implied that those changes have to happen before they can even begin to think about serious reforms."

"And you believe that?"

"Willy, why are you being so difficult about this? I don't either believe it or disbelieve it. My job is simply to take back to Washington

what the FSB's unvarnished assessment is. Not what I think it should be."

"Okay, Ethel, I understand that. But I can't buy the FSB making that kind of basic change -- from supporting Yeltsin to backing Cherkov -- without some consultation at a higher level. Pardon my bluntness, but why choose you as the person to deliver a message that's this important? If it's true, that is." *They had reached the vestibule where Willy stopped and stood silent for a moment, absorbed in thought. Then he asked, "Have you checked this Arbatov guy out with the Embassy?"*

"Of course. I met with Bill Henderson, the CIA station chief yesterday morning and he verified that Arbatov was my contact. Although," Ethel paused, a vague uneasiness suddenly seizing her. "Although, you know, Willy, I had a funny feeling about Henderson himself. He was pretty flippant about Yeltsin and agreed almost too readily with this new line. Like he already knew what Arbatov had told me." She took Willy by the arm and pulled him toward the exit. "Maybe your doubts are right, Willy. Maybe I should check this out more carefully. I do know someone else at the Embassy who might be able to help. Do you think I should call him?"

Willy extracted his arm and nodded thoughtfully, "Yeah, maybe you should." With a parting smile, but more subdued than usual, he waved his hand, dashed down the stairs, and hurried off toward the nearest subway into which he quickly disappeared.

Ethel phoned Michael Ashmore that afternoon. She had met Michael in Washington several years before when she was working for the Bureau of Intelligence and Research at the State Department and he was chief of the Soviet desk. He was now the Deputy Chief of Mission at the US Embassy in Moscow. Ethel had planned to see him at some point, but being Sunday, he probably wouldn't be at the Embassy. Luckily, she was able to reach him at his apartment. He invited her for lunch the next day.

"But Ethel," Ashmore frowned as he toyed with the gray, almost colorless meat he had just been served. "I've know Bill Henderson for years. Not well, perhaps. But it's hard to believe that he's involved in some sort of shady deal with this Arbatov fellow. Nonetheless," he paused, "I do respect your judgment in these matters and I could do some checking directly with the Agency at McLean. At least I could find out more about Arbatov and his reliability." As she started to interrupt, he continued, "And, of course, I won't mention anything to Henderson about it until we learn more -- if we do."

"Mike, I really appreciate your looking into this. Maybe I'm overly influenced by my own reading of the situation. But I don't believe that Cherkov is a liberal sheep in a hard-line wolf's clothing -- to coin a garbled metaphor!" Ethel stopped as she remembered Willy's doubts. "And besides, I don't think that this kind of information on a major change of policy would be leaked to someone like me to report on. Surely, the FSB would go directly to you or Henderson -- or maybe even to a higher level in Washington?"

Ashmore nodded back at her, more troubled than before. "That's what I've been mulling over in my mind, Ethel. Why the round-about way of handling this? Unless some group, some faction at the security service, wants to start weakening the US support of Yeltsin and knows that most of us here at the Embassy would regard that as unwise, or at least as premature."

Ethel interjected, "So they try to circumvent you and use me to convey a distorted assessment? But if that's the case, who is my real contact? And where?"

Sergey had not expected it. He was caught off guard when Arbatov phoned early that morning and told him to meet Dr. Matson in the park across from her hotel. He had wondered why Arbatov had called him personally, but he didn't question his superior. That bastard! Now, as he lay behind the fallen tree where they had carried him, he knew there wasn't much time left. The two agents had come up next to him, one on each side, guided him to the secluded grove of linden trees, and the knife had easily cut through his light jacket and shirt. He should have been more wary, he reflected. How stupid! He just had not expected it.

Sergey closed his eyes to the lulling enticement of rest. He needed to rest -- if only for a moment.

Willy had seen the whole thing, but had not been close enough to intervene. He had learned that Smirnov was Ethel's real FSB contact late Sunday afternoon after he left her at the art museum. Then it had taken him an hour or so to locate where he lived (there were three S. Smirnovs in the Moscow directory). He had decided that Sergey probably wouldn't try to contact Ethel until Monday or Tuesday -- the meetings were scheduled through Friday. Since Smirnov was part of the Russian team, it would make sense for him to approach her at one of the meetings. So early Monday morning Willy had stationed himself outside Smirnov's apartment building and followed him to the park. After the two thugs left, Willy ran to where Sergey lay. He was already dead.

That afternoon Ethel was surprised when the hotel clerk called her out of the meeting for a phone call. She was even more surprised when she heard Willy's voice: "Ethel, be careful. Your real contact was a guy named Smirnov. He's dead -- knifed in the park across the street from your hotel by some security henchmen from the FSB. I don't know who Arbatov is, but we were probably right in guessing that he's part of some faction that wants to see Yeltsin out and Cherkov in. Did you learn anything from your friend at the Embassy?"

"Only that he knew Henderson and had no reason to suspect him of collusion. But he said that he would call the Agency directly and try to find out more about Arbatov." With a sudden pang of sorrow at the thought of the handsome young Russian who had smiled shyly at her from across the table, she asked, "Was this Smirnov the same young fellow who is part of the Russian team attending our meetings?"

Ethel knew that he was, before Willy even responded. She had caught Sergey watching her more than once during the course of those long sessions. Then, during an afternoon break on Friday, he had approached her and suggested that just the two of them might meet over a cup of coffee to discuss "their personal views." Ethel had readily agreed, and had mentioned that Monday or Tuesday might work out, since she had already made arrangements to go to the Pushkin Museum on Sunday. At the time, she had thought that perhaps Smirnov was her contact, but when Arbatov called later she assumed that Smirnov simply wanted to exchange some personal views as he had said. She should have been more guarded; Ethel knew that now. But now it was too late. "Willy, how did you find out about all of this?" she asked. The line was dead.

Ethel had agreed to stop by at the Embassy to see Michael Ashmore before leaving for the States. Her democratization meetings had gone quite smoothly, despite everyone's concern and regret over the murder of the young Russian delegate, Sergey Smirnov. The police had initially ascribed it to a Mafia killing, but there was no evidence that Smirnov was connected in any way either with drugs or with other criminal activities. They soon were removed from the case, however, and the Federal Security Service took over.

Ashmore had called Ethel on Tuesday, the day after the murder, to inform her that Smirnov had indeed been her designated FSB contact, as she already knew from Willy. Arbatov, as leader of the anti-Yeltsin faction, had failed to persuade Sergey to provide a false evaluation of the government's stability and its chances for reform; so he personally decided to get rid of him and take his place. Henderson had long been sending critical reports on President Yeltsin back to Washington, and Mike now believed that he was also involved in the Arbatov plot. He told Ethel that Henderson had been placed under house arrest by some of the Embassy's marine guards who would escort him back to Washington later that week.

"Well, Ethel -- you can't say that it hasn't been an interesting or exciting visit, can you?" Mike Ashmore was relaxed and seemed genuinely pleased to welcome Ethel into his office. "I must apologize about Henderson. No one here had a clue, but he evidently has been working with the Arbatov group ever since Yeltsin came into office."

"What I still can't understand, Mike, is why they put together such an elaborate plot? Why not simply transmit their own point of view over here to the Embassy directly? Why involve an intermediary, like myself, particularly when I was serving as a member of an independent, non-governmental mission actually sent to support and strengthen democratization?"

"Partly because of that fact. Any report from you would be regarded as independent and unbiased. The Arbatov clique well knew that our Embassy staff is committed to the official US policy -- support for Boris Yeltsin. It wouldn't welcome a contrary report from a minority in the FSB. But if you reported back to Washington that your contact, an official representative from the security service, had provided an assessment of basic instability and mismanagement by the Yeltsin administration, then it certainly would be taken seriously. That is what Arbatov wanted Smirnov to do. When Sergey wouldn't falsify the more positive assessment, he was eliminated. Arbatov met with you and gave you the picture he wanted you to take back. Moreover, he knew that Henderson could be counted upon to make sure that your report would eventually reach the right people. A bit involved and elaborate, as you say, but it could have worked."

Ashmore paused to peer at Ethel over the top of his glasses. "Now, what I'd like to know, Ethel, is what made you so suspicious of Arbatov in the first place? As I gather from what you've said, Smirnov had not yet informed you that he was the real FSB contact -- right?"

As she glanced out of Ashmore's window to the street below, Ethel suddenly spied Willy. He was looking directly up at the DCM's window and pointedly held his forefinger up to his lips. "Yes, Willy," she thought, "I get the message." To Michael Ashmore she simply said, "Oh, I don't know, Mike. Just call it a woman's intuition!"

TREADMILL TO TERROR

Ethel frowned at the treadmill as her eyes began to adjust to the darkened hallway in which it stood. The fog-filtered light which managed to penetrate through the windows only dimly lit the long narrow room. She hadn't flicked on the light because it would only add to the heat she would generate when she began her half-hour, one and-a-half mile walking regimen. She and Roscoe had bought it almost a year ago, and much as she hated its demands on her time, she had forced herself to walk six days a week ever since. If the good Lord rested on Sunday, she figured, so could she. In her mid-fifties, Ethel had decided to lose the extra ten pounds she had put on over the past few years. When diet alone hadn't done it, she had finally succumbed to the monotony and boredom of exercise.

Turning on her tape recorder, she set the time, speed, and elevation on the treadmill, entered her weight to calibrate how many calories she'd burn up, and started walking to the Johnny Mathis tape she had rescued from a basement cabinet. Ethel and Roscoe listened to CDs or the radio when relaxing over cocktails, but these old tapes were okay for the walking. Now, if she could only get Roscoe to use "the walking machine," as he called it, they'd both be in better shape. When Johnny warbled, "Chances are, your chances are -- awfully good," Ethel thought, "Oh, no, they're not." Unfortunately, Roscoe had tripped and sprained his ankle while walking on the treadmill about three months after they bought it.

He swore then that he wouldn't go back on the damn thing -- and up to now, he hadn't.

Once Ethel actually got started, though, it really wasn't that bad. She hummed along with Johnny, Nat King Cole, and the Beachboys, strode briskly in step to the marches of John Philip Sousa, smiled at the lyrics from *The Sound of Music* and *Mary Poppins,* and thrilled to her favorite melodies from *Swan Lake* and *The Nutcracker Suite.*

She would imagine the female dancers in their feathery white swan dresses as they floated in time to the magical music of Tchaikowsky. Sometimes her mind wandered even further afield and she would suddenly find herself in the strangest of places. Like the time last September when Frank Sinatra sang *Give My Regards to Broadway.*

The traffic was as bad as Ethel remembered it to be. Broadway and 42nd Street looked like the mother of all traffic jams -- bumper to bumper cars and cabs and buses locked at the intersections, unable either to drive over to the other side or to retreat back behind the traffic lights which had just turned orange when they tried to cross.

"How long are we likely to be stuck here?" she asked the cab driver, shouting over the loud Latin-American music that pounded out from his radio.

He shook his head. "No compre'ndo. What you want, lady?"

She tried another approach. Pointing at her watch, which she held up for him to see through his rearview mirror, she asked, "How long? When to World Trade Center?"

The results weren't much better. "Si. I know. World Trade Center." He shook his head again and shrugged his shoulders. "Bad traffic. Rush hour bad. Sorry."

Ethel was due to meet Mel Friedman, the editor assigned to her by the publisher of a textbook she had written for introductory-level classes in International Relations. His office was located on Madison Avenue, but he had a meeting at the World Trade Center later that morning and they had agreed to meet there for breakfast at nine. Mel had been a great help to her with his professional editing, and they had become good friends in the process. The cabbie finally broke out of the snarled traffic and sped south on a one-way street, arriving at the south tower of the center at 8:45 A.M. Hurrying into the lobby, Ethel pushed the button for the elevator. She'd probably make it, after all.

Then it happened. A crashing boom reverberated from the north tower next door. Ethel and several others in the lobby rushed outside where they hoped to get a better look as what had caused it, but all they saw were clouds of thick black smoke which billowed out from the upper stories -- fairly high up around the 90th floor, Ethel guessed. There was little they could see except for the crowds of people running out of the building. Returning to the south tower lobby, Ethel heard the announcement that the "incident" had occurred in the north tower and the south building was safe. About fifteen minutes had passed, and she knew that Mel would be waiting for her. Maybe he would know what was going on.

Ethel impatiently stabbed her finger at the up button, but before the elevator could respond, a second crash echoed inside the lobby. A shudder ran though the entire building which began to sway perilously back and forth. It felt like the earthquake she had experienced when in Anchorage several years before, but because of the two explosions in succession, she knew it was something else. She anxiously waited for another announcement, but evidently the PA system had been damaged by whatever had happened. Several injured people began to flood the lobby as they descended in a daze from the floors above. Others, probably unable to use the stairs, were jumping from the upper windows -- engulfed in flames or covered in white ash.

Suddenly finding herself wobbling about on the buckling floor, Ethel realized that it was gradually giving way beneath her feet as it collapsed to the level below. Luckily, she was able to grab onto the door of the elevator which had just opened; the elevator shaft swayed with the rest of the building, but did not fall below the entrance level.

Pandemonium reigned. Shrill screams pierced her ears -- screams of fright from those above and screams of pain from those below whose bodies had plummeted down to break upon the debris on the lower levels. Blinded now by the smoke, Ethel inched her way toward the standing corner wall which she had seen only moments before it became enveloped in the dust rising from the fallen plaster of floors and walls. Shards from the plate-glass windows had shattered everywhere and left their red slashes on the faces and arms of those who had been standing in the vestibule near them.

Finding the corner, Ethel briefly caught a glimpse of what looked like a patch of open sky, quickly darkened by the plumes of rising smoke. She must be near an exit. Calm down, she told herself. Think. She realized that she had to get out -- away from the collapsing building. But she couldn't see where to move next, where to put her foot so that she too wouldn't end up two stories down.

At that moment, she felt the reassuring grasp of a hand under her arm and the blessed sound of a familiar voice. "Follow me, Ethel. I think I can get us out of here." She turned and gasped at the sight of the crooked smile, gray hair and ruddy face. A small camera hung from a strap around his neck. "Willy!" she almost screamed. "Oh, Willy, you don't know how glad I am to see you." As the comforting sense of relief flowed through her body, she began to cry.

Willy patted her clumsily on the back. "Don't cry, Ethel. Just face the wall and lean against it. Slide your left foot next to my right one. That's it. Now, bring your other foot over. Okay. Now, we'll just keep on going like this toward that opening in the wall over there and see if we can't get out of here." He kept his hand under her arm as they edged their way along the narrow piece of flooring still protruding from the one wall. Thank God for Willy, Ethel thought. He always showed up at the oddest moments in her life, but this time she wasn't even going to ask why.

They were well away from the south tower when it completely collapsed upon itself, killing everyone in the building and in the concourse below. Thirty minutes later, the north tower also collapsed. It took them almost an hour to make it across the fields of rubble -- first piled in smoking mounds at the base of where only hours before the World Trade Center had stood, and then strewn about in bits and pieces for ten more blocks. The roads were now crowded with fleeing people, police in cars and on foot, firemen and fire trucks -- all sirens blaring. Exhausted, Ethel could not comprehend what had happened. She only knew that she had to keep walking.

Ethel was walking quickly to the blaring music of the *1812 Overture* when the sound of Roscoe's voice suddenly startled her. He shouted to her from the family room and his tone of voice alone was enough to shock her out of her reverie. She noted with amazement that she had been walking for over an hour and had gone the equivalent of three miles. Her legs ached, and the acrid scent of smoke still permeated her nostrils. Her mind reeled with vague visions of falling buildings, floors opening up beneath her feet, and chunks of concrete and glass scattered about for blocks and blocks. And where had Willy gone? But the look on Roscoe's face gained her full attention.

"My God, Ethel. The World Trade Center has just been bombed! Two planes -- they flew right into it!" He switched up the volume as the newscaster continued. "--and we have no knowledge at this point of who was responsible, or how many people have been killed. For those who have just tuned in, let me repeat: two passenger airliners have crashed into the twin towers of the World Trade Center in New York City, and the upper parts of the towers have crumbled. Fire has spread from floor to floor and the New York Fire Department has sent all available men and equipment to the scene. The police are cordoning off all vehicular traffic south of 14th street, though survivors from the center are still fleeing on foot. Stay turned to Channel 12 for more news."

Ethel sat petrified. *She had been there!* She still smelled the smoke. Her legs still ached and her left arm was sore from where Willy had grabbed it to lead her out of that burning hell-hole. What was happening to her?

Roscoe was watching her with a worried frown on face. "What's wrong, Ethel? You've turned white as a sheet." He rose and walked to the bar. "You need something to calm you down. How about a drink?"

She started to shake her head in protest, but quickly changed her mind. "Yes -- it's much too early, but yes, I think I could use a drink."

They watched the TV reports and commentary intermittently for most of the afternoon, switching from station to station whenever the oft-repeated picture of the two planes smashing into the towers came on. Ethel could not help thinking about Mel Friedman, wondering where he had been when the planes struck and if he were still alive. Then she would tell herself that there was no reason to think Mel had even been at the World Trade Center, except for the weird dream or vision -- whatever it was -- that she had experienced while on the treadmill.

Trying to reassure herself and make some sense out of what she had felt and seen, Ethel reviewed the facts: One, she had not been in New York when the terrorist attack took place; she had been walking on her treadmill. Query: How could she have been at the World Trade Center? Two, she could not have heard the TV broadcast from the other room over the sound of the music that had been blaring from the tape recorder. Query: How did she know that the World Trade Center had collapsed? Three, if she had not been there, how could she have seen Willy and how could he have saved her?

The last question was less problematical to Ethel than the other two. Willy's appearances in her life were always unexpected, usually coming at times of crisis or when she faced a particularly insoluble problem. He refused to accept Roscoe's depiction of him as a figment of her imagination or, for that matter, any idea that he was less than *real*. In fact, because of Willy, Ethel had revised her own entire concept of what *reality* actually was. She now suddenly realized that she had to view her recent experience within the context of the ambiguity that Willy had introduced into her life.

She didn't mention any of this to Roscoe who had made it quite clear when she first met Willy that he was a non-believer in invisible guides or mentors. "Ethel," he had remonstrated with the patronizing air she detested, "you can believe in whatever you want, but don't expect me to go along with it." So, she never again mentioned her subsequent meetings with Willy, and Roscoe never saw him -- even when he was right there. Maybe she would see him again tomorrow and gain some understanding of what had happened.

But before it got too late that afternoon, she looked up Mel Friedman's number and called. The somber voice of his secretary chilled her to the bone. "Oh, Dr. Matson, I hate to be the one to tell you, but Mr. Friedman -- well, no one knows for sure, but he was going down to the World Trade Center this morning for a couple of meetings, and ... well, no one has heard from him since the attack. His wife is frantic." She paused as if waiting for Ethel to say something, but Ethel couldn't speak. "You've heard about what happened, right? I mean about ..."

Ethel finally regained enough composure to reply, though her eyes teared up and her voice quavered as she interrupted, "Yes, Dorothy, I know. We've both been glued to the TV almost all afternoon. How terrible for all of you. Do phone me when you know anything more definite, won't you?" She placed the phone back in its cradle and hurried to tell Roscoe. The next morning she woke early, flicked on a Tchaikowsky tape, and immediately started walking on the treadmill. If only Willy would come again.

The melancholy strains of Tchaikowsky's Symphony Number 6, "Pathetique," still echoed in the back of her mind when she saw him standing outside the Empire State Building, almost as if waiting for her. Wearing sunglasses and with his camera still slung around his neck, he looked like a typical tourist. "Willy! Oh, I'm so glad you're here. I was hoping you'd come."

"Well, we still have an unfinished agenda, haven't we, Ethel? You know I always come when you want to see me." He put his arm around her and hugged her briefly. "I understand your worries about Friedman, but he's okay. I'll fill you in on it all when we get up to the top." He guided her through the door toward the elevators. "This is about the only way we can get any view at all of what remains of the center. Everything is shut down below 14th street." Ascending quickly, the altitude popping Ethel's ears, they arrived at the observation deck in minutes and moved toward the perimeter. They gazed over to where the tall twin towers had once dominated the skyline. The smoke still

swirled upward, but little else could be seen except the jagged edge of the one tower.

"So, there it is. All that remains." *He was uncharacteristically quiet for a moment, just staring out at the scarred landscape. Then he turned back to Ethel.* "Well, I'm sure you've followed all the news reports. The government seems to be on top of things -- to the extent that's possible. And at least we know who did it. What else is puzzling you about this tragedy, Ethel?"

She looked him directly in the eye. "How did I know about the terrorist attack before it actually took place? I mean, how could I possibly have been here in New York and witnessed it all, when I was really just walking on my treadmill back in Madison, Wisconsin?" *His raised eyebrows and almost supercilious smile irritated her.* "Don't do that, Willy! I'm not going to get into another existential debate with you about reality. I can live with some ambiguity, but this is ridiculous! I want to know why this happened to me. I just don't believe that I could be in two places at the same time."

"Oh, come on, Ethel. Don't be angry with me. I'm not patronizing you. I'm simply surprised that after all this time and all the adventures we've had together, you still don't get it. 'Why?' is one of the most over-used questions in the English language. Even I don't know 'why.' Isn't it enough for you to possess this clairvoyance or ESP or whatever it is you have, and to learn from it? Just think of the insights you've gained from the experience you had. My Lord, Ethel, you were an eye-witness to the most horrendous terrorist attack the U.S. has ever faced. Do you have to know why?"

Before she could even respond, he switched the subject. "But you also want to know about Mel Friedman, don't you? He took a nasty fall from the mezzanine all the way down to below the lobby level. But he luckily survived with only a broken arm and a torn shoulder ligament -- at least they think that's all, though there might be some internal injuries too. He's at St. Vincent's Hospital for observation." *After a lingering look toward the smoldering ruins, they joined a crowd waiting for the elevator, but there was only room for one of them.* "Go ahead, Ethel. I'll meet you down below." *When she arrived at the ground floor, Willy had again disappeared.*

103

It was only mid-morning, so Ethel grabbed a cab to St. Vincent's where she hurried toward Mel's room. Thank God he had escaped. He was gazing out the window as she entered. A warm smile flitted across his lips when he saw her. "Ethel, God, it's good to see you. How did you know I was here?"

"Hi, Mel." Avoiding his question, she continued. "It's good to see you, too. I was frantic when I called your office yesterday and Dorothy told me you had been at the Trade Center when it all happened and they hadn't heard from you since the attack. I'm so relieved to know you're okay. Well," as she motioned to his bandaged shoulder and arm in a sling, "at least alive!"

He looked at her quizzically. "But you knew I was going to be at the center, Ethel. We were going to meet there for breakfast. In fact, I've been worried sick about you. After I fell, I lost consciousness for a while, but when I came to I thought I saw you clinging to the door of an elevator a couple of floors above me. Then some guy with gray hair and a camera around his neck was pulling -- or guiding -- you along the ledge next to the wall. But when you went around the corner, I lost sight of you. I gather you made it safely out of all the ruins. Some firemen came along and carried me to an ambulance. I guess we both were some of the lucky ones."

What could she say? She only nodded and breathed a sigh of relief when a nurse entered and suggested that she leave while they took a few more tests. She moved over to the side of his bed and gave him a hug. "I'll call when I can make it out here again,

Mel. We still have to meet about my text."

"You bet -- and lunch will be on me. See you then."

Ethel awoke back in her own bed the next morning. After her walk, she called Mel's office and listened to Dorothy verify what she already knew. Mel was alive and well; he had been taken to St. Vincent's Hospital after his fall at the World Trade Center. "His arm is broken, Ethel, and something's wrong with his shoulder, but they're going to release him this afternoon. You know how soon they dismiss everyone these days."

"Well, tell him I'm flying out to New York early next week to discuss the book. If you can make the appointment for him, I'd like to meet him at his office sometime late Tuesday morning. Then we can have lunch afterwards."

Roscoe looked up from his paper when she entered the family room. "So, who were you talking to so early in the morning?"

"I wanted to find out about Mel. And I'm glad I called. His secretary said he was hurt in the attack at the center -- a broken arm -- but he goes home today." She tentatively added, "I thought I'd fly out there next week. I'd like to see him, and I want to discuss the last revisions of my textbook anyhow. Do you want to come along?"

Roscoe rolled his eyes, but then smiled in resignation. "You just can't wait to see it, can you? Well, if you want to go and face all the security checks at the airport, be my guest. But no, I have no desire to visit New York -- or to see what's left of the towers."

Yes, she did want to go, and not only in her imagination. Willy had shown her that she truly lived in two "realities," and Ethel now knew she could handle the ambiguity of that word. In the fascinating dualism of consciousness and dreams, she might never know what would happen next, but she was sure it would be a grand adventure.

TWO RIDERS IN A WOODS

Ethel stared at the painting with a perplexed frown. The brilliant splotches of color screamed out at her eyes -- flashing reds and lustrous golds which merged into outrageous orange, Bisbee-blue turquoise stripes clashing with deep shades of purple, and dabbles of forest green emanating from the trees in the woods. The horses' flanks reflected the colors of the leaves and sky, shimmering in their velvet coats as they paced slowly into the forest, away from the viewer, but with their heads turned back -- one to the right and one to the left -- as if listening to something. Two Indian squaws sat passively on their backs, only their humped shoulders and the slight shadows of their bowed heads visible.

"Roscoe," she stated with a professorial tone of voice that brooked no opposition, "We simply have to buy that painting! I've never seen such vibrant colors. But it's the picture itself that absolutely intrigues me -- there's an air of mystery about it that I can't fathom. I haven't figured it out yet, but I love it!" She walked back to where the gallery owner was smiling at her enthusiasm. "What did you say it's called?"

"*Two Riders in a Woods.*" She smiled again. "Not terribly elucidating, is it? We don't know if it's early morning or mid-afternoon, we don't know where they've been or where they're going. Actually, we don't know anything about them -- just two riders in a woods." She pulled out a leaflet from behind the counter and handed it to Ethel. "This will tell you something about the artist who painted it. He's an up-and-coming young Apache who moved to Santa Fe from southeastern Arizona. I suppose that's where he became so fond of the Bisbee blue that he uses so much."

"Ethel, the last thing in the world that we need is another work of art," Roscoe complained. "Our walls are already covered with paintings, and our curio cabinet is chock-full of statues and vases and carvings. Where in blazes do you think we're going to hang it? Besides," he added, examining the painting critically, "this kind of Western Indian art hardly fits in with anything else we own and certainly not with our Queen Anne furniture and eighteenth century decor. Now, does it?" Roscoe was not as much opposed to the painting, Ethel knew, as to its cost of $1,500, actually marked down from $1,800. A good buy even at that, she thought, especially if Farrell (Desert Thorn) Webster were as "up-and-coming" as the gallery owner claimed.

"Could you keep it on hold for a couple of hours?" Ethel asked. Then, turning to Roscoe, she replied to his earlier question, "I know exactly where we can put it. We've always said that wall in the hallway next to the stairs needs something -- it's crying for color -- and our 'Two Riders' will be perfect." Ethel cocked her head at him and raised her eyebrows in mock skepticism, "As for 'fitting in,' since when have we had any kind of motif in what we collect? If anything, we own an eclectic hodge-podge of things that have no connection to each other except that we like them. Anyhow," she glanced at her watch, "let's discuss this over lunch. I'm famished."

Roscoe knew from long experience that once she had her mind set, Ethel could be as stubborn as a mule. He decided that he didn't want to spoil their pleasant two-week holiday with an argument. "Oh, let's buy the damn picture," he growled in submission. But to save his dignity, he added to the owner, "I assume you'll throw in the shipping?"

Knowing how to close a good deal when she had one, she nodded her head.

"*Two Riders in a Woods*" arrived at their home beyond the Madison beltway shortly after their own return. Now that it had come, Roscoe was as excited as Ethel, hurriedly cutting away the tape and bubble wrap that enveloped the canvas. "Well, she wrapped it securely enough," he grunted, as he removed the last piece of cardboard and propped the painting up against the back of the sofa for them to admire.

"It's gorgeous!" Ethel exclaimed. "You have to admit it yourself, Roscoe. Now, aren't you glad that you decided to buy it?"

Not unaware of her ploy to suggest that *he* had decided, Roscoe nonetheless nodded his head. "Yeah. I'm glad we bought it. Now, let's see how it fits over there in the hallway where you suggested."

That night before she went to bed, Ethel crept out to the stairway hall and gazed up at her new acquisition. It was different from anything else they owned, she admitted to herself, but it wasn't the Indian theme that made it so. It was the mystery of the subject matter itself that seized her imagination and continued to haunt her as she fell asleep.

The pow-wow lasted until the wee morning hours, and the incessant thumping of the drums kept Winter Rose fretfully awake. The Chiricahua Apache tribal council had decided to continue its struggle against the latest intrusion of Western settlers into their lands and were preparing for a dawn raid on the military fort that only recently been built for settler protection. In 1863, their Navajo brothers had already capitulated to the U.S. forces under Kit Carson, who had captured 8,000 of them and sent them on the "Long Walk" -- their forced deportation on foot to a reservation near Fort Sumner, New Mexico. By 1868, the Apache tribes had also been subdued and placed on reservations -- all but the Chiricahua who continued their attacks under the leadership of their great chief, Cochise. When he too succumbed to the inevitable and signed the treaty of 1872, only one small band of Chiricahua remained. Led by Geronimo, it carried on periodic raids against the settlers for fourteen more years.

Winter Rose knew little about these matters of war and fighting. She only knew that her father and brother were out there now, their faces daubed with paint, dancing the ritual dance of war. That was for men, she thought -- the raids and the hunting. It was enough for the women to gather their water and wood, to tend the fires of their hearth, to bake their corn bread and roast their game. Still, she couldn't help but fear for their safety and for that of Black Crow, her young warrior lover. Although he was pledged to wed her upon his return from the day's battle, she already bore his seed within her body. She brushed her straight black locks away from her face, turned over restlessly, and again sought the solace of sleep.

What a strange dream, Ethel thought, stretching her arms above her head and yawning loudly. Roscoe was already up -- she could smell the coffee. Passing the hall on her way to the kitchen, she stopped in front of the painting, and then paced back and forth, searching for new perspectives, perhaps new insights, into what it meant. She was still lost in thought when Roscoe came up behind her, a coffee cup in each hand.

"Here. Thought we'd both need this to get us through the mail that's piled up." He caught her puzzled frown. "What's the matter? Bad night?"

"No. Not really. I -- I just had such an odd dream last night. And then, while I was standing here, looking at the painting, it suddenly seemed different to me. As if it had changed somehow." She peered up at the canvas again.

Roscoe had lived with Ethel long enough to expect the unexpected, but this was a bit weird, even for her. He stepped back and studied the painting carefully. "Like how?" he asked, glancing sideways at her.

"Well, I don't know exactly. But look at the tops of those shawls -- there, next to the shadows of the two heads." She reached up and pointed.

"Yeah?"

"Doesn't the one look almost golden? As if there's maybe a strand of blonde hair peeping out?"

109

"Blonde hair? On a squaw?" Roscoe looked again and then moved back toward the dining room. "Nah. I think it's just one of those blotches of color he splashed all over the place. It's not meant to portray anything real -- but to convey a feeling, an impression. If anything, this painting is kind of impressionistic."

Ethel usually discounted Roscoe's artistic pronouncements, but there was some validity to this one. The painting was impressionistic. But it also clearly depicted two women on two horses -- and the artist had given one of them blonde hair. Why?

The small advance band of Chiricahua circled the military outpost to the other side and Black Crow cawed the signal that they were in place. As the first ray of sun bounced off the barrel of the sentinel's rifle, Geronimo silently raised his arm for the attack, and the mounted Indians swooped down on the unsuspecting fort. Though the Colonel in charge was a seasoned veteran of the long, chronic warfare with the Navahos, the men under his command were either raw recruits or aging veterans of the Civil War of over thirty years ago. They were ready enough to shoot at the Apaches as they entered the fort on horseback, but neither was prepared for the hand to hand combat that followed. The tomahawk-wielding Indians made short shrift of the entire brigade, with time to spare to collect the scalps of conquest.

Inside the Colonel's quarters, however, they encountered a problem they had not foreseen. The Colonel's daughter was living with him at the fort, while his wife was preparing more suitable lodging for them in the nearby town of Hurley. Geronimo, Black Crow, and his father were the first to arrive, and when they threw open the door to the living quarters, the Colonel's daughter stood defiantly facing them, a shotgun in her arms. As Black Crow lunged toward her, she pulled the trigger and the direct blast to his chest fatally cut him down. Black Crow's father raised his tomahawk to avenge his son's death, but Geronimo stopped him.

Though the Chiricahua had raided several farms and military outposts in the territory of southwestern Arizona, they generally had not engaged in frontal assaults on towns or villages. They carefully sought to avoid major pitched battles with large groups of settlers in which the Apaches' small numbers would put them at a relative disadvantage. "We'll take her with us. If we leave her here, either dead or alive, she will only bear witness to Apache involvement. We don't want all of Hurley following us back." Stopping further protest, he repeated firmly, "We'll take her with us."

And so it was that Melissa Starr arrived at the brush hut wickiup of Winter Rose. "Black Crow has passed over the great divide, and his spirit is no longer with us," his father told her sadly, as he pressed his arm around her shaking shoulders. "This woman is our prisoner. She will stay with you until we decide what to do with her. Give her food and water, and some bedding for the night. But watch her carefully." He did not explain further, nor relate the manner of Black Crow's death. Winter Rose ignored the woman, but nodded dully, comprehending only that her husband to be -- her brave warrior -- was dead. Her only future lay in the tiny embryo within her womb.

"So the Indians are probably Chiricahua?" Ethel asked.

Willy peered at the painting and nodded his head. "It's hard to tell definitely, because of the extravagant use of color, but the basic design of the blankets is that of the Apaches, particularly the Chiricahua." He glanced at Ethel curiously, "Why don't you simply call the artist and ask him?"

"I tried that, but he's the most incommunicative person I've ever spoken to." She frowned in irritation. "He said the painting itself 'materialized' in his mind as he was sketching it, and that the designs almost 'fell into place' of their own accord. He maintains that he did no special research on the Chiricahua, but most of his paintings do focus on the Apaches of Arizona and New Mexico. Besides, the gallery owner told us that he was a Chiricahua Apache himself."

Ethel wasn't sure exactly when or how Willy had arrived. Ever since she met him in that isolation tank several years ago, he had appeared sporadically in her life, usually when she was struggling with some kind of puzzling enigma -- like now. All she knew was that if anyone could solve the mystery of the two riders, Willy could do so.

"What does Roscoe think?" He looked at her innocently, but she could see the twinkle in his guarded glance. Willy never visited Ethel when Roscoe was around. When she had once asked him why, he answered with that wry smile of his, "Because even if I did, he wouldn't believe that I exist."

"Oh, Roscoe won't even admit that the one 'squaw' -- if that's what she is -- has blonde hair. But you can see it, can't you, Willy?"

Willy again turned his attention back to the women on horseback, and nodded. "You may have hit on something there, Ethel -- when you said 'if that's what she is.' I don't think that's a picture of two squaws at all. It's one Indian and a white woman -- or at least a woman with blonde hair." He pondered over his own conclusion, but finally repeated, "Yes, a woman with blonde hair. But what in hell are she and that Indian squaw doing in the woods on those two horses?"

The sun was setting, and as the bright colors of the painting were beginning to fade into the dusk of the hallway, they moved into the living room. When she asked Willy if he'd like a beer, he grinned and replied, "Is the Pope Catholic?" Ethel smiled and walked into the kitchen to fetch it. Returning with a bottle of Coors, a glass, and a bowl of pretzels, she found an empty room. As he so often did, Willy had again disappeared without so much as a word of explanation.

Ethel poured the beer for herself in complete frustration. She had never been patient with riddles, and Willy had come up with no answers to the mystery of the two riders. She was determined to solve it herself -- even if it required another confrontation with the taciturn young artist who had created the painting. She forced herself to relax, and gradually drifted off to her private realm of dreams.

The Council members seated themselves around the fire, speaking only in muted tones, while they waited for Geronimo to begin. As he rose, even the whispers stopped. "Our scouts have seen them gathering in the glen outside of Hurley. Men not only from there, but from all the farms and ranches nearby -- forty or forty-five of them." The Council was well aware that their little band of thirty Chiricahua warriors would be clearly outnumbered. Glancing at Black Crow's father, Geronimo could read his thoughts. "Somehow, they learned that we have the Colonel's daughter. Perhaps we should have left her there at the fort, but that choice is past. Now, we face the battle."

Geronimo divided the warriors into two groups -- twenty braves to ambush the settlers as they approached through the canyon, and the remaining ten to stay behind in the camp, guarding the women and children against any who might survive the ambush. The battle raged, but it lasted no longer than half an hour. Fought fiercely by both sides, the deaths and carnage mounted, but the Indians had the initial advantage of a surprise attack, descending from the hills onto the settlers trapped in the canyon below. As it became evident to the Chiricahua braves that they had not only repelled, but overcome the superior force of the enemy, they began to finish off the few wounded who remained.

Absorbed first in the battle itself and then later in their scalping frenzy, they failed to notice the small group of settlers who had remained at the rear of the action, apart from the main force. Not engaging in the general battle, this group of five men had zeroed in on Geronimo, separated him from the other braves, and surrounded him with their horses. One of them managed to land a forceful blow on his head, and as he reeled from the impact, they grabbed the reins of his horse and led him captive from the field. As they disappeared beyond the hills, the few Apaches who saw them regarded them as defeated cowards, seeking to save their own skins; they failed to see Geronimo in their midst. By the time the victorious Apaches had scavenged the canyon for the prizes of battle, the five survivors were well on their way back to Hurley with the greatest prize of all -- Geronimo.

It was not until they returned to the camp when the Apaches finally comprehended what had happened. The Council gathered once again to decide what to do, but only Black Crow's father had an answer. "We must send the woman back. Yes, we have won the battle, but at what price? We must offer to trade the Colonel's daughter for the release of Geronimo. Winter Rose can ride with her to Hurley with our offer. Our braves will follow them to ensure his return."

Willy arrived the next morning with a bouquet of bright yellow roses to apologize for his abrupt departure the previous evening. They were "winter roses," he ad libbed, after Ethel told him her dream about the Colonel's captured daughter and her horseback journey with Winter Rose back to Hurley.

"After I left you yesterday, I got to thinking about that painting, Ethel, and it seemed to me that the artist was trying to depict a story -- or perhaps a segment of a story. Now that you've told me your dream, I believe that he was painting the very story you've just related. Now, I don't know where he heard it or how he dreamed it up, but I don't think you're going to be satisfied until you confront him directly and find out." As always, Ethel followed Willy's advice.

"I know what you said, Mr. Webster -- or do you prefer being called Desert Thorn? I know that you said the painting 'materialized' out of nothing and that the design fell into place without any forethought on your part. It's simply that I don't believe you." In the silence that followed, Ethel feared that he might hang up on her without further ado; she listened for the click of a severed connection, but there was nothing. She then tried the tactic that Willy had recommended.

"Look, I'm not prying out of idle curiosity. We bought the painting because we loved it from the first moment we saw it. The colors alone are overwhelming. But the story it portrays is also overwhelming. If you are reluctant to tell it, let me." Then Ethel recounted the essence of her dreams: the killing of Black Crow, the abduction of Melissa Starr, the capture of Geronimo, and the proposed trade-off between them. "What I don't know is what happened then? Did the settlers trade Geronimo for the Colonel's daughter? And what happened to Winter Rose? Did she return safely to the camp?"

His voice struck her as hollow and far off. It sounded as if he were speaking from a great distance -- almost from a different place and time. "I don't know how you came to know this story, Mrs. Matson, for it is a tribal legend which has been passed down by word of mouth from one generation of Chiricahua to the next. It is written nowhere. But if you searched the graveyard at Hurley, as I have, you would find the grave of a Melissa Starr Babcock who died in 1919 at the age of sixty; she is buried next to her husband, Steven Babcock. In 1877 she was traded for the great Geronimo who continued his struggle against the American settlers for another nine years when he was finally hunted down by U.S. military troops and confined to a reservation in Oklahoma."

The voice stopped, and again Ethel thought that he had hung up. To urge a response, she asked, "And Winter Rose?"

He sighed deeply, and then continued, "Yes, Winter Rose survived and returned to the Chiricahua camp. The following spring, she bore Black Crow's child -- Black Thorn -- a sturdy boy who unfortunately, unlike his father, would never experience the free life of his forebears in the unfettered spaces of the Chiricahua mountains."

A long pause, but when he continued his voice was stronger, less hollow. "Black Thorn was my great, great, great grandfather. He and his progeny, my ancestors, were relegated to farming or ranching on the reservations of Arizona and New Mexico, where many of them continue that life today. Some of us, however, left the reservations and found our own paths in other places and in other trades. Fortunately, I found mine in painting. Strangely enough, *"Two Riders in a Woods"* is my only effort to illustrate our tribal legend. I'm glad you were intrigued by its symbolism -- the uncertainty of the journey ahead, with even the horses looking back for reassurance as they plodded on."

As she drifted off to sleep that night, Ethel thought about that symbolism. Up until Webster mentioned it, she hadn't really regarded the painting as symbolic of anything. To her, as to Roscoe, it was an impressionistic portrait of two riders in a woods. She had wanted to know the story behind it, but she had never ventured to delve any more deeply into its abstract meaning. Yet, the artist had touched upon something that went beyond the picture itself -- it *was* symbolic. In a subtle but vibrant way, it portrayed our human determination to strive on toward the future, despite the uncertainty of the journey ahead, but with part of us always looking back -- back toward the comfort and security of the past. Ethel couldn't wait to tell Willy. That night her dream was short, but sweet.

As the mid-wife placed the baby in her arms, Winter Rose wiped away the tears of her pain, hugged him close against her breasts, and lovingly smoothed his wet black hair. You are your father's son, she thought, and she named him Black Thorn -- the son of Black Crow. But he was also the son of Winter Rose, a thorn in her life alone. He would be the sire of many generations, and in the years to come his children and his children's children would sit around the campfire and tell the tale of how Winter Rose had carried him within her as she rode to save Geronimo, their great leader, from his captors.

Though cuddled in the warmth of her womb, Black Thorn had been aware of the slow movement of the horses as they carried his mother and the white woman on their fateful journey. He also heard the cheering of the braves when they saw Geronimo riding back with her, back to the safety of the camp. Yes, his father had been a brave warrior, but his mother had also earned the title "brave." She had saved the man who would lead the Chiricahua in the years ahead as they struggled to defend their lands and retain their own way of life. Even though in the end he would fail, it would be a noble effort.

RED ALERT

"Want to see the news?" Roscoe called to her from downstairs. Ethel glanced at her watch, put the computer in sleep mode, and nudged Eskimo to wake up. Crippled by his arthritis, the chunky dog reluctantly rose from the warmed carpet by her feet and lumbered after her from the library/den down to the family room. Ethel seldom watched TV during the day, but when she did she tuned into CNN. In the evening, though, they both preferred Mitch Connors at ABC for the world news roundup. Roscoe liked Connors' urbane mode of delivery, and Ethel was taken by his caustic comments on the international political scene which, she felt, were usually right on target.

Tonight he was again discussing the Israeli-built security wall which divided the West Bank between the Palestinians and the Israeli settlements which had encroached upon them. The Palestinians' claim for all of the West Bank went back to the 1976 war when Israel had wrested the territory from them. Though international law condemned the forceful acquisition of territory by warfare and the UN had adopted several resolutions calling for the return of the land to Palestinian authority, Israel had not budged, especially under the hard-line stance of Ariel Sharon. The newly-elected Labor Prime Minister, David Schur, was more amenable to a negotiated settlement, but he too had to avoid at all costs the appearance of bowing to the suicidal terrorism of the extreme wing of Hamas.

"So the wall still stands, both as a physical barrier and as a symbolic token of the deep divisions which exist between these two peoples." Connors turned to the map beside him and traced the snaky line that wriggled around to include the settlements in the Israeli occupied territory. "At the May meeting of the Quartet scheduled for next week, the focus of discussion will be this very wall. Both the UN and the European Union have taken the position that parts of the wall must be dismantled. Russia and the United States have not given advance notice of their policies." He paused and pointedly added, "Although it is assumed that the US will be more accommodating to the position of Israel -- as usual."

"Oh, brother," exclaimed Ethel. "I didn't expect that -- not even from Connors. He's straying pretty darn close to the shady edges of what's accepted – or not accepted --as *politically correct*. I don't think ABC's sponsors will be very happy with that remark. Why, ..." At that moment all hell broke loose on the set of "World News Roundup." Three muffled shots reverberated from the baffling of the studio walls as Mitch Connors grabbed at his chest, the red blood spurting through his fingers. A surprised expression flitted across his face just before he slumped forward in his seat, his head hitting the table in front of him. Screams echoed from off the set and the camera went wild, recording flashing scenes from all over the studio. It then focused on two hooded men who were waving pistols at the cameraman --- just before the screen went blank.

"My God, they shot Mitch Connors!" Roscoe cried.

Ethel grabbed the remote and flipped the channel. With beads of sweat standing out on his forehead, Robert Edwards on Channel 6 was white-lipped and teary-eyed as he reported, "We have no further news at this time. For those of you who have just joined CBS, a terrorist attack has taken place within ABC studios -- on the set. Anchor man Mitch Connors and a cameraman have been shot. Initial reports indicate that Connors' wounds might have been fatal, but we can't confirm that at this time. Security guards shot and killed the two unidentified armed men who initiated the attack, but the police who have now arrived on the scene have reported that a note found on one of the bodies implicates them as members of a

U.S. "sleeper group" of Al Qaida. CBS has sent a camera crew over to ABC and will report to us live as soon as they arrive there and are admitted."

As Edwards faded off camera and a scheduled ad appeared on the screen, Ethel switched back to ABC. Still blank -- with a voice overlay saying, "This is a temporary shut-down only. ABC news will continue momentarily. Please stay tuned." She flipped again, this time to CNN: "... and the police have cordoned off the entire area. The two gunmen have been killed, but it is believed that three others were involved in this attack." A crying woman handed the announcer a slip of paper. He read, "General Hospital has verified that Mitch Connors was dead on arrival at the emergency room."

Ethel switched off the TV and walked over to the small wet bar in the corner of the room. "I'm having a Scotch. How about you?" Roscoe nodded and she poured him his usual martini on the rocks. Wisconsin's May had not yet brought any spring warmth to Madison, and Roscoe turned on the gas fireplace. They both settled down across from the blackened TV and stared at the empty screen.

Ethel was the first to speak. "I suppose we should have expected something -- it's been over three years since 9/11, with no major terrorist attacks in this country. Oh, we had the Madrid train bombing and those attacks on the Saudi government buildings, but nothing over here." She rubbed her chin in the quaint professorial gesture she often used when thinking aloud. "Of course, we've all been saturated with the violence and suicide attacks in Iraq and in the Israeli-Palestinian conflict. We've had enough violence to last us a lifetime. But, still, we might have expected something over here. Something big."

"Didn't you even speculate once about some sort of attack on the media?" Roscoe asked. "It seems to me that one night when you had some of your students over, you tried to stretch their thinking as to what would really grab the attention of the media. And then you mentioned that an actual televised attack on a TV personality would do it." As she nodded her head ruefully, he added, "Of course, no one could have predicted that some group might really do that. It's not as if you were writing their script for them."

"No," she smiled. "I wasn't writing any script. Still, I wonder if I ever mentioned it in DC at any of those meetings of the NABIT that I went to. I just don't remember." The NABIT was the National Advisory Board on International Terrorism, a non-governmental advisory group made up of academics, former intelligence operatives, retired Foreign Service Officers, and a few current members of the central intelligence community. As an advisor to the State Department's Bureau of Intelligence and Research, Ethel had also been appointed to the NABIT. She paused before going on. "But now that it happened, it seems so obvious, doesn't it? I mean, you already have the attention of millions of people -- I don't know what the viewership for ABC is, but it must be in the millions. Everyone watching an actual terrorist event taking place right there on their television screens. See it from the comfort of your own home!"

Another pause. "But what I don't quite understand is why Al Qaida targeted Mitch Connors? Of all the U.S. commentators, he's probably the most sympathetic -- well, not sympathetic, but fair -- in his reporting on terrorism. Y'know?"

That next morning, while Roscoe poured over the extensive newspaper coverage of the ABC terrorist attack, Ethel took Eskimo for his morning outing. As she had half expected, Willy was waiting for her in Wingra Park, sitting on his favorite bench and feeding the squirrels from a bag half full of peanuts. Willy always appeared at those junctures in her life when something dramatic or puzzling had happened or was about to happen. She had first met him when she ventured into the isolated atmosphere of a sensory deprivation tank, but after that, his visits occurred both in her dreams and in day-time reality -- although Willy didn't like to distinguish between the two.

"I thought you might be here, Willy." She smiled as she settled down beside him, holding the dog's leash in anticipation of any surprise attack on the unsuspecting squirrels. "Roscoe and I were watching ABC when it happened. What do you make of it all?"

Combing his fingers through his rumpled shock of white hair, Willy shook his head in a gesture of bewilderment, sorrow, or anger -- or a combination of all three. "I don't know what to make of it yet, Ethel. Obviously, another major set-back to our intelligence gathering and clearly designed to shake us from our complacency. But why Connors? If it was Al Qaida, why strike at the one national newsman who's had a reasonably balanced approach to covering terrorism, particularly regarding the Israeli-Palestinian conflict?" He raised his shaggy eyebrows as he looked quizzically at her. "What about you? After all, you're the academic expert on this stuff, not me." He never missed the opportunity to poke a little fun at the consulting Ethel occasionally did for the State Department.

"I wondered about the same thing, Willy. I mean, why Connors? But why did you say if it was Al Qaida? CBS reported that a note found on the body of one of the terrorists clearly implicated Al Qaida. Maybe they'll find out more when they capture the other three who supposedly were involved. I imagine the local police have brought in the FBI by now, and hopefully they're including the CIA -- that is, if we learned anything from 9/11."

Willy didn't immediately respond. In his usual fashion, he had narrowed down his initial question about what she thought of the attack in general, to the specific problem she too had identified: Why Mitch Connors? And then he had introduced that intriguing "if" -- if it was Al Qaida, he had ventured. But if not Al Qaida, who?

Ethel was silently pondering this, when Willy returned to the last thread of their conversation. "Have you ever heard of Metsada?"

She had heard it mentioned by one of her colleagues at the State Department's Bureau of Intelligence and Research as part of Israel's intelligence organization, but its exact fit eluded her. "Isn't it connected with Shin Bet?"

"No, no." Willy shook his head again, this time almost impatiently. Shin Bet is the Israeli's General Secret Service -- their domestic intelligence service. They sometimes refer to it as Shabak. But Metsada is the clandestine operations command of Mossad, the Israeli secret service that operates overseas. It's kind of like the Operations Directorate of the CIA -- you know, the dirty tricks people."

"Okay. So?"

"Well, ever since Prime Minister Sharon appointed the new director of Mossad, there's been a huge increase in its budget. But more important, since 9/11 Israel has started to take a much more aggressive approach to the war on terrorism -- including the staging of targeted killings overseas, probably by Metsada. When Sharon first came into office he didn't support those killings, but since about 2002/2003 he's changed his stance to allow what they now call "preventive operations." The U.S. emphasis on our own war on terrorism as a primary focus of our foreign policy and the Bush adoption of "pre-emptive warfare" have encouraged the Israelis to move in the same direction."

"But when you talk about targeted killings overseas, Willy, surely you don't include the United States, do you?"

Willy shrugged. "Something to think about, Ethel, something to think about." And then, before she could reply, he was gone.

In response to the ABC terrorist attack in May, the fall meeting of the National Advisory Board on International Terrorism had been moved up to June. Meeting in one of the large conference rooms of the Old Executive Office Building, it was chaired by the Deputy Director of CIA, Brent McDonald. Contrary to her usual punctuality, Ethel was the last to arrive. Slightly disoriented, she nodded at her colleagues around the table and quickly glanced at the agenda as McDonald began.

After a half-hour briefing, he concluded. "So, that's the long and short of it," he summarized. "The security people at ABC somehow failed to prevent the three accomplices from leaving the building, and neither the local police nor the FBI contingent assigned to the case has been able to trace them. Despite the note they found which implicated Al Qaida, Bin Laden himself has now denied that they were responsible -- but we're discounting that. As for our own response, although we had advance rumblings of a 'major terrorist attack' impending, there was nothing specific enough to go on in terms of preventive security measures -- kind of like what the intelligence community faced prior to 9/11."

He glanced around the long oval table at the group assembled. "As you know, the President has put the country on red alert. We'll discuss possible targets tomorrow. But what we want from you now is whatever creative ideas you might have on why Al Qaida attacked ABC -- and especially Mitch Connors."

Abe Zablonski, a former CIA operative, led off. "Well, we all know that one of the intermediate goals of all terrorist organizations is media exposure -- the more, the better. Not only does such publicity 'terrorize' a larger number of people than the immediate target, but it also helps to magnify the size and strength of the terrorist group, many of whom are actually quite small. What better way to insure complete media coverage and a direct and unforgettable impact than to commit the act on live TV in front of millions of viewers?" They all nodded in agreement.

"Yes, the tactic was ingenious in that regard -- just like the bombing of the World Trade Center," McDonald agreed. "It's surprising now, in retrospect, that none of us ever thought of it. In previous meetings we talked about biological and chemical terrorism -- even nuclear -- but as far as I can remember, none of us ever mentioned the possibility of using an airplane as an armed projectile or committing an assassination on live TV."

Ethel squirmed uncomfortably in her chair. Roscoe was right. She had raised the possibility of a terrorist attack against the media in her class on international terrorism -- to a bunch of kids! Why hadn't she ever mentioned it to this group where it might have had some impact on official thinking? And even if everyone had rejected the idea as too far-fetched, at least she could now feel that she had made the effort. "I'll never make that mistake again," she vowed to herself.

At that moment, Phil Porter, an INR colleague of hers, indirectly raised the "if it was Al Qaida" question that Willy had plagued her with in the park: "I can understand Al Qaida targeting the media, but why Connors? He's been labeled a Palestinian sympathizer by the Israelis and, although he condemned Al Qaida and Osama Bin Laden for 9/11, he never demonized them. In fact, he always tried to put their struggle into some kind of political perspective. And now Osama himself has denied responsibility. If that note indicating Al Qaida involvement *hadn't been found, we never would have thought of them as the obvious perpetrators, would we?"*

Zablonski didn't buy it. "Yeah? Why not? Al Qaida didn't have anything against anyone in particular at the Trade Center either, did they? They declared this war on the U.S. as a nation, and they're going to fight it wherever and whenever they get the chance. I don't give a hell of a lot of credence to Osama's denial. If it wasn't Al Qaida, who was it?" A pregnant pause, while heads nodded in agreement and shoulders shrugged.

Then, breaking the silence, Ethel spoke up. Armed with her new resolution, she spoke quietly but firmly. "What about Metsada?" They all stared at her as if she had suddenly gone out of her mind.

Calmly and with her most serious professorial air, Ethel continued. "Now, I know this isn't politically correct, but since we're all bound to secrecy concerning what goes on here, I'd like us to do some thinking outside the box. We all know that the Israelis have embarked on a more aggressive policy toward terrorism -- not only in Israel and Palestine, but elsewhere, as well. We also know that Metsada is their chosen instrument for overseas assassinations. Finally, we know that Mitch Connors has been a thorn in their side for years. What could be more appealing to them than to silence him and then blame it on Al Qaida -- all in one single act?" This time, the silence was unbroken.

Phil Porter and Ethel left the meeting together on their way to brief the Assistant Secretary for Intelligence and Research and his three Deputy Assistant Secretaries on the NABIT discussions they had just had. As they strolled down the mall toward the State Department, Phil chuckled, "Well, you sure as hell woke everyone up with that bombshell, Ethel. Whatever gave you the bizarre idea that Israeli intelligence might have been involved?"

"But it makes sense, doesn't it, Phil?" Ethel countered, not about to damage her credibility even further by mentioning her imaginary friend, Willy. No one at the meeting had responded to her unorthodox analysis, and after a few concluding remarks, the chairman had ended the session and suggested that they all meet again for a wrap-up the next morning. "I know it's the mode these days to blame Al Qaida for every act of terrorism anywhere in the world, and usually they're more than

willing to claim credit for whatever they've done. But this time they were quick to deny any involvement whatsoever. That note found on the one body -- whatever it said -- could have been a Metsada subterfuge. If the assassins had escaped, they could have planted it somewhere else in the studio. Unfortunately for them, they didn't get that chance."

"I don't know, Ethel. It's just so damn far-fetched. Hell, Israel is our closest ally in the Middle East; we pour billions into their economy every year, not to mention the weaponry we provide. Do you really believe that they would undertake clandestine terrorist operations against us -- right here in America?"

"What I'm saying is that we should at least keep our minds open to that possibility. To the Israelis, their struggle with the Palestinians is a life and death matter. Anyone who assists the Palestinians or challenges what Israel regards as necessary measures for its self defense is an enemy. We might not have considered Mitch Connors as a threat to Israeli security, but I can see how the gung ho leadership of Metsada might have. So -- what's more rational than to eliminate that threat by a highly publicized act of terrorism and at the same time to blame that act on America's number one terrorist bane -- Al Qaida?"

Phil frowned and pursed his lips as he pondered her argument. But he didn't refute it. He took her arm protectively as they approached some construction along Constitution Avenue. "Always some damn road repairs," he complained, trying to guide both them and their conversation onto safer ground.

But Ethel wasn't going to be diverted. "What bothers me is the absolute refusal of the NABIT members to even envisage the possibility that it might not be Al Qaida, but perhaps, just perhaps, the clandestine work of Metsada -- or terrorists hired by Metsada."

Phil smiled wryly. "What bothers me even more, Ethel, is whether any of those NABIT members are buddy-buddy with anyone in the Mossad. Your suspicions would not be music to their ears, you know. I hope they can all keep their mouths shut."

"Well, I hope that Brent McDonald will at least include my theory in his final report to the powers that be in the intelligence community. I'll be sure to raise it when we talk to the INR brass, but it would be comforting to know that someone in the agency might give it some attention, too."

Arriving at the 21st Street entrance of the State Department, they dutifully got out their security identification tags and entered.

The next morning Ethel awoke back in her own bed in Madison, Wisconsin. She smelled the coffee all the way from the downstairs kitchen and glanced at her watch; it was already eight o'clock. Roscoe had probably been up since seven. Ethel tried to think through the events of the preceding day, or, as she was beginning to realize, the events of her night-time dream. But it seemed so real -- so completely believable. Of course, that was what Willy always told her: your dreams carry as much reality as your day-time life. You just have to interpret them in a different way. She jumped from bed and hastily put on some slacks and a cotton shirt. She had to find Willy!

"Hi, honey. Where are you dashing off to?" Roscoe looked up from the morning paper as she grabbed a portable cup of coffee to take with her to the park. Eskimo was already at the door, his tail wagging.

"I've got some ideas I've got to think through before the NABIT meeting next week. They moved it up to June, you know." That part of the dream was true -- she had received the notification from Brent McDonald in late May. But there had been no meeting yesterday, and she had been right here in Madison all day long. She blew a kiss to Roscoe as she and Eskimo bolted out the door.

When they reached the park, Willy was nowhere to be seen. There were two young girls taking turns at pushing a baby buggy along the winding path and an old priest sitting alone on a bench by the lake. As Eskimo dashed up to him, he turned toward Ethel and she recognized Willy. "Now what?" she asked, sitting down beside him while he patted Eskimo on the head. "What's with the priestly garb, Willy?" She scrutinized him with a critical eye. "I think I liked you better as a monk

-- when we visited the Potala Palace in Tibet. You somehow don't look like the father confessor type."

Willy sat back and cocked his head at her in his inscrutable Willy fashion. *"Ah, but that's just it, Ethel. If I'm going to play the father confessor role, I have to look the part. And I know you're about to confess your brilliant theory that you outlined to the NABIT yesterday afternoon."*

"But that was a dream, Willy. A realistic one, I'll admit, but still just a dream."

"Ah, was it?"

"Well, I know for certain that I was here in town yesterday and not in Washington, D.C. -- not at the NABIT and not at the State Department."

"All right, Ethel. Let's not quibble over existential reality again. Let's assume that it was a dream. But, as you now know, dreams have their own reality -- and their own lessons to teach. What lessons did you learn from your meeting?"

This was what Ethel had been waiting for. She had her own theory about all that had happened (or all that she had dreamed), but she needed to bounce it off of Willy. Much as Roscoe admired her professorial career and her professional consultations in Washington, he was less enamored about some of her esoteric thinking and philosophical essays she occasionally dabbled in. No, she couldn't turn to Roscoe for any advice about her dream lessons. In contrast, she knew that Willy thrived in the nether world of her imagination and would be a worthy recipient of her confession. His black vestment and clerical collar seemed rather comforting, after all.

"Well, I think I learned three things, Willy. First of all, the more I heard from McDonald and the others, the more I came to doubt that Al Qaida murdered Mitch Connors. It was all too much a matter of dogma with them, too much reliance on that one, single, implicating note. And then there was Bin Laden's own denial which supported my doubts. Secondly, the more I thought about the logic of Metsada's involvement, which..." she smiled and patted Willy on the shoulder, *"which you suggested in the first place, the more sense it made -- despite the incredulity that all those NABIT experts expressed."* She paused. *"What do you think?"*

Willy was smiling at her now, but not yet ready to respond. "You said you learned three lessons. What was the third?"

Ethel smiled back. "The third is the most important lesson of all: to keep my mouth shut!" Willy's bushy eyebrows rose up in surprise. "When I suggested that Metsada agents might have been the terrorists behind the Connors murder, I did it as a sort of atonement for not having ever raised the possibility of a terrorist attack directly on the media -- even though I had thought of such a possibility and even discussed it with my class. I regretted my silence and vowed not to repeat it. But I chose the wrong time and the wrong place to publicize my theory -- our theory -- about Metsada. I never should have voiced those suspicions so openly in such a large group. And when I actually do meet with the NABIT next week, I won't repeat that mistake."

Willy's smile had turned to a frown. "But surely, Ethel, you're going to discuss these ideas with someone. Aren't you?"

"Yes -- of course. When I get back home I plan to phone Brent McDonald and ask for a private session with him sometime before or after the advisory group meeting. I'm also going to call Phil Porter and ask him to set up a meeting with Mel Gilbert, the INR Assistant Secretary. In both cases, I'll set forth my suspicions and the reasons for them as best I can. What they do with it all, though, is up to them."

Willy stood and stretched. "Bravo! Quite a confession, Ethel. And I absolve you of one of the greatest sins of all: not knowing what you can do, and not knowing what you can't do. It's pretty damn hard to figure it out sometimes, but in this case I think you've got it right. Do your best to make your case, but let the decision-makers make the final decisions. What the hell, Ethel -- that's what they're paid for." He put his arm around her shoulder, grinned, and gave her a big hug.

Feeling a tug on her wrist, Ethel walked over to untangle Eskimo's leash from a nearby bush. When she turned back to say goodbye, Willy was already gone. He always did that, she thought, shaking her head. She wondered why.

FORTUNE COOKIES

Ethel grabbed her coffee cup off the tray as the plane again lurched downward from its cruising altitude. Her empty paper plate flew into the aisle, but her fortune cookie fell on her lap. "Well, at least I finished that taco salad before this rough weather hit us." Roscoe was less fortunate; his coffee spilled across his plate and tray and was dripping onto his trousers. He dabbed at it with his napkin, but the damage was done.

Shaking her head, Ethel handed him her napkin. "Here, use this one, too. You might as well forget about your salad. Most of it landed on the floor." Both of them had ordered the airline's "international cuisine delight" as their noon snack, but the odd combination of a taco salad and fortune cookie as *international* failed to impress Ethel.

When the pilot managed to maneuver the plane up above the storm, two of the stewardesses scurried down the aisle, picking up the debris and throwing it into huge plastic bags. "Oh, would you hand me that fortune cookie?" Roscoe pointed to the floor.. "It's all wrapped, so it should be okay." He turned to Ethel, "You have yours?"

She nodded as she crunched on part of her cookie and removed the fortune from the other half. "Hey, listen to this: 'Your journey may lead you astray. Take advice from an old friend.' Hmm. I don't like the sound of that. What's yours?"

"Strange one: 'Some mysteries are never solved.' Weird." He shook his head as he glanced around at the filled seats. "Boy, they sure like to pack 'em in, don't they?"

"Well, these cheapie tour flights are always pretty full. What with the crowded planes, the tight seats, and the lousy food snacks, 'getting there' is not half the fun!"

Just then the plane suddenly dropped about two feet -- napkins, plastic glasses, and paper plates again went flying through the aisles. Having started its descent toward Miami, it had re-entered the storm on its way down. Then it veered to the north-east, pulled up slightly, and held steady at the new altitude. The pilot's voice came over the intercom. "We've just passed through a zone of turbulence, folks. Nothing to worry about. But it does extend all the way down to Miami where all in-coming flights are being consigned to a holding pattern over the city. Our gas is down and we've been re-routed directly to Bermuda. Those of you taking the Bermuda cruise can board your ship there; the others will have to wait while we re-fuel before heading for Miami."

Knowing her fear of bumpy plane rides, Roscoe grinned at Ethel as he took her hand in his. "Well, that's a stroke of good luck. We don't have to take a separate flight to Bermuda and our cruise ship will pick us up right there."

But as they began their final descent, the turbulence returned -- with a vengeance. As the plane careened violently back and forth and then plummeted headlong toward the water, Ethel could sense a sickening fear permeating the cabin, not alleviated by the pilot's message. "Everyone fasten your seatbelts -- immediately! Follow the emergency directions for a crash landing. Crew members take your assigned seats." The plane hit the water with a deafening thud. Ethel blacked out.

Ethel gently touched her head and smiled gratefully at Willy as he wrung out his handkerchief and held it against the slight bump on her forehead. Her consciousness was gradually returning. Only the two of them were afloat in the small lifeboat. "Where's Roscoe, Willy?" She scanned the empty horizon and saw nothing except their plane bobbing on the waves. Then the panic grabbed her. "Where is Roscoe?"

"He's okay, Ethel. He's okay. He was searching for you when he climbed out of the other side of the plane, but one of the stewards had carried you out on this side where he couldn't see you. They pulled him into a motorized lifeboat and took off toward shore -- at least toward where they must think the shore is. But we don't have a motor and I decided to wait here near the plane where any rescue boat might have a better chance of finding us." He glanced over at the plane. "Even though it's sinking fast."

Ethel knew better than to ask Willy how he had gotten there. It was just another one of his strange appearances in her life.

"But where on earth are we, Willy? All I remember is the plane diving down toward the water and the captain telling us to prepare for a crash landing. Then I must have fainted -- or maybe lost consciousness when I hit my head. I suppose we're between Miami and Bermuda somewhere." She again scanned the horizon. "But where?"

"If I have it figured right, Ethel, we're right smack in the middle of the Bermuda Triangle." He took off his navy blue captain's hat (Willy always dressed for whatever adventure he embarked upon) and pushed his fingers through his thick white hair, scratching his scalp along the way. "Yes, that's it -- the Bermuda Triangle."

"The Bermuda Triangle?" She put her fingers to her forehead, but winced. "You mean where all those ships and planes have disappeared?"

"That's it. The area between Miami, Bermuda, and San Juan, Puerto Rico. And you're also right about "all" those ships and planes. Over 2,000 ships and boats and some 75 aircraft have been reported missing or lost in these waters." Willy shaded his eyes to peer toward the horizon where he pointed out to Ethel the indistinct outline of a distant ship. "Our rescue may be on the way, Ethel. It's heading in this direction."

The U.S.S. Cyclops picked them up in the late afternoon of March 7, 2008. Their rescuers told them that it was headed for Baltimore; it had left Barbados a few days before and was loaded with manganese ore. They were ushered into the quarters of the captain, George W. Worley, who was clearly proud of the 522 foot collier which he commanded. "It will give those Germans a run for their money," he boasted. It was only days later when they understood his meaning.

Captain Worley seemed suspicious about their account of their plane crash, particularly since the plane had sunk by the time the Cyclops arrived on the scene. He also questioned them closely about their planned cruise of the Caribbean which they said they were going to take out of Bermuda. "How you can possibly take a vacation cruise in wartime is beyond me," he criticized. "Or that the cruise people are even offering one."

Though mainly grateful for their deliverance, Ethel and Willy soon began to wonder about the Captain's sanity. "What Germans?" Ethel repeated to Willy when they were by themselves. "What wartime?"

Willy tried to engage the other officers in conversation, but they took their cue from the Captain and said little. "I don't know what's going on here, Ethel, but we seem to be in some kind of time warp. This ship should have been retired years ago; I'd figure it was probably built in the early 1900s. And everyone is doing everything by rote, as if they've done it hundreds of times. Captain Worley himself is at worst demented or at best simply weird. You remember your fortune cookie? Well, your journey has already 'gone astray,' so here's the advice of an old friend: Get off this ship just as soon as you can!"

After a lot of cajoling and some monetary inducement, however, Worley did agree to drop them off in Bermuda where they arrived early the following morning. "I can't bring the Cyclops any closer into shore and we don't have time to wait for a tender, so we'll have to send you in your own lifeboat" The few vacationers on the beach where they landed took little note of them, and after Willy escorted Ethel to the dock where her cruise ship awaited, he quickly took his leave. But his parting words were: "If I were you, Ethel, I'd say as little about your rescue as you can. Meanwhile, I'm going to do a little research of my own on the U.S.S. Cyclops. Perhaps I'll see you later on the cruise."

"My God, am I glad to see you, Ethel!" Roscoe held her tightly in his arms and kissed the bump which had turned to a light purple bruise on her forehead. "As soon as we arrived here in Bermuda, we contacted the authorities and they dispatched two small motor boats out toward where the airliner went down; they also sent a helicopter to survey the whole area, but they found nothing. Evidently, our plane sank quite fast, so it was difficult to find exactly where it went down. A few other lifeboats made it in to shore -- but not with you." He hugged her again. "What happened? How did you get here?"

She remembered Willy's advice. "Oh, I worried about you, too, Roscoe! I was frantic. But I did hope, and pray, that you found a lifeboat. I think what happened is that we somehow got out on opposite sides of the plane and couldn't see each other. I was unconscious for some time, and I think that someone must have pulled me out of the plane and placed me in a small lifeboat. Then I drifted for a long time -- again, I must have slipped off in sleep -- until I saw this ship on the horizon. I yelled, but of course they couldn't hear me. Somehow, they must have seen the boat, though, because they picked me up and brought me here -- where I belong." She cuddled in his arms. "But I don't remember the name of the ship."

"Well, the cruise will go as planned except for a few days' delay. They're still missing a few passengers, but they're hopeful of finding more lifeboats or even some individuals with life vests. What seems to be a mystery is why our plane sank so quickly. They'll probably also want to identify the ship that rescued you. You sure you can't think of its name?" Ethel shook her head in what she hoped would be her last little white lie.

"Hi, Ethel." The unruly shock of white hair framed a familiar face that was beginning to redden with sunburn. Willy sat down on the deck chair next to her. "Were you able to keep all the curiosity seekers at bay? Or did you enlighten them with the name of the Cyclops?"

"You told me not to say too much, so I was the soul of secrecy." She laughed aloud, "Besides, there's not too much I could tell them. Besides the name, I mean." She raised her eyebrow and tilted her head. "So, what was the deal?"

Willy relished his role as professor -- particularly when he was able to explain something to Professor Ethel Matson. He grinned with anticipation. "Well, first of all, you have to remember where we were: in the Bermuda Triangle where a couple thousand ships and boats and a large number of planes as well have 'disappeared' or have been reported 'lost' or 'missing.' The U.S.S. Cyclops was one of those. It vanished with its 309 crew members in the area of the Bermuda Triangle in early March, 1918. It had sailed from Rio de Janeiro in mid-February loaded with manganese ore, docked in Barbados on March 3rd, and then left Barbados for Baltimore on March 4th. It was due to arrive in Baltimore on March 13th. It never did."

"But Willy ---"*He raised his hand to silence her.* "Hear me out, Ethel. Yes, we saw it in early March, 2008 -- ninety years later. But do you remember how I mentioned that the officers and crew seemed to be almost in a trance, performing their work as if by rote? That's because the Cyclops has made that same voyage at least every year for ninety years!"

Ethel interrupted. "And that explains Captain Morley's references to the Germans. He thought he was still in the middle of World War I!" *She pursed her lips and frowned.* "But what really happened to the Cyclops? It couldn't have just disappeared into thin air."

"That's exactly what the historians have been trying to figure out ever since. All attempts to locate any wreck or remains of the Cyclops have been in vain. One theory is that it was sunk by a German sub, but according to German records, no submarines were stationed in that area at that time; nor did the Cyclops ever send out an SOS. Some naval experts have argued that it perhaps capsized or simply broke apart in heavy seas, but if that were so -- Where is the wreck? Where is the evidence?"

Ethel shook her head in frustration and doubt. "But we saw *that* ship, Willy! We met the Captain, the officers, the crew. Was that just another dream? Something I dredged up from my imagination because of that blow on my head? Or was Hamlet right? Maybe there are more things in heaven and earth than are dreamed of in our philosophy?" Maybe Roscoe's fortune cookie was right: "Some mysteries are never solved!" *Willy smiled his enigmatic smile -- but he didn't answer.*

ONE MISTY, MOISTY MORNING

The wind had picked up since she left the old Dunster Hotel, and it blew sharp bits of icy mist against her face. The sky was leaden, with no portent of relief. Ethel pulled her jacket shut and buttoned it up tightly to her chin. The snow was falling heavier now and beginning to cover the sidewalk, though Ethel knew it probably wouldn't last. "C'mon, Eskimo, let's head back -- Mommy's getting cold." Her eight-year-old Malamute limped along at his own slow speed, the arthritic pain in his front leg hobbling the prancing pace he once had. "Oh, I know you can't go much faster, old boy, but you don't have to stop and look in every shop window along the way, do you?"

Ethel frequently carried on this kind of a monologue with Eskimo, but unlike her daughter, Chris, she couldn't usually engage him in any kind of two-way communication. She had succeeded once when he rescued her from a snowstorm accident, and she had certainly tried since then, but somehow she couldn't "loosen up and open up," as Chris put it, to his thoughts or messages. He now glanced up at her, his deep brown eyes sparkling and his mouth open in a canine grin. Back home in Wisconsin where the snow piled up in fluffy drifts, Eskimo would shove his nose down deep into a snow bank and then toss it up in the air to fling the flakes in a white shower over his head and shoulders. His Alaskan heritage, she supposed. But here in England the snow seldom got that deep.

They turned the corner at the ancient wool market place to circle their way back, when up ahead Ethel saw the dark form of another intrepid pedestrian approaching them from midway up the block. After three months in this quaint Somerset village, she had come to know many of the residents, but this old man with his bent back and shuffling gait didn't look at all familiar. As he neared them, she was struck by his strange apparel -- a well-worn leather coat that covered his leather pants reaching almost to his ankles and just touching his over-sized leather boots. Peering out at her from a leather and fur hat of the kind the Russians often wear, his wizened face wrinkled even more into a broad grin.

"How d'ye do?" his aged voice cackled as he touched his fingers to his hat in an old-fashioned greeting. He stooped to pet Eskimo and scratch behind his ears. "And ye?" he said to the dog. "Yer leg really bothers ye, don't it, ol' feller?" Eskimo cocked his head and stared back with the look he always had when Chris talked to him. "Yes, indeedy, boy, ye got a bad achy leg there, hain't ye? Want ter tell me 'bout it?' Eskimo whined. After a moment, the old man nodded at the dog, pulled himself up into a semi-straight position, and turned his head to Ethel. "How long's he had the 'thritis, Missy?"

"Oh, for years now." She wondered how he knew it was arthritis, but didn't ask. "We picked him up from a humane society shelter when he was just a puppy; they said his former owners kept the dogs in a damp basement. We think he got it from that."

"Could be. Sure'n it could be. But 'tis a shame, ain't it?"

Yes, we feel so sorry for him. I know from his limp that his leg aches, but he likes the snow so much, he wants to walk in it -- even if it does hurt."

"Yes, indeedy. 'Tis exactly what he told me." The man stooped to pet Eskimo again; then raising his hand up to his hat, he turned to go. "Aye, ye've got yerself a mighty fine dog there, Missy. And I'd add, if ye permit, he has hisself a mighty fine mistress!"

Ethel grinned at his quaint compliment, but before she could respond, the old man had already disappeared down the winding street into the misty fog. It was then that she remembered the old English rhyme which she had learned as a child:

"One misty, moisty morning, when cloudy was the weather,
I chanced to meet an old man, clothed all in leather.
He began to compliment, and I began to grin --
"How d'ye do?" and "How d'ye do?" and "How d'ye do?" again!

A semi-retired professor, Ethel had started to write fiction three years ago. She had been encouraged by the publication of a couple of short stories, and recently embarked upon the writing of a novel. Loving England, she placed its story within the setting of Exmoor and the wild scenery of the Doone Valley with its nearby villages of Dunster and Oare. She had begged Roscoe to come along, now that he had taken early retirement from his stock brokerage firm, but rural England had never fascinated him.

"You go, Ethel. Since you're not teaching this semester, you could take a week or two. But you'll have to make some arrangements for Eskimo. I'm not going to be tied to a dog-sitting job when I've just freed myself up from my work at Brady's." He added as if to placate her, "When you're ready to come home, I'll join you for a week in London."

What to do about Eskimo presented a major problem, as their regular dog-sitter had moved and Ethel refused to leave him at a kennel. When she checked the web, though, she found that English hotels were far more dog-friendly than American ones, and the Dunster Hotel was a life-saver. The quarantine procedures and shots had been lengthy and time consuming, however, delaying her departure from the summer until November -- and the dismal weather of an English winter.

"A couple of weeks" was not long enough, Ethel knew, but she never dreamed it would take over a month to complete the research, immerse herself in the local atmosphere, and develop the story outline which she planned to embellish and finish back home. It was now mid-December, and she had bundles of notes and was almost done with her preliminary summary. She planned to meet Roscoe in London the following week. They had made advance reservations at the Thistle Victoria Hotel next to Victoria Station -- not one of the smaller, more quiet hotels where Ethel preferred to stay, but one that was well located for tube and bus transport around London and, more importantly, one that did accommodate dogs.

Back in her room/suite combination, Ethel settled down in her lounge chair to review the two-page plot summary she had drafted last week. It would still require some fine tuning, but she was satisfied with its general theme and sequence of events. She had been enthralled by the story of *Lorna Doone* when she read it in high school many years ago, and on her first visit to England she had insisted on including a tour of Exmoor, especially the edge of Somerset which encompassed Oare Parish and the Oare Church of St. Mary the Virgin. Oare was mentioned in the Doomsday book and the Oare Church had been a parish church for at least eight hundred years. But Ethel's interest arose more from its role in the Lorna Doone legend popularized by the novelist, R. D. Blackmore.

Her own novel would draw upon that legend as a backdrop to a modern romance. Reading through the hard copy of her outline, she crossed out words and sentences as she went along, also adding short cryptic notes which she could refer to later when she revised and expanded the text on her computer:

Summary: A young American student of British literature, Jonathan Riley, is visiting Exmoor, researching material for his thesis on the works of R. D. Blackmore, the British novelist. Jonathan is particularly intrigued by Blackmore's novel of "Lorna Doone," and combs through the Oare parish records for historical evidence regarding the infamous Doone family and their lovely "princess," Lorna. He finds a booklet by Sir Atholl Oakeley which outlines the history of the Doones and features a picture of Lorna herself on its cover -- a copy of a famous painting of her. (Note: Insert here the story of the outlaw tribe of Doones, how they came to the valley, Lorna Doone's romance with John Ridd, and the attempted murder of Lorna in Oare Church.) *Riley becomes mesmerized by the legend of Lorna and, not admitting it to himself, he falls in love with the enchanting woman in the portrait.*

One foggy day, while taking some notes in the Oare Church, he happens to glance out the west window and glimpses a young woman strolling in the churchyard. Aware of someone watching her, she stares back at him for a long moment, and a puzzled expression flashes across her face before she turns away and disappears around the corner. Since the woman bears a marked resemblance to Lorna, Jonathan hurries from the church to speak with her. But outside, she is nowhere to be seen -- like a phantom, he thinks, enveloped in the mist.

Jonathan, by now obsessed with his infatuation, embarks upon an extensive search for the elusive woman in the churchyard -- but all to no avail. (Note: Describe some of his exhaustive trips to Dunster, Porlock, Lynmouth and Lynton, Parracombe, Blackmoor Gate, Simonsbath, Exford, Whedon Cross, and Oare, none of which bears any fruit.) *Discouraged and despondent, the young student hikes through the Exmoor hills toward the Doone Valley where he makes a final effort to find the woman he now calls "Lorna." On the moor Jonathan meets ...* (Note: Who? The ghost of Lorna? The woman who looks like Lorna?) Ethel put down her pen and pondered over the note she had inserted over a week ago. She knew how she wanted to end her novel, but she was still no closer to creating this crucial link to the hero's final discovery of his love.

The next day was a rerun of the day before -- overcast and misty. They were again passing the wool market in Dunster when Ethel spied the old man sitting on a bench inside the open structure. "How d'ye do, Missy?" he cackled as she approached, with Eskimo wagging his tail enthusiastically. "And how be ye, ol' feller?" he said to the dog as he ruffled the neck fur behind his ears. Tilting his head up toward Ethel, he smiled his wrinkly smile and handed her a small paper bag. "Jist a few chewy treats for the laddie. A wee bit, only -- fer his 'thritis." Sensing her hesitation, he assured her, "Natural herbs. Ye might try 'em. Their names be listed on a note inside, should ye want to get some more."

Thanking him warmly, Ethel turned to leave, but Eskimo was reluctant to part from his new friend. "C'mon, boy. Time for lunch, and --" she added, flourishing the bag, "some new treats!" That did it. She smiled and waved her goodbye as they headed back to their hotel. The next day she hired a car to drive them to Taunton; from there they took a train to London where Roscoe met them at the Thistle Victoria Hotel.

"I could hardly believe it myself!" Ethel bubbled excitedly. "Yesterday he was limping along like he usually does, but this morning he scampered from his rug on the floor and actually jumped up on my bed. Just like he used to do!"

"And you've done nothing different -- except for giving him those herbal chews?" Roscoe asked dubiously.

"Nothing. Only a few of the treats that the old man gave me in that bag. Here, you can see them for yourself." Ethel took the bag out of her purse and handed it to Roscoe. "I hesitated to give him any at first -- not knowing exactly what they were -- but when I checked the list of herbs he had written down, they all seemed harmless enough."

"So now you're convinced that this leather-coated character has some kind of mystical powers to cure arthritis?" Although Roscoe raised his eyebrows in his most skeptical manner, his instant smile tempered the irritation Ethel was beginning to feel. She grinned back, but grabbed the bag of herbal chews and put it back in her purse.

"I never said he had *mystical* powers. What I said was that all of our traditional cures -- the glucosamine and the piroxicam -- haven't done much good. And then all of a sudden I gave him those herbs and -- well, you can see for yourself!" Eskimo had just trotted over to the corner and brought his rubber ball back to them to throw. As he chased it across the room, she added, "He hasn't actually *run* after that ball for three years."

That night when they went to bed, Eskimo nestling at their feet, Ethel knew how she was going to solve the mystery of the elusive modern "Lorna." Much as she looked forward to their visit to London, she could hardly wait to get back home to write it.

On the moor, shrouded in morning mist, Jonathan meets an old man dressed in leather breaches covered by a long, old-fashioned leather coat. He wears big leather boots and a leather cap with flaps that are pulled down over his ears. "How d'ye do?" his voice rasps, and raising his hand to his forehead in an awkward kind of greeting, he falls in step with the young American. "So -- be ye searchin' then for the Valley of the Doones? Over there, beyond that craggy tor it be. I be headed there myself." (Note: Jonathan asks him about what happened to the rest of the Doones after the fateful attack on their mountain retreat, led by John Ridd. Fill in here with the bloody raid on Doone Valley, the final demise of the Doone clan, and the death of Carver Doone, their leader.)

"But were there no survivors?" Jonathan asks, and the old man simply shakes his head. "Nay, there be none, lad, at least in these moors -- nor any with the name of Doone. When the Doones were killed or driven from the valley, only Lorna remained behind, by then happily wed to John Ridd. But she -- perhaps ye didn't know? -- she were truly a Dugal of the Scottish highland clan. Ne'er a Doone at all. She'd been kidnapped by the Doones as a wee lass. The 'Lorna' ye be lookin' for is a great, great descendent -- many times -- of Lady Lorna Dugal and farmer John Ridd. She lives on the Ridd farm down in the valley. Down there below, lad. Kin ye see the smoke from the chimbley?" At this point, two paths diverge into the valley. The old man points to the one leading to a small cottage at the bottom of the hill, surrounded by rich farmland. Bidding farewell, he takes the other path himself, soon shrouded in a sea of fog and mist.

The novel ends with Jonathan knocking on the door of the cottage. The phantom from the churchyard opens it, a welcome smile on her lips. Amazed at the similarity between the portrait of Lorna Doone and the woman who now appears before him, Jonathan stands speechless: they could have been identical twins. She smiles again and then, taking him by the arm, she leads him inside the cottage. "Come in, then won't ye? Sure and I'm sorry that I fled from ye at the Oare churchyard. But I was afrighted when I saw yer face." Her brow furrowed as she again stared at him with puzzlement and wonder. "Yer the livin' image of

*John Ridd, ye know. The parsonage history book has a sketch of him
-- with the first Lorna. Did ye not see it, then?"*

*He shakes his head and stammers, "No. Just the one of Lorna --
Lorna Doone."*

*"Well, the old man of the fog and mist told me ye'd be coming. I've
been waitin' for ye for a long, long time, John."*

Just how long, he wonders -- and how did she know his name?
(Note: Don't explain too much. End it with a touch of mystery
-- about the mystical role of the old man of the fog and mist on that
misty, moisty morning.)

It was almost midnight when Ethel printed out a copy and put
the typed sheets in a folder. Roscoe had already gone to bed; she'd
show it to him in the morning. He wouldn't like it too much, she
suspected. Having dealt all his life with numbers, he felt more
comfortable with clear-cut factual accounts than with the semi-
mystical writings of his aspiring novelist wife. "So, who was this old
man?" he would ask, knowing that she had based the book character
on the real one she had met in Dunster. "How did he know that
Riley was looking for Doone Valley?"

Ethel shrugged to herself as she wondered how she might
respond. She didn't know the answer; but that wasn't the point,
was it? She had simply used the old man as an external force -- *Deus
ex machina* -- a necessary link between her hero's quest and his final
discovery of a real Lorna. A strange link he might be, perhaps, but
he filled the role she needed. Just as her own old man of the fog and
mist had somehow found a cure for Eskimo's arthritic pains, even
though she would never know how he did it. That was the beauty
and charm of mysticism, after all -- one didn't have to have all the
answers.

FAMILY SECRETS

"Now, before we mail all this stuff, are you really sure you want to put on this Mueller family reunion of yours?" As an only child with two distant cousins whom he seldom saw, Roscoe was not enamored with Ethel's new-found enthusiasm for family ties. She had started it all with her tentative exploration of her family tree, the roots of which had gone back to her great, great grandfather, Hermann Mueller, who came to America from Germany at the age of two when his parents settled in Wisconsin in 1842. Though Hermann became a farmer, his son, Carl, became a cheese-maker, as did Ethel's grandfather, Frederick.

After a few years, however, Grandpa Frederick bought a tavern in a small town north of Milwaukee which he successfully ran until 1920 when it all came to an abrupt end. It was then that the National Prohibition Act and the Eighteenth Amendment to the Constitution established prohibition as the new law of the land. As Grandma Mueller told it, many of Frederick's fellow tavern owners secretly began to manufacture moonshine in illegal stills, but Grandpa closed down the tavern and returned to his father's cheese factory for the rest of his working life.

While fleshing out the branches which included her cousins, Ethel had suddenly thought how nice it would be to have a family reunion. Most of them lived in Wisconsin or at least in the Midwest, so having it near where they lived in Madison made sense. She knew Roscoe didn't like the idea too much, but he wasn't adamantly opposed either.

"Oh, Roscoe, we've been through this a dozen times. Yes, I really do want to have this family reunion. I haven't seen some of my cousins since Mother died, and that was over ten years ago. Besides," she threw him a quick grin, "Fred promised to help with the expenses – such as they are. There's only the rental of the hall at the country club and these mailings; they all have to pay in advance for their buffet dinners and they're on their own for their drinks when they get there."

"Yeah, well, I'll count your brother Fred's contribution when I see it. Considering the way you two get along -- or don't get along -- it's surprising that he's even coming."

Cocking her head slightly, Ethel nodded. "I know. I wasn't so sure either as to how he'd react, but he seems genuinely interested in doing this. After all, he said, he is named after Grandpa Mueller. He and Ann are driving up a couple days ahead of time to help. Although I don't know what else there's to do." She sealed the last envelope and placed it on the pile. "As far as I'm concerned, that's it."

Frieda Mueller crossed her arms over her formidable bosom and frowned down at her husband as he sat at the rickety table next to the furnace and poured a shot of the pale liquid from the unlabeled bottle into his glass. "So how long do you intend to go on making this Schnapps, Frederick?"

"As long as our friends and neighbors want to buy it, I suppose." He took a sip from his glass and smacked his lips loudly. "Ach, Frieda, don't go making such a fuss about a little moonshine. I closed down the tavern, didn't I? And we're renting it out to Henry Krueger as a grocery store." He nodded toward the stairs. "That door up there from the store to the stairs is padlocked; Krueger has no idea that this still is down here in the basement."

He poured a shot into another glass which he offered to her, but she refused. "Hell, Frieda, I'm not selling the stuff over the counter – just to friends. Now, what's the harm in that?"

"And you don't think that Krueger wonders what you're doing down here in the furnace room when you come and go through that back cellar door?"

"He works up front at the counter most of the time – can't see me 'come and go.' Besides, I told him I was storing a lot of the bottles and other bar equipment down here." He grinned up at her. "Just in case they ever repeal that damned prohibition law."

"Well, I don't like it, Frederick. I don't like it one bit." Frieda finally sat down in the chair he had pulled out for her. "You've read about how those federal agents are snooping around all the former taverns and bars. And when they find any vats or stills where anyone is making moonshine, they bust 'em up and send the owners to jail." She relented and took a sip of the Schnapps. "Not bad." But the frown returned. "Still, it's not worth it, Frederick. It's just not worth it."

Ethel awoke with her Grandma's admonition echoing in her ears. She turned over and peered at the clock on her night-table: just 7:05 AM, time to get up for her Friday schedule. Roscoe was already downstairs; she could smell the coffee. She had a nine o'clock class to teach, but was then free to get ready for the big family reunion tomorrow. Fred and Ann had arrived Wednesday and were coming over for supper to review the list of those attending the reunion and to help with any last-minute preparations.

Late that afternoon, after she passed around the cheese and crackers, Ethel sat down with her glass of Scotch and turned to her brother. "Fred, when Grandma Mueller died and Dad closed up the estate, she still owned that old tavern in Milton that Grandpa used to run, didn't she?"

"Yeah, she rented it out, but she owned it. Why?"

"Well, I had this strange dream last night about Grandma and Grandpa when they closed it down because of prohibition. Only in the dream, they didn't really close it down completely. Grandpa had a still down in the basement under the tavern – under the part that Mr.

Krueger ran as a grocery store. Do you remember if there was a back outside entrance to that basement? Or what was down there?"

"Not really. Dad asked if I wanted to go along with him to look the place over before he advertised it for rent, but I never went." He paused as he tried to stretch his memory. Their mother died ten years ago, but their father had died some ten years before that. "But, you know, I do remember his saying there were a lot of old bottles down in the basement – and a huge laundry tub." He laughed, "Or an old-fashioned still maybe? Dad wondered at the time what Grandpa used it for."

"You know," Ethel mused, "Grandma always made such a big thing about how Grandpa didn't cheat on prohibition like a lot of the other tavern owners – according to her, he closed down the tavern and went back to that cheese factory. Still, I wonder…"

Fred got up to fix himself another drink. "Well, we'll never know, will we?"

But Ethel thought to herself, "Maybe no, maybe yes…" That night as she lay in bed, she closed her eyes and tried to bring back into the focus of her inner mind the basement scene of the night before.

The thunder paused for a moment and they finally heard the knocking on the back cellar door and then the slow footsteps of Police Chief Mike Cleary as he approached the furnace room.

"Hello, Frederick." Nodding to Frieda, "Good afternoon, Mrs. Mueller."

"Hello, Chief." Frederick was standing by the still and gestured to the empty chair next to Frieda. "What brings you down here on such a rainy day?"

"Oh, just a friendly visit, Frederick. A kind of friendly warning, you might say."

He shook his head when Frederick handed him a shot glass of liquor, but then he took it just the same. "Thanks. Might as well taste the evidence before they come and smash it all to hell." Smiling at Frieda, he shrugged his shoulders and downed it in one swallow.

Frieda's face turned white, but she said nothing. The Chief put his glass on the table, looked at the still, and shook his head. "I don't know who turned you in – the call went directly to the feds in Milwaukee. It didn't come to us. But by courtesy protocol they have to let us know if they're going to make a raid in our territory. An agent "Fisher" is coming -- could be tonight or tomorrow morning." He paused, then got up to leave. Frederick smiled and shook his hand. "You have my thanks, Mike. I don't know exactly what we can do about it all, but thanks for the advance warning."

As the Chief walked toward the cellar door, he added, "You've always been a straight shooter, Frederick. You've run a decent establishment and never gave us any trouble. I don't personally go with this prohibition stuff, but the law's the law. If this Fisher fellow calls on me, I'll have to come with him."

Frederick nodded and Frieda, now recovered, added, "We understand, Chief."

When Cleary shut the door, Frederick collapsed in the vacant chair while Frieda rose from hers. "I think I know what we can do." She whispered now, even though the Chief was already on his way. "Get that big pail from the laundry room. We're going to get rid of this so-called evidence!" And for the next hour they took turns in dipping the pail into the huge vat and throwing the moonshine down the laundry room drain. When they finished that, they carried all of the full bottles to the car. They then filled the vat with water and soap. "We'll bring some dirty clothes from home, Frieda explained. "This will be our 'soaking tub' for your cheese factory clothes. Those clothes absolutely stink! And we'll just say that our tub at home isn't big enough."

Frederick kissed her with the love he had always felt for her -- and he added an extra hug of admiration for the quick thinking he had not fully appreciated before. But as she hugged him back, she thought to herself, "I wonder if it will work."

The reunion consumed so much of Ethel's time on Saturday that her pursuit of the mystery of the moonshine operations of her grandfather was temporarily put on hold. Her dream – or vision? – of the visit of Chief Cleary and the sanitization of the still remained vivid in her mind, but she had neither the time nor the energy to try to figure it all out.

Ethel and Roscoe drove over to the country club an hour early to greet her relatives as they arrived. Chris and Kathy, their two daughters, drove with them, but Chris's husband, Russell, and their daughter, Leska, waited for Fred and Ann to pick them up. When the four of them finally got to the country club, most of the other guests were already seated. Just like Fred, Ethel thought; he had to make everyone worry. But with an effort she swallowed her irritation -- after all, he had managed to come.

The pre-dinner program of family remarks and remembrances went as well as Ethel had hoped. There were three branches of the Frederick Mueller tree -- Frederick's three children: Ethel's father, his brother, and his sister – all deceased. Ethel had asked her cousins from each branch of the tree to introduce their spouses and children and grandchildren, if there were any; then to say a few words about each. She had figured it might take an hour, but they were finished in forty-five minutes.

The champagne flowed freely (an added touch that although Roscoe had resisted, Fred had insisted on), and the steak and salmon entrees were excellent in presentation as well as taste. After the dessert and coffee were served, Ethel stood, and clinking her glass with a spoon, she soon had the attention of the group. "As I wrote in the invitation, we have the hall rented for the rest of the evening. There's no need for anyone to rush off. But before we all do break up and" – with a grin – "before all our champagne glasses are empty, I'd like to propose a toast:

"Here's to Frederick and Frieda Mueller, better known to all of us cousins here as Grandpa and Grandma Mueller." As she raised her glass, the toast echoed through the room: "To Grandpa and Grandma Mueller."

Ethel continued, "Though they are the more immediate founders of this family, our family tree goes all the way back through Carl and

Hermann Mueller to Hermann's parents who came to America from Germany in 1842. Some of us remember Grandpa best from his days as tavern owner and bartender at the Western Home in Milton. Then prohibition came and he closed the tavern. But he did salvage and leave behind a few bottles of home-made Schnapps that my father found at Grandma Mueller's house when she passed away and he helped settle the estate. Now, I'm not saying that Grandpa made it and I'm not saying that he didn't. But for those of you who aren't going to ask specifically where it came from, I have three bottles here that I'm willing to share for this occasion. Come on up after your dessert and have a sample. It's pretty good!" The applause this time filled the hall.

Agent Fisher cast a suspicious eye at the huge vat in the furnace room filled with dirty water and stinky clothes. His frown then deepened and his eyes narrowed even more as he addressed the man with the handle-bar mustache and his formidable wife. "So, you say that this is a 'soaking vat' that you use for the clothes you wear in your cheese factory? That you need one, and your laundry room at your home doesn't have one?"

It was one of the wildest stories Fisher had ever heard, but he hadn't been able to find one bottle of moonshine in the whole building and that vat sure stunk of cheese.

Noticing his wrinkled nose, Mrs. Mueller answered, "Well, you can smell it for yourself, can't you? Nothing will get rid of that smell except for a good soaking. And the smell spreads everywhere. We have a new house now and to save steps we put our laundry room on the first floor. So we didn't want to use that. We thought that as long as we own this building here with this big tub, why not use it?"

Agent Fisher looked over at Chief Cleary, but the Chief simply shrugged his shoulders. "So, where did you get this vat in the first place? It looks like a God-damn still to me – with all those pipe attachments. Doesn't it, Chief?" Cleary shrugged again.

Frederick chimed in. "Well, I wouldn't know, Agent Fisher. When we bought the tavern, that tub was already here. But I wouldn't be surprised if maybe it once was used to make liquor. You know, back in the old days there were a lot of taverns where people made their own beer and liquor. I don't mean illegally, like now, what with prohibition and all. But longer ago, you know."

Frieda switched the topic. "Have you any other questions, Mr. Fisher? This smell is getting mighty strong even for this place and I'd hate to have Mr. Krueger start to complain — he's our renter upstairs. I'm about ready to empty out that dirty water and put in some fresh. Unless you have something else, that is?" Frieda gave him her sweetest smile and rose from the chair where she was sitting. Frederick moved to her side, and Chief Cleary edged toward the door. All eyes were on Fisher.

"No. No, I don't have anything else, Mrs. Mueller. We get these reports, though, and we have to look into them. I hope you understand." He shook hands with both Frieda and Frederick and followed Cleary to the door. As they walked outside, Frieda heard him say, "Well, if that wasn't the damnedest thing I've ever run into! And that smell! But do you believe them, Chief?" Cleary shrugged for the third time, but he hid his smile.

Ethel woke and turned slowly toward the clock before she remembered it was Sunday. She had at least another hour before the late church service. A slight ache in the middle of her forehead reminded her that she had perhaps sipped one too many "samples" of the Schnapps. And then she wondered, where did those bottles of Schnapps come from that her father had found? And who made it? Though her brother Fred might remark, "We'll never know," she thought she knew. As she remembered her dream, she smiled to herself. Quite a man, her grandfather was. Quite a woman, her grandmother. And quite a strange family secret!

INSIDE THE DIORAMA

"But, Grandma, he *did* move! I saw him!" Leska pointed at the fierce looking Indian chief whose spear protruded from the shoulder of the buffalo at the edge of the exhibit. The dimly lit diorama portrayed the five Indian hunters pursuing their buffalo game across an arid stretch of sand and cacti. In the lead was the feather-plumed chief, with one hand extended in the direction of the spear he had just thrown and the other clutching his reins and tomahawk. Frozen in time, the scene was like a three-dimensional snapshot, Ethel thought -- the motion all implied, but not real.

Although the individual figures were solidly embedded in the wood and plaster of the diorama, the stage itself rotated around in a circle when anyone pressed the button at the side which said, "For motion and music, press once to start." Soft drum beats echoed in the now almost empty hall and the sound of hoofbeats could also be heard.

"Well, he sure looks like he's moving, Leska, but see -- he stays right in the same spot. All of the other Indians, and the buffaloes, too. The stage moves around, but not the figures. That's what a diorama is supposed to do -- make the viewer think that it's real, or like this one, that the Indians and buffaloes are actually moving."

Ethel saw the frustration in her granddaughter's face as she shook her head and muttered to herself, "But he *actually did* move. I saw him." At eight, Leska was already the spitting image of Chris, Ethel

151

and Roscoe's eldest daughter, and showed many of the traits that Ethel herself had passed on to her progeny -- especially the firmness of her opinions and her persistence in expressing and defending them. Roscoe called it "being stubborn," but Ethel saw it as "not being wishy-washy" or as "standing up for oneself."

Deciding to change the subject, Ethel took Leska's hand and gradually guided her away from the diorama toward the butterfly exhibit at the end of the hall. "Let's find your Mom and Dad and see what they've been up to. I think they're still inside with the butterflies." She glanced at her watch and frowned, "Grandpa will pick you up and drive you and your folks back to our place; I have to stay here for a late afternoon meeting of the Friends of the Museum. I'll join you back home for supper. Grandpa's going to fry some hamburgers on the grill."

Chris and Russell emerged from the butterfly enclosure as they approached. "All of these exhibits are always so neat! We don't even have a museum near us in Alaska; we have to go to Anchorage if we want to visit one. Leska, you missed all the beautiful butterflies -- a couple landed right on my head. Were the Indians and buffaloes worth it?"

"Yeah, Mom. I even saw some of them move!" So much for reality, Ethel thought.

Ethel found herself inside the wigwam with the wounded Indian chief lying on a cot beside her. She had seen it all: The chief had just thrown his spear when a warrior next to him shoved him off his horse and into the path of the buffalo that followed. He landed on its horns. Ethel, standing at the edge of the diorama had been scooped up by another Indian and dropped at the entrance to the wigwam. She must have passed out, because when they carried in the wounded chief, they woke her and nudged her into the tent. They brought hot water and some clean rags and made it clear that she should dress his wounds. She bathed the gash in his side and bound it with the rags, but the blood still seeped through. Her first-aid course in college had hardly prepared her for this.

She felt weak and disoriented -- as if she had awakened from a deep sleep. When she got up, she staggered slightly, but managed to move to the open flap that served as a kind of door. There, outside the tent, a group of some fifteen to twenty Indian braves were seated in a circle around the fire, humming and singing to the beat of a tom-tom while what seemed to be a medicine man danced before the fire. At once, she recognized the brave who had pushed the chief onto the horns of the buffalo -- his red-feathered plume bobbing up and down in rhythm to the tom-tom's beat. He saw her, too.

Ethel backed into the tent, pulled the flap down, and sank to the ground next to the chief. What should she do? What could she do? If only Willy were there, he'd know what to do. Willy usually appeared when she had one of these nightmares or "altered consciousness" episodes. Where in heck was he?

Just then the flap over the entrance was pulled back and the red-plumed Indian who had pushed the chief strode into the tent. He nudged the supine body roughly with his foot, and the chief groaned, but did not move. The warrior yanked Ethel to her feet, shoving her toward the entrance. Next to the fire there was now another pile of wood stacked around a small platform with a pole standing upright in the middle. Ethel had seen enough Western movies in her youth to understand what that meant.

She screamed out now to the other braves. "Don't. Oh, please don't! Do any of you speak English -- can't you understand? This man here," -- she pointed to the brave who was pushing her toward the platform -- "this man here tried to kill your chief. I saw it all. He shoved him into the path of that buffalo. He knows that I saw him do it and now he wants to kill me. Please, please – can't any of you help me?"

But none of them moved forward to help her. Their blank stares confirmed her fears that none of them could understand her. Even the medicine man stood quietly by, unmoved and unmoving. As they bound her to the post, she fainted again.

"You're unusually quiet tonight, Ethel. Boring meeting, or so absorbing that you're still thinking about it?" Roscoe passed her the plate of freshly-grilled hamburgers, followed by a basket of rolls and a dish of sautéed onions. "Here, dig in. We all had some appetizers with drinks before you got here."

Ethel vividly remembered her adventure into the diorama. Her meeting had ended early and she had taken a short detour up to the second floor on her way to the parking garage. With only the night lights on, the diorama was even less lit up than earlier and most of the Indians and buffaloes appeared only as dark shapes against an equally dark background. Though she saw no one there, someone had pressed the activation button and the stage was rotating slowly in the darkness with the dull thud of the drums punctuating the silence.

She had to force herself to return to the conversation at the table. "What? Oh, I'm sorry, Roscoe, but I had the strangest kind of daydream at the museum and I just can't get it out of my head." She turned to her granddaughter and continued, "I went back to that diorama, Leska. You know, the one with the Indians and buffaloes? And I had the oddest feeling that I was actually *inside* the exhibit, right alongside all the action -- part of the action, in fact." She shook her head and shrugged. "Just weird."

Leska nodded knowingly. "I told you that Indian chief was moving, Grandma. He threw his spear right at that buffalo. And then that other Indian -- the one with the bright red feathers -- pushed him off his horse. I saw the whole thing."

"But you just mentioned the chief, Leska. You didn't say anything about the other Indian at all. Are you sure you saw him moving too?"

"For Pete's sake, let her be, Ethel." Roscoe had little patience for Ethel's "flights of fancy," as he called them. "The child has almost as much imagination as you do. Don't encourage her any further." He turned to Chris. "Right, honey?"

"Oh, I'm not going to get mixed up in this one, Dad. When it involves things like reality -- or *imagination* -- I have my own battles to fight."

Ethel nodded sympathetically, while Roscoe rolled his eyes; Russell and Leska just grinned. They all knew that Chris faced a barrage of letters to the editor every time she published one of her articles on animal communication.

"Okay by me. But I'm beginning to think this whole family is short a couple of marbles -- all except Russell and me, of course." Roscoe effectively terminated the conversation by rising to get some more burgers from the grate.

"So be it," Ethel thought. But before she climbed into bed that night she once again examined the red feather that she had found in her purse when she returned home from the museum earlier. Where had it come from? Tonight she had to return to the diorama -- if only in her dreams.

Ethel was bound tightly to the post in the middle of the small platform which was surrounded by kindling wood and straw. The other Indians had now joined the medicine man in his dance around the fire which blazed brightly only six or eight feet from her. As the brave with the red feathers approached her with a burning stick in his hand, Ethel searched wildly about for some escape. But there was none.

It was at that moment that Willy emerged from the chief's tent with a pistol in one hand and with his other arm supporting the chief who shuffled slowly beside him. The chief held his hand to his side, but with Willy's help he managed to stay on his feet. The blood from his wound had spread on the bandage Ethel had tied around him, but the strips of cloth held it firmly in place. The shot into the air from Willy's gun echoed loudly through the canyon and brought the music and the dancing to an abrupt end.

All eyes focused on the chief as he pointed to the brave with the red feathers and uttered a few sharp words. The other warriors immediately seized him and stood by the fire, awaiting further orders. Two of them released Ethel who ran sobbing to Willy's side. Smiling, the chief nodded his head to her and patted her gently on her shoulder. He then spoke again to the gathered warriors who now tied the captive brave to the post in Ethel's place. They lit the straw and wood and as the flames rose around the raised platform, Willy guided Ethel back to the chief's tent.

She fought to control her sobbing, but the tears nonetheless streamed down her cheeks. "Oh, Willy, thank God that you came! There was no way out, no escape. I really thought it was the end." Flashing his broad crooked grin, Willy gave her a warm hug while she wiped her eyes on her sleeve and sniffled audibly. "But how did you get here? How did you know where I was?" She knew better than to ask -- Willy seldom answered her questions -- but her emotions were now in control. Rationality had left her when she was pulled into the diorama. When? She didn't know. Time had no meaning.

As she had expected, Willy avoided the question. "If you're feeling better, Ethel, let's see if we can find the chief and get the hell out of here."

"But, what about that gun, Willy? I never knew you carried a gun. Why..." At that moment the Indian chief entered the tent and motioned for the two of them to sit down. Joining them, he passed a long carved pipe to Willy who accepted it with a deferential nod and puffed on it briefly. He then returned it to the chief and spoke quietly, but intensely, with him before he and Ethel got up and were escorted out of the tent. As they passed the smoldering funeral pyre, little remained of the tethered Indian but his charred body and ashes. Willy bent and scooped up a red feather lying on the ground next to the embers and handed it to Ethel. Reaching the edge of the diorama, they stepped off into the darkness of the museum.

"Well, you're the late one this morning, Ethel. Bad night?" Roscoe looked up from the kitchen table as Ethel entered.

"No, not really. Just another strange dream." Ethel occasionally resorted to such little white lies whenever she had one of her subconscious adventures or ran into Willy in a new "journey of the mind." As she sat down she turned to smile at Leska, "But it reminded me that before I left the diorama yesterday, I took another close look at the Indian chase. And, you know what? That Indian chief -- the one who was knocked off his horse by the Indian with the red feathers -- remember? Well, he was back on his horse -- sitting there just as proud as could be. Just as if nothing had happened."

"And what about the Indian with the red feathers?" Leska persisted.

Ethel frowned slightly and pursed her lips together as she searched for the right answer. "He was gone, Leska. He just wasn't there." She handed her granddaughter the charred red feather. "But I found this at the edge of the diorama." She paused and then smiled again, "I don't think he'll ever bother the chief again."

Leska looked at the feather thoughtfully and then shook her head slowly. "No, Grandma, I don't think he will."

THE DANILOV BRAIN

"So?" Roscoe's eyebrow arched halfway up his forehead, and a slight quiver of his lips betrayed the smile he was trying to hide. "So, what are you going to do with it?"

Ethel set the metal container on the kitchen table, tapped her chin, and stared at it. "I don't have the slightest idea." She glanced up at him and let a wide grin burst forth. "I don't know, Roscoe. I haven't heard from Michael in years -- and now this. We're second or third cousins and I never even knew his grandfather. Why he would want me to have his grandfather's brain -- pickled or not -- is beyond me."

The large package had arrived that morning by UPS. The accompanying note read: "This is the brain of Ivan Danilov, the grandfather of Michael Petrov, who has just passed away. Mr. Petrov's will specifies that it should be sent to you as his closest living relative. It has been preserved in cryonic stasis since the death of Mr. Danilov several years ago. The inner cylinder must be kept filled with liquid nitrogen and the dry ice in the outer canister must also be replenished every few days. An electric freezer is being sent separately for longer-term storage. Please feel free to contact us if you have any questions. Thomas Downe and Associates, SC, Attorneys at Law." A clipping of the Petrov obituary was enclosed.

Ethel picked up the newspaper clipping. "It says here that Michael was seventy-eight when he died. Assuming that he was thirty-five or forty when his grandfather died, that brain could have been preserved for about forty years or so." She got up from the table and carried the container to the garage door. "For the time being, I think we'll keep Mr. Danilov's brain in the garage. Meanwhile, I'm going to Google up some information on cryonics."

That afternoon Roscoe listened carefully while Ethel read the blurb she had found on the Cryonics Laboratory in Michigan: "The Cryonics Laboratory offers the latest technology in cryopreservation services. As soon as possible after legal death, the patient (or his/her brain) is infused with a substance to prevent ice formation, cooled to a temperature where physical decay essentially stops, and is then maintained indefinitely in cryostasis. When and if future medical technology allows, our patients hope to be rejuvenated, revived, and awakened to a greatly extended life in youthful good health, free from disease or the aging process."

"Google also posted a site which included an open letter by several scientists supporting cryonics. Here, listen to this: 'The purpose of cryonics is to save lives and restore health. Today's medical technology can't always keep us alive, let alone healthy. Cryonics should be able to preserve life and restore health in all but the most extreme circumstances. Tissue preserved at the temperature of liquid nitrogen does not deteriorate, even after centuries of storage. Therefore, if current medical technology can't keep us alive we can instead choose to be preserved in liquid nitrogen, with the expectation that future medical technology should be able to both reverse any cryopreservation injury and restore good health.'"

Ethel continued, "There seem to be a number of these cryonics places in the United States -- the West Coast, of course, but also cities like Scottsdale, Albuquerque, Denver, and surprisingly, there's a Cryonics Institute right here in Wisconsin, a few miles from Janesville. But there are more in Europe, especially in Russia and the Ukraine where they say that the science of cryobiology has a long history. I suppose that's how Michael's grandfather learned about it. When I checked the family tree I found out that he came to the States from Russia as a young man."

Roscoe knew what Ethel had in mind, but asked anyhow, "And what do you intend to do with Mr. Danilov's brain, Ethel? Find out if it's still working? I suppose you could drive over to that institute near Janesville and hear what they have to say. Actually, it might be interesting. Unfortunately, I'm tied up with some real estate deals the next couple of days or I'd go with you."

She gave him a quick hug. "That's okay, honey. I don't mind driving alone -– and I really do want to find out more about this whole subject. I'll go tomorrow."

As Ethel rounded the bend leading to the on-ramp for the highway from Madison toward Janesville, she saw a familiar figure at the curb, his arm and thumb extended. "Willy!" she exclaimed as he entered the car. "I'm so glad you decided to join me. The strangest thing has happened -– I know you'll be as fascinated as I am." Willy always appeared when Ethel was embarking on one of her strange adventures or was wrestling to discover the key to some new dilemma or mystery.

After she related the happenings of the previous day and told Willy that she had managed to make an appointment for ten-thirty, she asked if he had ever heard of the institute. He sat for a while in silence, his white hair ruffled against the head rest and his eyes closed. Then, rather abruptly, he asked, "What do you know about this Cryonics Institute, Ethel? And what do you hope to find out?" Willy often preluded his own answers with questions. When she shrugged in response, he continued, "Well, it happens that I have heard of it, but only in very general terms -– nothing specific. It's a private institution, well-endowed, but it's extremely secretive, with little published about it in the public domain." He frowned and added, "That's why I'm surprised to hear that even Google knows something about it."

Ethel knew better than to ask how Willy had heard of it. She wouldn't get a straight answer if she did. So she returned to his second question. "I'd like to know the current status of their research in this field–- I mean, you know, how close they think they might be to actually bringing some of these frozen bodies back to life." She shrugged again and added, "Well, of course I'm skeptical myself, but I'd like to hear their spin on it. And, of course, I'd like to know the condition of Danilov's brain. Has it been safely preserved, and what should I be doing with it, if anything."

"Good enough, if they care to share any of that information. But don't be surprised if they're a bit reticent. Next to national intelligence, nothing is more secret than scientific research."

Now off the highway, they followed the directions that the institute secretary had given Ethel and soon found the small winding road marked "Private Use Only."

Willy nudged Ethel's arm as they glimpsed the massive stone edifice through the trees and around the next bend. "Let me off here, Ethel. I want to sniff around a little on my own. Don't worry, I'll be somewhere along this road when you leave." He hopped out before she could protest. "See you later."

A uniformed guard opened the gates as Ethel approached and waved her through. Definitely expecting me, she thought, and well organized. Once parked, she checked the note she had scribbled down during her phone conversation. "Dr. Petrovich," she said to herself. She repeated it to the man who opened the door.

"Yes, he's expecting you, Dr. Matson. This way, please. Let me help you with your package."

The room was more like the office of a businessman than that of a doctor. Dr. Petrovich rose from behind a solid cherry desk to greet her. Short and compact, he sported a neatly trimmed mustache and beard and was dressed in casual slacks, but with a white shirt and tie. He motioned to some comfortable easy chairs which were positioned on an oriental rug next to a low wooden-inlaid coffee table. "Coffee? Or would you prefer tea?" It was all very civilized, she thought, but somehow it didn't fit in with the topic they were about to discuss -- a topic which Ethel still felt to be a bit macabre. She fidgeted with the metal canister the attendant had carried in and then placed carefully on the table in front of her.

"So, Dr. Matson, what field of medicine do you practice?"

"Oh, none," she smiled apologetically. "I'm the PhD type of Doctor."

"So your current interest in cryonics is a personal one, not professional?"

Ethel motioned to the container on the table. "Purely personal. As I mentioned to your secretary yesterday, I received this package containing the brain of a distant cousin's grandfather who, I figure, must have died some forty years ago. My cousin recently passed away and willed me the brain. I'm interested in the current state of cryonic research and also what I should or should not do with Mr. Danilov's brain. I came here because I saw you listed on the Internet and we live over in Madison -- it's only an hour's drive."

Petrovich listened attentively, nodding his head when she finished. "Well, as you may already know from what you found on the internet, many of us who specialize in cryonics believe that technology will ultimately be able to transform human life and postpone death indefinitely. The science of cryobiology, the study of the effects of extremely low temperatures on cells, has contributed significantly to cryonics, as has the study of cryoprotectors, chemicals which help to freeze cells with minimal damage. Both had a long history in the Soviet Union."

He paused, but then continued as if by rote. "It was not until 1964 when an American physicist, Robert Ettinger, published his book, *The Prospect of Immortality*, that cryonics became more popular in the United States. Now there are over 150 bodies frozen in cryonic stasis, about one-half at the Cryonics Laboratory in Michigan which was founded by Ettinger in 1976; though in his eighties now, he's still involved in it. I studied with Ettinger several years before starting our own institute here. Unlike his laboratory, however, our institute does not store any bodies or body parts. Once we have successfully frozen them, we ship them to Ettinger. We're purely engaged in research on the freezing process itself."

Dr. Petrovich rose and reached over toward the metal container. "May I?" he asked perfunctorily, and Ethel nodded. He opened the top carefully and slowly pulled out a glass cylinder. A cloud of moisture rose up from the dry ice, and Dr. Petrovich wiped off the condensation on the cylinder. Ethel leaned forward to get a better look at the rounded piece of gray matter rotating slowly about inside.

"It's preserved in liquid nitrogen. As I mentioned, there are several bodies that have been frozen, but as far as I know, only half a dozen human brains, two in Krioris near Moscow, the first cryonics company outside the US." He looked over at Ethel as he replaced the cylinder inside the canister. "That's why I'm so interested in this Danilov brain. Would you have any objection to our keeping it here for a few days -- just to determine if it is still *in stasis*? That is, what you might call *alive*."

Ethel hesitated only a moment. His request seemed reasonable enough. After all, they were the experts, and what did she intend to do with the brain -- living or dead? She only wished Willy were there. "Sure, I suppose that would make sense." Then, as an afterthought, "Can you give me some kind of receipt, or something?"

Petrovich flashed a quick smile, but without humor. "Of course, Dr. Matson. Whatever you wish." He stepped over to his desk, wrote a few lines in long-hand, and passed the paper to her. On official Cryonics Institute stationery it simply said,

"Received of Dr. Ethel Matson, one human brain -- condition to be determined."

Willy was waiting around the bend where Ethel had dropped him off. He didn't comment specifically on her leaving the brain with Dr. Petrovich, but he did express his general disapproval of the institute. "I don't like the whole set-up, Ethel. I got in through a basement door, found a white lab coat in one of the staff closets, and bluffed my way around the various laboratories to see what I could find. I saw at least twenty different doctors or technicians, and I didn't even get up to the second floor. Why would they need so many technicians if they're only engaged in research? There were several huge storage rooms stacked with metal containers like the one with Danilov's brain, but much larger -- large enough to hold a human body. That's why I was surprised that

Petrovich told you that they don't store any bodies here. I just don't believe him."

"But why would they be so interested in Danilov's brain if they already have so many bodies, presumably including the brains? Surely they could remove some of them from the bodies and experiment as to how long they could remain alive without a body, couldn't they?"

"That's exactly what I was thinking when I spied the lab's library at the end of the corridor on the first floor. They have an entire room filled with books and articles on cryonics, Ethel, and the Ettinger Cryonics Laboratory up in Michigan is clearly recognized as the premier cryonics research facility in the country. They also had biographical data on the major players in the field. I only had a few minutes, but I looked up the name Danilov and found what I had expected. Michael's grandfather was a pioneer in the study of cryonics and in fact is credited with freezing the first dog at a cryobiology institute in Ukraine when it was still part of the Soviet Union. It was frozen for over eight hours and then revived – quite a feat for the time. However, it seems that the mainstream cryobiology researchers were not too keen on the life-preserving theory of cryonics, and Danilov was not encouraged to stay. It was then that he immigrated to America."

Ethel caught the implication immediately. "So Dr. Petrovich and his colleagues are probably less interested in the status of Danilov's brain than in its contents. If they find that it's still in a state of stasis, they could perhaps remove a brain from one of the bodies you think they have in storage and implant that of Danilov. If they can successfully resurrect Danilov in someone else's body, they could bring him up to date on the cryonics of today and tap his vast background and knowledge of the subject for the benefit of Petrovich's institute."

"Whoa, Ethel. That 'if they can resurrect' is a big ' if.' Don't tell me that your one hour with Dr. Petrovich convinced you of the reality of the cryonics theory. After all, it's still only a theory and although several bodies have been frozen, none as yet has ever been unfrozen and returned to life."

Ethel sidled to the right as they approached the Madison exit. Once off the highway she parked and turned to Willy. "No, Willy. I don't believe that frozen bodies can be resurrected – at least with the technology we now have. But I'm pretty certain that Dr. Petrovich believes it and that he's going to test his theory with the brain of Ivan Danilov, Michael's grandfather. And I'm not sure that I want to be an accomplice in that experiment." She frowned as Willy reached for the door handle. "Don't go, Willy. We still have to figure out what we're going to do to stop him." But by that time Willy was out of the car, waving goodbye over his shoulder.

He invariably pulled his disappearing acts at the most inconvenient times. Ethel wanted to call out after him, but knew it would be in vain. Oh, well, he'll come back. He always did.

"No, Dr. Petrovich, I don't understand." Roscoe listened as Ethel's voice took on the irritated, no nonsense tone he knew so well. "I have simply asked for the return of the Danilov brain which I left with you just yesterday and for which, by the way, I have your hand-written receipt. I don't understand why that should be so *impractical* as you suggest." She listened impatiently, tapping her chin as she shook her head. "Yes, I know that you want to do some experiments to determine if it is still *in stasis*, but I have decided that I want to give more thought to that and, in the meantime, I don't want to risk the brain being damaged."

Another two minutes in silence and then she exploded. "I'm sorry that you feel that way, Dr. Petrovich, but I can assure you that I am not ignorant of the importance of your research, nor oblivious to its possible long-term benefits. But until I can feel more assured that Mr. Danilov's brain will not be damaged, or ..." she hesitated for only an instant, but then continued, "or not be transferred to some host body, I must demand its return. I plan to drive over this afternoon and expect to pick up the brain at that time." She hung up without a goodbye.

"So what made you change your mind?" Roscoe frowned. "It's not like you to vacillate like this, Ethel. If you had doubts about that institute why did you drive over there in the first place? You might have expected that they'd have to keep the brain to determine if it was still alive. Why all the doubts now?"

She couldn't mention Willy again -- they had had the argument about "that figment of her imagination" too many times already. A little white lie would have to suffice. "Oh, Roscoe, I don't know exactly what it is. but all the way home I had this uneasy feeling that something wasn't right at that institute; that maybe they might want Danilov's brain for some reason other than disinterested research. Then, when I got home I looked him up on the net, and sure enough he was a pioneer in cryonic research. I think they want to steal his brain and use it for their own work." Well, so she hadn't found that information on the web, but Roscoe needn't know that it was Willy who had clued her in.

That afternoon when she took off for Janesville she fully expected to see Willy along the way -- but Willy wasn't there. She'd have to handle this one on her own. Dr. Petrovich himself met her at the door and greeted her with the utmost civility. Overly effusive, she thought, but she could hardly indict him for that. "I'm extremely disappointed in your decision to take back the brain before we've had the opportunity to thoroughly examine it, Dr. Matson. I can assure you that the testing we do would not damage the brain in any way." He smiled broadly in her direction as he motioned her to a chair opposite his desk, but his eyes never met hers. "Are you sure that we can't persuade you to change your mind?"

"I'm afraid not. I've given the matter serious thought, and I don't think my cousin would have approved of any kind of experimentation on his grandfather's brain." She shrugged, "After all, if he had been concerned about its condition, he could have had it examined himself. He had it in his possession for about forty years and he lived in Michigan, where I think you said the Ettinger lab is located."

Dr. Petrovich opened his mouth as if to speak, shook his head, and closed it again. Then, pushing a button on his phone console, he spoke curtly into the receiver. "Yes, bring it in. Yes, the one we were discussing." A door opened behind Ethel and a white-coated lab assistant brought in the canister and set it on the desk. Dr. Petrovich lifted the cover and pulled out the glass cylinder, the motion again causing the gray matter inside to rotate slightly in a slow circular motion.

"Just to keep the record straight, Dr. Matson, I'd appreciate your signing this little note which I had prepared for you. He handed her another sheet of Cryonics Institute stationery: "Brain of Ivan Danilov received from Dr. Michael Petrovich, condition undetermined." Ethel signed where indicated.

"Thank you, Dr. Petrovich. I'm sorry to have caused you this disappointment, but I hope you can understand my point of view."

"Of course." Less cordial now, but polite. "I understand, even though I don't agree." He extended his hand for a perfunctory shake and saw Ethel to the door.

Ethel spied Willy right around the bend in the road. She peppered him with questions as soon as he opened the door. "So when did you get out here? And how did you know I was coming?"

"Well, after our conversation yesterday, I pretty much figured you'd try to get the brain back -- probably as soon as possible."

As he carefully placed the large paper bag he was carrying in the back seat, she asked, "And what is that?"

"That, my dear, is Mr. Danilov's brain."

Ethel was so shocked that she stopped the car and even ignored the irritating supercilious smile that spread across his face.

"What? Willy, I have his brain right behind me in that canister. I got it from Dr. Petrovich just ten minutes ago!"

"No, you got what Dr. Petrovich said was Danilov's brain." He settled back and motioned her to drive on. "As we suspected, those larger canisters do contain bodies, including brains, which have been preserved in cryonic stasis. Before you arrived, the good doctor ordered a brain to be removed from one of those bodies and placed in the canister he gave you. The implantation of Danilov's brain into that body was to take place tomorrow morning. Earlier, when I first got there, I managed to

hide in a closet in the lab they used, and I found Danilov's brain in the original canister it came in. That's what's in the paper bag."

"You stole Mr. Danilov's brain?"

"Hardly, Ethel. After all, it wasn't theirs, was it? It was willed to you by your cousin and only loaned to them for their research. When you changed your mind, it was their obligation to return it to you. The fact that they gave you a substitute brain in an apparent attempt to defraud you doesn't lessen their culpability -- actually, it increases it."

"But surely when they find that it's missing, they'll guess that I took it."

"How could you? You were with Petrovich the entire time you were at the institute and he himself saw you leave with the canister he gave you. Right?"

Her reply was hesitant. "Yes -- I guess so." Her frown deepened as she shook her head. "But what in heaven's name am I going to do with two brains, Willy?"

Willy simply motioned for her to pull over to the side. As he climbed out, he added, "Oh, you'll think of something, Ethel. You always do!"

As soon as the phone rang, Ethel knew it was Dr. Petrovich. "No, I'm sorry, but I haven't changed my mind, Dr. Petrovich." Pause. "Well, I don't really know what I'm going to do with it. For the time being, I'm simply going to keep it." A longer pause. "No, I don't understand how the situation has changed. Perhaps you can enlighten me?" The line went dead.

Roscoe smiled as she slammed down the receiver. "I take it he didn't mention that he had a body all ready to receive Danilov's brain? Or that the one he gave you was a substitute?"

She shook her head. "He can't figure out who took the Danilov brain from the lab -- but I think he suspects that I had something to do with it."

"Well, you did sneak back in there and abscond with it, didn't you?" Ethel had decided not to tell him about Willy stealing the brain. Roscoe didn't believe in Willy. She had made up the story about sneaking back in through the basement door Willy had mentioned and taking it herself, but she didn't want to get into any details. Roscoe might be gullible, but he wasn't stupid.

So she finessed the issue and quickly changed the subject. "Now that Danilov's brain is safely back in my possession, I think I know what to do. I'm going to return the brain Petrovich gave me. I'll say that now that I've had more time to think it all over again, I feel that he should go ahead with his planned experiments.

Obviously, I won't mention that I know about the substitution or what he was going to do with the real Danilov brain. He can put the one he gave me back in the same body it belongs to -- I don't care."

"And the real Danilov brain?"

"I'm going to contact the Ettinger people, tell them about Danilov, and see if they want his brain." When Willy had told her about his research on Danilov in the library, he had also mentioned that the Ettinger Cryonics Laboratory was the premier cryonics research facility in the United States. If she had to trust anyone with Danilov's brain, Ethel was inclined to trust them far more than Dr. Petrovich.

"So what did the Ettinger people have to say?" Ethel hadn't seen Willy since their second trip to the Janesville facility the previous week.

"Well, I finally talked to Dr. Ettinger himself and he was absolutely elated. It seems that Dr. Petrovich didn't tell me the whole story about his leaving the Cryonics Laboratory in Michigan. It's true that he studied there with Dr. Ettinger, but after a few years they learned that he had secretly begun to set up his Janesville facility with many of the same chemical processes and equipment developed by Ettinger -- he had even recruited some of the staff members. So they asked him to leave. And there is no relationship between the two institutes. As far as Ettinger knows, Dr. Petrovich is engaged in the same kind of research that is done in Michigan and which would involve the freezing of whole bodies, not just body parts."

"Ettinger was very familiar with Danilov and his work and, like Petrovich, he believes that if Danilov's brain can be revitalized in another body, his contribution to the further development of cryonics would be enormous. He couldn't thank me enough and urged me to send it just as soon as possible."

"So it's gone?"

"I sent it UPS that afternoon. They received it the following day."

Willy looked over his shoulder at the canister in the back seat. "And that?"

"That, my dear Willy, is the substitute brain which Dr. Petrovich so kindly gave me on our last visit. I'm returning it as promised."

"That's above and beyond the call of duty, Ethel. Why not just send it -- or, better yet, let him drive over and pick it up?"

"Ah, but then, Willy, I wouldn't have another chance to snoop around his institute. After all, we haven't found out yet where he gets all those bodies!"

PIRACY AT SEA

"Piracy at sea continues into the present day. Partly because of the decreased ability of European navies to project their power abroad and the small-sized navies and limited patrol capabilities of poor countries, piracy in recent times has increased in areas such as south and southeast Asia, the coasts off Latin America and Africa, the Indian Ocean, and the Red Sea." Ethel read aloud to Roscoe from the Google excerpt she had brought along on the cruise. "Modern pirates now favor small motorized boats, often disguised as fishing vessels, which can easily overtake cargo containers and even some of the smaller tourist ships when they are passing through straits or other restricted areas. Modern pirates are less interested in the cargo, than in the belongings of passengers and crew members, as well as any valuables in the ship's safe."

Roscoe was not impressed. "Well, Mexico is hardly that *poor* a country, is it, Ethel? At least compared to many others, and I doubt if the Mexican navy would allow such piracy nonsense right here off the coast of Cancun where so many of their tourist revenues come from. Whatever got you going on this kick anyhow?"

"Oh, I don't know -- interesting, though, isn't it? I read about that ship that was hijacked last fall by so-called *pirates* off the coast of Africa and was surprised that piracy is apparently still alive and flourishing. So I looked it up in Google." She handed him the two pages. "Here, read the whole thing if you like. I'm going back to my Sudoku."

They had just begun their January cruise -- down the eastern coast of Mexico, through the Panama Canal, and then up the western coasts of Costa Rica and Guatemala. Having left the cold and snow of Wisconsin behind them, they were thoroughly enjoying their vacation on *The Pearl Princess*, the sun and warmth of the Caribbean, and the prospect of their transit through the canal. As usual, Ethel had read up on all the places they were about to visit, but she was especially impressed by the magnitude of the task of building the canal. "I can't wait to see it."

She could sense that Willy was there before he spoke. She thought he might show up sometime during the voyage -- there were few trips she had taken when he didn't appear. His white hair ruffled in the breeze and he firmly pulled his blue captain's cap down on his head to hold it in place. "Quite a sight, isn't it, Ethel? I mean, I'm sure you've gone through some other canals and locks before these, but look at how close to the sides that huge ship ahead of us is moving along. And so much of the engineering depends on gravity alone -- just letting the water seek its own natural level." He grinned as he added, "But where is the good Roscoe? I can't imagine him missing all this."

"Oh, he's sitting out on our balcony." She shrugged at his raised eyebrows. "Yeah, we did it up right this time -- reserved a cabin with a large window and balcony and made sure it was located on the starboard side of the ship so we can see the shoreline when close enough. But I kind of like to watch the hustle and bustle of the crew and passengers." She cocked her head and smiled, "And what brings you here, Willy? What kind of exciting new adventure are you about to stir up?"

"C'mon now, Ethel. You know it's you who stirs up all the trouble. I'm only an innocent bystander, or as Roscoe thinks, a figment of your lively imagination." His eyes twinkled in anticipation of another round in their ongoing debate about the nature of reality and imagination. "Why, I don't think he'd believe in me if he saw me right now with his own two eyes. But maybe you're not ready yet for such a serious discussion. I saw the steward down below on the lower deck. Are you up

to your usual Scotch?" He was off before she could nod her head. When she saw Roscoe approaching from the other direction, however, she knew Willy wouldn't be back. At least not that afternoon.

"Do you remember seeing that boat when we passed through the canal, Roscoe? Ethel handed him her binoculars and pointed back beyond the stern. "No. Further back – almost on the horizon. Can you see it now?"

He raised the binoculars slightly and fiddled with the adjustments. "Yeah, I think so. I mean, I see some kind of boat back there, but it's too far away to say whether or not it was one of those passing through the canal when we were. Why?" He frowned at her silent shrug. "Does it look familiar to you?"

"No. That's what bothers me. Where did it come from?"

"Hell, Ethel. There were dozens of ships routed through that canal when we went through and we only saw those right in front and behind us. But there could have been dozens more just off the coast or, for that matter, sailing up from South America." He gave her the glasses back and returned to the brochure he was reading. "You know, these rain forests in Costa Rica really sound interesting -- I'm glad we signed up for that land tour tomorrow. They charged enough extra for it, but it may be worth it."

Ethel smiled indulgently. "I'm sure it will be. It's one of the things that sold me on this particular cruise." It wasn't that Roscoe was exactly what she'd call "tight," but he was certainly frugal. She'd never forget the time they bought that horse painting in Arizona. Now that it hung in their foyer back home in Madison, he loved it as much as she did. But she had pulled out all stops to persuade him to buy it in the first place. The same thing with this cruise. He had fought her tooth and nail, but now, a good seven days at sea, he was enjoying every minute of it. She again focused the binoculars on the horizon behind them.

All those who had signed up for the land tour boarded the small motor boats that were going to take them to Puerta Caldera. There they would proceed by bus to the nearby nature preserve and rain forest. During the night, Roscoe had developed one of his sinus headaches and at the last minute decided not to go. Ethel offered to stay with him, but he wouldn't have it. "Why should you miss the tour, just because I'm feeling lousy? We probably won't get a refund, and there's nothing you can really do anyhow, Ethel. I'll rest in the cabin now, but later I'll watch you take off from our balcony."

Turning back to wave at Roscoe, Ethel noticed that the motorized fishing boat she had seen on the horizon was now approaching the cruise ship they had just left. As it pulled up next to The Pearl Princess, she could hear the shouting back and forth, but couldn't make out what anyone was saying.

"I wonder what's going on back there," she murmured to Willy who had jumped into her boat to join her right before it took off for the harbor.

"I don't know. But it looks like they're in some kind of trouble and want to board our cruise liner. See the gangway being lowered down to their boat?" Willy picked up Ethel's binoculars to get a better look, but their own little motor boat had already gone a good distance toward the shore, and as they swerved into the harbor he couldn't see the liner at all. "Damn. Lost sight of them." He paused in thought. "But I wonder..."

"What? What do you wonder?"

"Well, I was just wondering why a fishing boat would try to get help from a cruise ship when it was already in sight of a nearby harbor where presumably it could find whatever assistance it might need? Unless..."

"Unless they didn't need any assistance in the first place," Ethel finished for him. "Unless the crew on that 'fishing boat' wanted to board our liner for some completely different reason." Ethel looked back toward the pilot who was slowing down to dock at the narrow passenger pier. A somewhat dilapidated tour bus waited on the shore with its motor running. "Willy, we have to get back to The Pearl Princess. You may think I'm daft, but I think those are pirates out there trying to take over our ship!"

Ethel wasn't too far off the mark. Antonio Morales Guzman was a Colombian drug lord, who occasionally engaged in what the press labeled "acts of piracy." With drug sales to the States through Mexico temporarily impeded (though not cut off) by increased border vigilance, Morales now and then turned to robbery at sea or modern day piracy to supplement his income. Tourist ships were easy prey, he learned, and loaded with wealthy patrons, well-endowed with both cash and jewelry. Moreover, although cruise ships carried larger crews than cargo vessels, the crew members tended to be selected for their language skills, cooking ability or general affability toward passengers, rather than for any knowledge of security procedures or arms and weaponry.

The Pearl Princess was a relatively small cruise ship, with less than two hundred passengers and about eighty crew members. Morales' own well-armed and well-trained pirate gang spread out quickly over the three main decks and, with their loaded weapons in full sight, they soon persuaded the liner crew to follow their instructions. They secured most of them in the exercise/health facility located on the lower deck. Morales then had the captain announce over the loudspeaker that all passengers should assemble at their lifeboat stations where his pirate band collected both cash and jewelry. Another group of the drug-runners searched the cabins for any valuables stashed in suitcases or dresser drawers. The flimsy safes provided by *The Pearl Princess* were little match for some well-placed bullets. The ship's main safe proved to be an equally soft target.

Roscoe proceeded to B-16, Foreword Deck D, the designated lifeboat station where he and Ethel had assembled with their fellow passengers for instructions their second day on board. He never carried that much cash on him, but the burly pirate who seized his billfold soon emptied it of all that he had, plus credit cards. Roscoe was secretly pleased that he had placed their extra cash, travelers checks, and Ethel's jewelry in their safe, not thinking they would break it open. But when he returned to his cabin, obeying the gentle nudge of a rifle stock, he was dismayed to see the safe empty.

The whole operation took less than ninety minutes. "Lock the good captain in his cabin," Morales ordered. "Check on the rest of the crew in the health facility, and be sure those doors are secured." *The Pearl Princess* was not damaged in any way -- it wasn't Morales' style. But it floated serenely at anchor, only a short distance from the harbor of Puerto Caldera and only thirty short miles from the rain forest where Roscoe believed Ethel was enjoying her pre-paid land tour.

Meanwhile, Ethel and Willy located the main harbor office, though Willy chose to remain outside. Senor Umberto Perez, the Costa Rican harbor master, was not easily disturbed by the many real and imagined problems of gringo tourists, but this Americano woman was reasonable enough and seemed to know what she was talking about. Moreover, when he tried to radio The Pearl Princess, he failed to make any contact with it. "So, you say that you saw these men from the large motor boat walk up the gangplank to your cruise ship's deck?" He paused to tap his chin with the pen he had used to scribble a few notes while they were talking. "Perhaps they had some troubles with their boat and simply were asking for help?"

"That's what we thought at first," Ethel interrupted. "But if they needed help, why didn't they just sail into the harbor here? Why board a tourist ship at sea?" When he didn't answer, she continued. "Now, I know this may sound far-fetched, but I've been reading that in recent years several acts of piracy have taken place not only off the coast of Africa, but in these waters as well. Do you think they could actually be pirates?"

Glimpsing the raised eyebrow of the harbor master, she toned down her rhetoric. "Well, it's probably too early to speculate about that, but ---" she paused, assumed her most professorial look, and added in Spanish, "but perhaps you could send a patrol boat out to The Pearl Princess just to check on what actually happened?"

"Si. We can – and will – do just that. You are quite correct, Senora Matson, about the increase in acts of piracy. We here in Costa Rica have had at least two recent attempts to seize cargo ships after they left the canal." He shrugged and added, "As you know, Costa Rica has no

navy, but up to now these bandidos or "pirates" have not been so bold as to attack or -- how do you say it? -- take over a tourist cruise ship." He tapped his chin again and picked up the phone. "I'll order a cutter with an armed crew to leave immediately. If you would like, you may join it." There was no time to locate Willy.

The cutter reached The Pearl Princess only thirty minutes after Morales and his pirate band had left it. The gangplank they had used to board and leave the ship was still in place, and Ethel and the harbor master quickly scrambled on board. By this time, the passengers had released the captain, the stewards and the rest of the crew who filled in Perez with all the details. In the distance, the pirate ship could still be seen. Perez turned to Ethel with a courteous smile, but politely cut off the question she was about to ask. "I'm sure you would like to accompany us, Senora Matson, but I fear that under the circumstances that will not be possible.

Hurrying over toward the cutter, Perez turned back to Ethel. "Hopefully, we will capture these bandidos of the sea and when we do, we will stop back here before returning to the harbor."

"Whatever made you suspect that they were pirates in the first place, Ethel?" Roscoe's headache had disappeared with the pirates, and he was eagerly awaiting the return of the harbor cutter from its pursuit of the marauding ship. "They managed to pretty well strip everyone of all cash, credit cards, jewelry -- even travelers checks. I guess they emptied the ship's safe as well. But thanks to you, we may recover it all." He put his arm around her and hugged her warmly against his chest.

Ethel wanted to tell him that it was actually Willy who had suggested to her that she try to get the harbor master to investigate, but she decided to leave well enough alone. Roscoe had not seen Willy jump into her boat when she had left for their rain forest tour, so he wasn't even aware that Ethel's "imaginary friend" had been around. She wondered where he was now. Roscoe was still on a roll. "I didn't mind so much about the cash," (like hell, he didn't, she thought), "but I did feel bad about that garnet ring." He frowned,

"If they don't get everything back, I wonder if our insurance will cover it?"

"Oh, forget about the money for now, Roscoe. The important thing is that you weren't hurt -- that no one was hurt -- and that those pirates will probably be caught and get the prison terms they deserve. At least, I certainly hope so!"

When harbor master Perez finally returned to *The Pearl Princess* some two hours later, he was followed by the pirate boat under Costa Rican control and by another harbor cutter which had assisted in its capture. After consulting with Perez, the captain of *The Pearl Princess* announced that everyone should begin to line up in front of the purser's office where they would try to restore all the stolen goods to their rightful owners.

Roscoe left immediately, while Ethel stayed behind to say goodbye to Senor Perez. He smiled warmly as he shook her hand. "We learned that these bandidos of the sea are actually Colombian drug runners, Senora – engaged in a little piracy on the side. We appreciate your assistance, Senora Matson. If you had just gone on to take your rain forest tour, by the time you returned to your cruise ship, the bandidos would have been too far away to catch." He bowed his head slightly and saluted his farewell.

Standing at the rail as Perez returned to his boat, Ethel suddenly saw Willy waving to her from the second cutter. He shouted, "I want to see the end of this story, Ethel. I'm riding back to Puerto Caldera with them. I'll see you in Madison next week. But make sure you get your garnet ring back." Now, how did he know that her garnet ring had been taken, she wondered. But then, that was vintage Willy. She shook her head as she made her way down to the purser's office where she was sure that Roscoe was waiting – probably first in line.

BELOW THE SURFACE

The waves slapped loudly against the sides of the Loch Ness Cruiser as it plowed resolutely through the turbulent waters. His eyes squinting into the distance and his hands firmly on the wheel, Captain McGregor headed toward the rocks where the most recent sighting of "the Loch Ness monster" had been reported. His flamboyant brochure featured grainy photos of what was described as a long-necked sea serpent, frequently seen in the bay off Glen Urquhart. The captain himself had promised his American tourists that they would surely catch a glimpse of "Nessie" on their tour.

Standing near the captain, Ethel peered ahead with the high-powered binoculars she had bought especially for this trip; she saw nothing but the lake. Roscoe had long since retired to a canvas chair on the forward deck. Now asleep, he was completely oblivious to the chatter of his fellow passengers who crowded against the rail in front of him, their eyes focused on the swirling eddy which the captain pointed out to them.

"There! To the port side, lass." McGregor nudged Ethel's glasses slightly to the left to guide them in the right direction. "Did ya see 'er?"

Though she desperately wanted to believe in "Nessie," Ethel's common sense kept her from letting her emotions cloud her judgment. "Well, I do see the circles of roiling water over there, but I'm afraid that I don't see any sea monster, Captain McGregor – not even her long neck." Once again, she raised her binoculars to her eyes and searched the horizon. For what? Did she really expect to see the famous sea serpent of Loch Ness? More important, she reminded herself, did such a creature even exist?

Ethel had found the dog-eared booklet entitled "The Monster of Loch Ness" in a used bookstore and read it before she and Roscoe embarked on their trip to Scotland. Now, as the boat left the shore, she took it out of her purse and again perused its contents. Though most of it focused on the monster, the author had also devoted several pages to the lake itself: "Loch Ness is a long narrow loch, a little over 24 miles long and an average of less than a mile wide. It covers nearly 14,000 acres and its maximum depth is 975 feet, most of it below sea level. Tradition opines that the loch holds huge caverns with their entrances below water level, but inside sloping upwards above the surface of the lake, thus sustaining oxygen dependent life."

Their failure yesterday to sight the monster (if there were one, Ethel thought), had not deterred her from another cruise with the good captain McGregor. Roscoe had begged off "because of the bad weather," but Ethel knew that he really was more interested in scouting around the quaint little shops of Fort Augustus than in searching the seas for the legendary sea serpent. She hadn't seen anyone else venture on board. Though Ethel didn't mind traveling alone, she was nonetheless happily surprised when Willy joined her on the rear deck. Since Roscoe didn't believe that Willy existed, he seldom appeared when Ethel's husband was around. But Ethel had become comfortable with his sporadic visits, and was no longer surprised when he suddenly showed up.

"I thought I saw you on shore when we docked yesterday, Willy, but you were nowhere in sight when we got off the boat. I'm glad you could make it today."

"Actually, the lake is a bit rough for my taste, Ethel." He grabbed the rail as the boat pitched forward into the oncoming waves. "But I knew you wouldn't leave Loch Ness without at least one more try to find Nessie."

"So, is there a Nessie, Willy?" She grinned and shook her head. *"I suppose that's a silly question, isn't it? If anyone were to believe in sea monsters, it would be you."*

"And you, too, Ethel. Underneath that professorial objectivity of yours you've always been a true romantic at heart." Glancing up at the gathering storm, Willy pulled a skipper's hat from his jacket pocket and settled it firmly over his white, curly hair. But when the ship lurched again, the two of them began to move toward the raised platform at the front of the boat where the Captain beckoned.

Peering into the thick fog ahead, Captain McGregor stood at the wheel in front of the cabin, expertly guiding the boat toward something that only he could see. *"C'mon up here, mates. I think she just went down up ahead here -- by these huge boulders. I've sighted 'er near 'em before. It's where the locals say the big underwater caverns are."* He grinned. *"And where our Nessie lives."*

Ethel scanned the waters near the outcropping of boulders toward which they were heading – but again she saw nothing but the fog and the rocks. The boat was dangerously close to the looming stone mass, she thought, when suddenly the hull   shuddered with a sickening scrunch. The jolting halt to their forward motion thrust Ethel and Willy to their hands and knees. *"My God, Willy – we hit the rocks!"* Grasping the wheel, McGregor stayed on his feet, but Ethel and Willy slid sideways on the deck, stopped from falling overboard only by the frail wooden railing to which they clung.

"Any more news on the Loch Ness Cruiser?" Roscoe was frantic. It was the third time he had asked the police officer the same question. The local police from Fort Augustus had given him a lift up to Glen Urquhart which was located to the north and near the mid-point of the shoestring lake. It was there that the tour ship had been impaled on the outlying rocks and now sat suspended.

"As I told you, Mr. Matson, we haven't heard a thing since that first SOS signal from Captain McGregor. Their radio could have been damaged by the crash, or...." His voice faded as he noted the fear in Roscoe's eyes. "Look, I'm sure they're going to be all right. As long as the boat hangs on to that rock, they're above water and, if they weren't hurt by the crash itself, they should be okay."

"But can't you do something? Don't you have some kind of rescue teams trained for these kinds of emergencies? Can't you send another boat out there -- to see how they are and to bring them back here to shore? Or maybe a helicopter?"

"As I said, sir, we alerted the Loch Ness Phenomena Investigation Bureau in Fort Augustus when we got the SOS call from Captain McGregor, and they are sending one of their boats over here to Urquhart Bay just as soon as they can get one geared up. As you yourself suggested, they need to locate some trained personnel and, if possible, take a doctor along in case of any injuries. As far as a copter is concerned, the closest would be at Inverness and we've already phoned them." He paused and then patted Roscoe on the back. "One of our squad cars is returning to Port Augustus – why not ride back with them and rest a bit at your motel? We'll phone as soon as we have any news."

"Thanks, officer, but I feel a little closer to the action here, and if -- when Ethel returns -- I want to be here. Do you have any idea when that ship will come?"

"Shouldn't be too long, sir. We'll let you know when it's on its way."

It was then that the bumping began -- the bumping that just wouldn't stop. Though the prow of the boat seemed tightly wedged between two gigantic boulders protruding from the water, the whole boat still shook violently after every muffled bump. And each time Willy and Ethel tried to stand, the lurching of the boat sent them back to their knees. "It's like there's something down there," Ethel yelled to McGregor. "Maybe it's just the waves pushing us against the rocks – or maybe – maybe it's something else."

"It's Nessie," McGregor shouted. "She's tryin' to free us from those boulders." He cackled a nervous laugh. "Yep, that's what the ol' gal is tryin' to do, all right!"

But Willy didn't laugh. "Well, whatever it is, if it keeps on, it could easily break up this whole damn boat." He pointed to a crack between them and McGregor . "See that crack in the deck over there? This whole back section is pulling away! If she goes, we'll be going with her. We're safer if we can swim to those rocks." He grabbed Ethel by the arm and helped her over the railing just as the boat began to crack apart.

Captain McGregor tried to yell over the sound of the splintering boat: "Stay on board! Git up front here. Come back! These rocks should hold us fast -- even if 'er rear does break off." But as the crack widened and finally split the boat in two, the rear section tilted precariously backward and slid into the water with both Ethel and Willy hanging on to the wooden rail.

Both the boat and McGregor disappeared from their view, as into the water they descended, clinging tightly to the railing and gasping for their last breath before they sank into its swirling depths. Then, suddenly, the turbulence died down, and they were borne more slowly but steadily along toward an open cave that beckoned before them. They could feel the pressure of the force that was moving them, but they couldn't see it. When they reached the cavern mouth, the rail broke from the rest of the rear and they were pushed though the opening and back up to the surface. There they saw the source of their rescue.

As she deposited them on the narrow shelf that lined the walls of the cavern, Nessie finally appeared to them in full view. Her long neck curved gracefully up toward the ceiling and her humped back reached almost as far. She looked much like the faded photographs in Captain McGregor's brochure -- gigantic in size, a small head for such a huge body, and a long scaly tail. But despite her size, neither Ethel nor Willy was afraid. They sensed a basic goodness in the huge sea monster which had rescued them, and only felt saddened when she slipped back into the water and swam away.

The helicopter arrived before the rescue boat and whirled its way toward the shattered remains of the Loch Ness Cruiser. The co-pilot was shouting from the open door, but the wind swept the words from his mouth. Though the Captain heard nothing, the hefty rope that lowered a plastic seat next to the raised platform on which he stood was explanation enough. McGregor staggered his way to the chair, slung himself into the seat, and was slowly pulled up to the copter's door. As the copter circled above the front of the boat, still firmly stuck between the two boulders, the Captain searched the waters below. He only saw the shadow of what might have been the legendary Nessie -- or, he admitted reluctantly, it might just be the broken rear of the cruiser.

Roscoe rushed over to the copter when it landed, but it was only Captain McGregor who stepped down from the cockpit. "Where's Ethel?" he shouted, grabbing the Captain by the lapels of his jacket. "What happened to Ethel?"

"She went down when my boat broke apart -- along with that curly-haired gen'leman she was talking to. I told 'em to stay on board. They were tryin' to make it to the rocks, I think, but ---" He shook his head slowly. "I saw 'em go down with the poopdeck when the boat split." Seeing the despair in Roscoe's eyes, he added, "But hang on, sir. There's still hope. Folks 'round here say there are some big caves out there -- under the surface of those boulders. Maybe they got inside."

"Where in hell is that rescue boat anyhow?" Roscoe exploded. He turned to the police officer and asked, "Can't you find out if it's on its way? Maybe you could radio them to circle around out there when it gets here?"

"We just heard they're on their way, Mr. Matson. And, yes, we've let them know that Captain McGregor is safe on shore, but that two passengers are still missing." He scanned the horizon with his binoculars and then handed them to Roscoe. "There she is!" Pointing with one hand, he guided Roscoe's glasses with the other. "Do you see her?"

As Roscoe watched, the rescue boat from Fort Augustus made its way toward the remains of the Loch Ness Cruiser.

"So, what now, Willy?" Ethel shivered in the damp cold of the cavern, while Willy explored the cave's perimeter. He walked carefully around the narrow shelf onto which Nessie had shoved both them and the railing to which they had clung.

"I don't see any other entrance or exit besides the one we came in. If we want to get out of here, we'll have to use the same one." He cocked his head and then placed his ear tightly against the wall of the cave. "You can hear – or maybe feel – the vibrations of the storm outside, but I think it's letting up. We might want to take a chance that McGregor got off an SOS before the boat broke up and that they sent another boat or a helicopter to get us to shore."

"But we can't just swim out of here, Willy, and tread water out there while we wait for a boat we don't even know is on its way." The despair crept in, despite her efforts to hide it. "And yet, we can't just sit here, either. Oh, Willy – think of something!"

Willy had made a full circle of the cave and was back next to Ethel and the broken railing. He sat down, put his arm around her shoulder, and gave her a half-hearted hug. "Hey, it's not all that bad, Ethel. We still have this wooden rail to hang onto and, who knows, maybe old Nessie will guide us to shore. I don't think she brought us to this cave just to abandon us here." He added thoughtfully, "No, I think that Nessie is not the 'monster' she's made out to be. Somehow, she's going to get us out of here."

They sat together on the ledge and waited, the minutes dragging by until over an hour had passed. As they talked, he tried to divert her attention. "Just think what a story you'll have to tell when you get back home, Ethel. I can see it in the Madison Journal now: 'Local Woman Rescued by Loch Ness Monster.' She will rescue us, you know. Why, even Roscoe will be impressed." His effort to distract her was unsuccessful. But before she could reply, Willy shook his head, put his finger to his lips, and again placed his ear against the wall. "It's a helicopter, Ethel! They did send one to find us!"

At the same moment, Nessie's head once more emerged. She grasped the railing in her mouth and carried it slowly toward the side of the

185

ledge above the cavern's mouth, where she waited for them to follow. They hurried into the water and, holding tightly to the rail, they descended below the surface as she propelled them toward the dimly lit opening. But the rail was buoyant and clumsy to move, and by the time she guided them through the underwater mouth of the cave and up to the surface on the other side, the copter had already picked up McGregor. Having surveyed the surrounding waters and finding no one, it was on its way to Glen Urquhart. Ethel and Willy waved and shouted, but all to no avail. This time, the shadow of despair descended on them both.

But Nessie had not abandoned them. Carefully grasping the railing with her mouth placed between the two of them, she pushed them toward the nearest boulder and lifted them, rail and all, onto its flat top. As she again departed under the surface of the water, she flipped her scaly tail in a final farewell. In the distance they could see the rescue ship from Fort Augustus approaching them at full speed.

The police drove Roscoe from Glen Urquhart to the port at Fort Augustus where the rescue boat had already landed. He rushed to take Ethel in his arms and still held her hand in his as the squad car drove them from the police station to their motel. Willy had said his goodbye to Ethel on the boat when it landed and soon disappeared into the crowd which had gathered to see the rescued Americans. With his skipper's hat and navy jacket, Willy looked like a crew member from the rescue boat and no one bothered to stop him. By the time the police sought to question "the other passenger," Willy was long gone.

Now that Ethel was safe, Roscoe shrugged aside his anxiety and started asking the inevitable questions. "But why did you insist on telling that story about the Loch Ness monster, Ethel? Now, these locals, including the police, may believe there's some sort of sea serpent out there – though I think they were skeptical. But don't expect me to believe in her. I'm perfectly willing to accept the fact that **you** believe in Nessie, but that doesn't make her real." He looked at her intently. "You know, you could have hit your head when the boat broke up and maybe you had some kind of hallucination. Or, maybe your always fertile imagination just went completely wild!" Then he squeezed her hand and hugged her again. "I'm sorry, hon. I didn't mean to preach. If only that other passenger had stuck around, maybe he could have shed some light on what happened."

Ethel returned his hug and smiled as she remembered Willy's last words before he jumped to the ground from the boat's gangplank. "My only regret, Ethel, is that I can't be around to watch Roscoe's face when you tell him about our little adventure. If he finds it hard to believe in my existence, just think what a problem he'll have with Nessie!"

UNCERTAIN OMEN

Although her emotions had been totally shaken by the phone call, the reality of Gary's death only began to penetrate Ethel's conscious thinking as her plane ascended out of O'Hare and banked east toward New York. As usual on her short trips to attend the board meetings of Transatlantic Research and Analysis, Inc., Ethel had planned to meet Gary for dinner on Monday night. The cab ride from La Guardia to the Yale Club took thirty-five to fifty minutes, depending on arrival time, and she figured that dinner at seven should work out fine. She had sent him an email with the dates, but surprisingly there had been no reply. A week ago Roscoe suggested that she phone him to confirm; so she did call, but only got his voice recorder and simply left a message.

Then, on Friday, Evelyn phoned. "It's Evelyn Manthis," Roscoe murmured as he handed Ethel the phone. "Isn't that Gary's daughter?" Ethel shrugged as she took the phone. Evelyn's voice betrayed her tears, and Ethel's heart started pounding when she heard the news. "It's Evelyn, Ethel." She hesitated, then added, "Gary's daughter."

"Yes, Evelyn. I remember -- though it's been ages since I've seen you. Is anything wrong? You sound upset."

"It's Dad, Ethel." Another pause. "I don't know how to break this gently. Dad was killed in a car accident last week." She rushed on then before Ethel could even think of a reply. "I've been trying to notify the relatives and all his friends, but wasn't able to get to his apartment in New York until earlier this week. I listened to your phone message and got your number from that. I could have tried to reach you earlier at the college, I suppose, but I know you retired and -- well, I just wasn't thinking real good."

"No, that's okay, Evelyn. I'm just so terribly sorry. I don't know what to say. How did it happen? How is your Mom taking it?" Gary had told her that Susan had Altzheimer's, and now lived in an institution near Evelyn in Minneapolis. "Does she understand what happened?"

"Well, we're not sure, but we think so. At least at times. He was visiting here -- Dad was -- before the accident, and she knew who he was then. But later, when we tried to explain what happened, she was pretty mixed up. She knows that she's not in their home in Washington any more, but she doesn't know where she is. And she sometimes talks about him as if he's still alive and working in New York."

Gary and Susan had split up in the late 1990s when he retired early from the State Department and took a job as a consultant in New York. She had stayed on in their home in DC until the Altzheimer's deteriorated to the point where she couldn't live alone any longer. They finally decided on a nursing home near Evelyn.

"What about your brother and sister?" Ethel was never good at names, and couldn't for the life of her think of them. They chatted on like that for a while until Evelyn could speak about the accident itself.

"He drove here from New York -- it was funny, considering all his international work at the Department, but he never liked flying. So, anyhow, he stayed with us for about three days and then left to drive back through Canada. He was passing a car somewhere in Ontario and -- well, he didn't allow enough space and they had a head-on collision. The other driver was killed, too. But I guess it was Dad's fault. He always did drive too fast." She stopped and all Ethel could hear was the low hum of some music in the background. After a few more condolences, they hung up.

Ethel had met Gary Manthis more than twenty years ago when he came to the University of Wisconsin – Madison as a "diplomat in residence" -- fairly high-level foreign service officers who take a year's sabbatical at various university and college campuses around the country. They teach classes, give lectures, and engage in research, if so inclined -- all designed to give them a break from the hurly-burly of their everyday work in order to devote their time to thinking about the more academic and esoteric aspects of foreign policy. Since Ethel taught the international relations and American foreign policy classes, Gary joined her as adjunct lecturer and they became fast friends.

When Gary learned that Ethel had once thought about the foreign service as a career, he alerted her to a new program that brought academics to the State Department for two or three years to engage in a hands-on experience at the policy-making level. Roscoe's stock brokerage job was flexible, so she applied, was accepted, and spent 1993 to 1995 in Washington in the Bureau of European Affairs. Gary retired a couple of years later, but they kept in touch -- through his separation from Susan, his move to New York, and Ethel's own retirement soon thereafter. Her appointment to the board of Transatlantic Research and Analysis brought her to New York two or three times a year when she usually managed to see Gary for dinner. Not this time, she thought bleakly.

As the plane started its descent, another thought began to nag at her mind. The board meeting was tomorrow, but she didn't plan to leave until Wednesday. She had another friend in New York whom she frequently saw on her visits there, and she had also tried to contact her before this trip. Although Ethel had talked to Gini two months ago and planned to meet on Tuesday night for dinner and the musical, *Chicago*, she had not been able to reach her since. Two emails had gone unanswered and only a recorder had responded to Ethel's phone call. Ordinarily, Ethel wouldn't have worried -- Gini often spent long weekends with her daughter and son-in-law in Connecticut. But Gary's death intruded on her usual calm. She tried to shake off the sense of foreboding by telling herself she would call Gini as soon as she got to the Yale Club. Ethel had also brought along Gini's daughter's number.

"This is Gini," the familiar voice said. "I'm not at home right now, but if you'll leave your number and a brief message, ..." Ethel dutifully left her message -- again. But then she began to fret. It just wasn't like Gini not to have tried to make some sort of contact. She knew Ethel would be leaving for her board meeting in the morning and probably would be gone most of the day. Ethel had to know where and when they were going to meet before she left in the morning. But nothing opens in New York until about ten, and she'd have to be at her meeting by then. She decided to call Gini's daughter that night. It was only 5:30, and she might still be at her office.

Ethel knew that Gini's daughter was a lawyer, but she didn't expect the run-around she got when trying to reach her. Finally, the officious secretary left it at this: "Look, Tracy has already left for the day and I'm not at liberty to give you her home phone or her cell number; but I'll try to reach her for you and call you back in fifteen minutes. Is that okay?" Ethel had little choice. After twenty-five minutes she was growing frantic, but then the phone rang. It was Tracy herself.

"I'm truly sorry, Ethel. I know we haven't met, but Mom talked about you so much that I do feel I know you." She paused. Just like Evelyn Manthis, Ethel thought, her stomach turning. "Ethel, I don't know how to tell you this, but Mom passed away this last Friday." Silence -- on both ends of the line.

"But what ... how? She wasn't ill, was she?" The rest of the conversation simply laid out the facts: a pain in the chest and a trip to emergency, a problem with the aorta and a necessary transplant, seeming recovery, but then the fatal turn-around and her death. "I knew she had the tickets for *Chicago*, but I couldn't find your phone number anywhere and I didn't know where you'd be staying when you got here. I was just hoping that you might have my number and call. But I didn't want you to hear it from my secretary or someone else; I wanted to tell you myself." This time they both cried together. Ethel managed to get her home number and address before hanging up.

By this time she was utterly drained. It was not only a double blow to her emotions, but an absolutely weird coincidence. Two close friends had died within a week of each other and both had planned to have dinner with her on this visit. She felt both empty because of their loss, and strangely tied to their passing. It wasn't a matter of cause and effect; she didn't believe that dining with her was somehow the kiss of death. But she did sense a sort of warning -- a message about her own mortality.

Ethel had always believed that death was just another stage in the progress of life, and that one's essential "being" continued after death. What she now realized was the vagary of death; that it can come at any time, under any guise -- on a Canadian highway, in a New York hospital, or even on a plane ride home. After all, wasn't there an old wives' tale that bad things always come in threes? She wasn't looking forward to her flight home, but she did manage to move up her reservation a day early. She left for Chicago early Tuesday afternoon, right after her meeting at TRA.

Roscoe met her at the airport and she unburdened her feelings and uneasy apprehensions to him for most of the way home. "Yeah, it's weird all right," he agreed. "But I wouldn't make too much out of it, Ethel. Coincidences do happen, you know." As he pulled into the driveway, he added, "And I never did believe in omens or buy that stuff about bad things coming in threes. After all, here you are -- safe and sound." Ethel nodded, but an uneasy premonition hung on. She spent most of the rest of the day unpacking, sending sympathy notes to Evelyn and Tracy, and phoning their own kids to fill them in on her miserable trip.

It wasn't until early Wednesday evening when her doubts were confirmed. Roscoe had flicked on the TV news and the smoldering wreckage of the plane burst its image onto the screen. The overlay voice continued, "... and observers said that the plane had just taken off from LaGuardia when the smaller aircraft suddenly veered into its path and the two collided." Back to Mike Spencer in the studio: "For any of you who have just tuned in, American Flight 207, from LaGuardia to O'Hare, has just crashed after hitting another aircraft upon take-off. As of now, we have no further details, but from the looks of things, it's unlikely there are any survivors. Now back to the scene of the crash." The sirens could be heard in the background as the smoke swirled upward from the wreckage.

"Oh, my God, Roscoe. That was my flight!" Her face went white. Roscoe took one look and rushed to the bar where he poured her a healthy shot of Scotch. Ethel gulped half of it down before she could continue. "If I hadn't switched my reservation to come home early, I'd have been on that plane!" She didn't need to say the rest: "And if Gary and Gini hadn't died, I never would have changed my flight."

Premonition? Omen? In her own mind, she would never know for sure.

"RECALCULATING"

"Damn! There she goes again!" Ethel was no longer just frustrated and irritated; she was getting downright angry. "Vicky," as she had named the voice on her GPS (global positioning system), had once again announced that she was recalculating Ethel's highway route from Denver down to Phoenix. Ethel had already spent a couple of days reminiscing with an old college friend in Denver, and was now heading south for Arizona where Roscoe was expecting her.

"Recalculating." Vicky's voice came through loud and clear. This was the third time she had changed the route and Ethel was now thoroughly confused. She had been reluctant to disregard the neatly high-lighted map that AAA had provided her, along with the Trip Tick that outlined each segment of the trip. But Roscoe had sworn by the GPS which he had given Ethel for Christmas and had made her promise to use it.

"It's so much easier to use than trying to follow those maps while driving, Ethel. And safer, too. You can just listen to the verbal instructions and keep your eyes on the road." He pulled out the map and spread it on the dining room table. "Now, look here. It's pretty much of a straight shot over to Denver from Wisconsin – you can simply follow the map for that part if you want to. But from Denver on, there are a lot of different highways which may or may not be clearly marked and your GPS will give you plenty of advance notice as you approach them." He patted her back in the patronizing way she hated, and added, "I know you're not too fond of these electronic 'gadgets' as you call them, but just give it a fair trial." She had promised -- and now here she was.

Instead of flying, Ethel had decided to drive out to Colorado and Arizona for their winter vacation in order to take Eskimo along with her. She had heard too many awful stories about dogs cooped up in too-hot or too-cold airplane baggage compartments to take him along on a flight. Since Roscoe couldn't get away for the three to four extra days of driving time both ways, he had flown alone directly to Phoenix and had reluctantly agreed to Ethel driving by herself – except for Eskimo in the back seat.

"Turn right onto Alternate 69 in one mile." That reminded her: it was time for a pit stop, anyhow. Taking the next exit to Alternate 69, she stopped at a filling station, where she walked Eskimo until he did his job. She then pulled out the map which she had dutifully stored in the glove compartment when she left Denver. Vicky had led her out of Denver on a different route than that high-lighted by Triple A, but at least she could find it on the map. Her problem was that the two previous "recalculations" had put her on Highway 69, a mountainous and winding road that she couldn't locate on her map. The sun was already beginning to descend toward the horizon, and now she was on *Alternate 69*, clearly a secondary road. Where in hell was Vicky leading her?

Surprisingly, the gas station proprietor wasn't able to guide her back to the highways high-lighted on the map, but he recommended a "nice motel a few miles up the road" that had a restaurant and would take dogs. Since Vicky had also directed her to Alternate 69, Ethel drove on to "The Lost Oasis" a mile or so further on. The motel had what looked like a half-way decent short-order restaurant attached, so Ethel pulled in with a sigh of relief and registered for the night. She figured they should be able to make Phoenix by the end of the next day.

Willy was nursing a beer at a small window table on the opposite side of the room from the motel entrance, but Ethel recognized him immediately when she entered. His curly white hair was complemented nicely by his navy sweatshirt. No longer surprised by his sudden appearances, Ethel walked over and sat down in the empty chair without waiting for his invitation. She smiled as he looked up. "So what brings you to the 'Lost Oasis' on this God-forsaken road to nowhere, Willy?"

"Probably the same thing that brought you here, Ethel. I'm lost." He waved to the waitress and ordered Ethel a Scotch on the rocks. "I assume you're not driving any further tonight?"

She shook her head. "Nope. I'm bushed physically and completely pissed off psychologically." Ethel did not normally use that kind of language, except sometimes with Willy and when extremely upset. This was one of those occasions. Willy simply raised his eyebrows and waited for her to continue.

"I've been using a new GPS outfit that Roscoe gave me for Christmas and it's driving me crazy! Vicky (she's the GPS voice) keeps recalculating the route and now I'm on this damn country road that I can't even find on my map. So what brought you here?"

"Like I said, I'm lost, too. I don't belong to triple A and I don't have a GPS, so I printed up a route from Denver to Phoenix from my computer's Map Quest program. But just a ways back I found myself on Highway 69 which I couldn't find anywhere on my map either. So I exited to a filling station right off the highway on Alternate 69 and they directed me here – probably the same thing that happened to you."

Ethel nodded. She knew better than to ask why he was traveling from Denver to Phoenix in the first place. He often just showed up on various trips she took. "So we're both here on an Alternate Highway 69 that neither of us can find on our maps?"

"So it appears, Ethel. So it appears. But let's have something to eat, get a good night's sleep, and see what tomorrow will bring." He paused. "Just in case I'm gone when you get up, go back to 69 south. I'll catch you somewhere along the way."

Ethel awoke at 7:30 – a bit late for her. As she had suspected, Willy had already left. Over the years she had become accustomed to his periodic appearances – as well as his equally unexplainable disappearances which she no longer tried to understand. Though her husband regarded Willy as a figment of her imagination, Ethel knew that he was far more important than that. Roscoe could dismiss him if he wished, but Ethel valued the insights he provided and the wise advice he frequently gave. She knew that Willy would appear again somewhere along route 69.

When she dropped off her key, however, she decided to check on her planned route to Phoenix. The motel clerk immediately responded: "Oh, I wouldn't take 69 if I were you, miss. It's pretty crooked and hilly and there's no town or gas station for miles and miles. I'd take the road right outside here – Alternate 69; it's a newer and better road and goes through Ghost Town Junction – a real nice tourist town that used to be known as just Town Junction. Further on, it rejoins the regular highway about a hundred miles south. Ethel had no desire to stop at a ghost town, but she didn't like the idea of long stretches of highway with no towns or filling stations either. She was sure Willy would find her no matter which route she took.

As Ethel started out on the alternate route, Vicky simply said, "Follow Alternate 69 for ten miles to Ghost Town Junction. Then continue on Alternate 69 for one hundred miles to Highway 69, south." Ethel still couldn't find either Highway 69 or Alternate 69 on her map, but at least Vicky seemed to know where they were going. The day was cool, but sunny, and Eskimo was resting quietly in the back seat. It was only 8:15 and although she couldn't figure out the exact mileage, Ethel guessed that she could easily make Phoenix before nightfall. Her mood improved considerably, although she did wonder where Willy had gone.

Ghost Town Junction turned out to be a few shops, a one-time hotel turned tavern, a gas station, and several shoddy houses lined up along three or four crossroads which intersected Alternate 69. Since Ethel had not filled her usual bottle of water when she left the motel, she stopped at the tavern. She pushed tentatively at the door which swung wide open. "Hello! Anyone here?" Her words echoed back to her from the wooden walls and tin ceiling. The place was empty. "Hello?" She tried again. Shrugging her shoulders, she stepped behind the bar, filled her bottle with water, and left fifty cents on the bar. Maybe a little tight, she thought, but what the hell.

Before leaving, Ethel noticed the antique sign over the bar: "Wilhelm Weinhold, Prop." Now, that was interesting! Her grandmother's maiden name was Weinhold, and her mother and father had gone out West for a month to visit a Weinhold great uncle (was it Wilhem?) on an early "pre-marriage honeymoon." Her mother had told her that they decided they didn't want to wait to get married until their return home, so they were married at her great uncle's home. To satisfy her parents, she said, they later held a second wedding ceremony back in Wisconsin. When she had her first baby some eight months later, however, it had still scandalized her parents and other relatives. But Ethel couldn't remember if Colorado was the "out West" state where they had gone. Maybe she should just look around a little bit more before dashing on toward Phoenix.

Only one of the three shops was open – a typical tourist variety store with everything from cowboy hats and walking sticks to Indian jewelry and Mexican vanilla. But Ethel's hopes faded when she saw the teen-age salesgirl chewing gum behind the checkout counter. "I don't suppose you know anything about the people who own the tavern over there, do you?" The girl shook her head. "Do you know when they open?"

"Yeah. In about fifteen minutes or so – at ten o'clock. They serve coffee and doughnuts." She thought a minute. The owners – their name is Anderson."

As Ethel walked back to her car to take Eskimo for a stretch before the tavern formally opened, she grinned to see Willy pull up behind her in his Porsche. Where he got his money she didn't know – and never asked. It was as much an enigma as Willy himself.

"So where did you dash off to so early this morning?"

"Well, the motel guy recommended this alternate route – as he must have done to you, too – but I wanted to check out 69 for myself. He was right. It was pretty hilly and had one s-shaped curve after another, so I came back this way figuring I'd meet you somewhere along the way." He looked around the abandoned streets. "Not much here, though, is there." It was a statement, not a question. "On the other hand, maybe you'll discover all kinds of things and even solve some old family mysteries." He laughed at her quizzical look. "You know, about your mom and dad's 'honeymoon' out West."

Before she could ask him how he knew anything at all about her folks' honeymoon, the doors of the tavern opened. The Andersons had arrived. Willy and Ethel introduced themselves and ordered some doughnuts and coffee. When asked about the Weinhold sign, Mrs. Anderson said that it had belonged to some previous owners who had operated both a tavern and a hotel in the building in the early 1920s when Mr. Anderson's grandfather had purchased it. "We have some old pictures too, that they left behind. Maybe you'd like to see them – you know, since you might be relatives and all that?"

Among others, the pictures showed Ethel's mother on the back of a horse with her father holding the reins, the two of them hugging each other in the doorway to the tavern, and – much to Ethel's surprise – a wedding picture with bridal gown, suit and tie, minister and all. So her mother had been telling the truth all along! Her mom and dad had been married in Town Junction, Colorado on what everyone had thought was a "pre-marriage" honeymoon – a secret for all those years.

As Ethel and Willy peered at the old faded photographs, Ethel pondered, "Why didn't my mother just insist that she was telling the truth? Why did they go through another wedding ceremony back in Wisconsin when they returned?" Once again she turned to Willy, "I'm almost more confused now than before. What do you think, Willy?"

"Well, she probably did tell them, Ethel. But maybe her parents just didn't believe them – or wouldn't accept their 'out West' marriage as valid. Eloping, you know, was at one time almost as bad as having sex before marriage. Maybe it was just simpler to have a second wedding back home where everyone could see them tie the knot." Willy shook his head as he added, "I don't know, Ethel. but I do believe one thing.

I think that your GPS Vicky was determined to set the record straight when she recalculated your route to include Alternate Highway 69. You never would have come this way on your own if the GPS hadn't told you to, would you?"

No, she wouldn't, she thought. She owed Vicky's "recalculating" a real thank you. Too bad she couldn't ever explain it all to Roscoe. He'd never believe her.

WINDOWS

Caught in the noon-day traffic, the bus came to a complete stop in front of a small apartment building. Roscoe had driven their car to his business appointment, and Ethel was enjoying her open-air bus tour of Miami. Folding her map and putting it on her lap, she stared across the sidewalk into an open apartment window where a man and woman were arguing so loudly that she could overhear everything they said.

"You're doing it all for spite – just for spite!" The woman slammed a letter on the table next to them. "I won't give up Jessie -- certainly not to you -- so now you're trying to take her by those false legal charges. You can't stand it that I found someone else."

"Yeah, a great new daddy for Jessie he would be. A child molester!"

"Oh, come on, David. You know damn well that happened over twenty years ago when Jon was only sixteen. It was simply two kids having sex, but because the girl was under age and her parents pressed the case, they cited him."

"Well, whatever you think, that letter says you have to appear in court and the judge will decide whether you keep Jessie or not. We may be divorced, but she's my kid, too. Now that I have a steady job, I think I've got a pretty good chance to get her. After all," he added with a sneer, "I don't have any 'child molesting' on my record."

"David, be reasonable. Jessie doesn't *want* to live with you. She and I have had our problems, too, but she's gotten over that teen rebellion stage and really wants to stay with me. I've talked to her about it, Dave. Why don't you just ask her?"

The bus started to move before Ethel could hear his reply. Pursing her lips, she frowned slightly and shook her head. She picked up her map and was just about to return to it when someone slid in and sat down in the seat beside her.

"Hello, Ethel. What are you up to?" It was Willy.

"Eavesdropping, I guess you'd call it," she smiled back. Ethel then related the conversation she had overheard through the open window. "I wonder what they'll do? It's kind of like watching a reality TV serial and having the announcer tell you to return tomorrow for the next episode. Except who knows where they'll be tomorrow?"

"Well, you can always write your own script, you know." Willy pulled out a bag of popcorn from his baggy briefcase and offered her some. "C'mon. Have some. Pretend you're at the movies."

Ignoring the popcorn, she frowned again. "What do you mean, pretend I'm at the movies?" After several encounters with Willy, Ethel was no longer surprised by his unexpected appearances and unusual insights. "These were real people, Willy."

"There you go again – real versus unreal. Sure, they're real if you believe them to be real. It's all in our minds anyhow, isn't it?" He paused for a moment. Then, cocking his head to one side, he continued. "I thought we had gone around that corner – that you had come to realize that reality is ultimately only a matter of our subjective perspectives. So, if you want to learn how the story turns out, all you have to do is watch another episode – or look in another window." He patted her affectionately on the shoulder as he got up to leave. "I'll be back later to hear the conclusion!" And then he was gone.

The rest of her trip was uneventful, until the bus stopped at a central mall "for twenty minutes of shopping" before continuing its tour. Uninterested in any shopping, Ethel wandered slowly down the crowded street. But in passing a corner drugstore, she was distracted by the woman and child sitting at a table by an open window. It was the same woman she had seen in the apartment! Pretending to look at the window display which partially concealed her, Ethel listened to their conversation.

The girl was on the verge of tears and speaking loudly, her emotions out of control. "I don't care what the courts might say, Mom! I'm not going to live with Dad. It was bad enough when he was still at home, fighting with you all the time. But now that he's gone, you and I – well, you and I are getting along okay – and school is okay, too." She stopped to dry her eyes with a crumpled tissue. "I just don't want to go with him and start out all over again at some school somewhere else."

"And you don't have to, Jessie. That's what I'm trying to tell you. You just have to be willing to tell the judge – or whatever sort of mediator they have there – what you're saying now. The other thing that your Dad is telling them about Jon is simply not true, and I'm sure we can explain that and clear everything up. But you do have to appear and tell them how you really feel. You can do that, can't you?"

"But that's the problem, Mom. I think Dad may be right about Jon. I don't like him – and I don't trust him. No, wait!" She put up her hand to stop her mother's reply. "Wait and listen. I know that you care for him or think that you love him and all that, but he's different when he's with me alone. I don't want to live with Dad, but I don't want Jon around either. He came onto me, Mom. He really did!"

Ethel waited, now absorbed in the drama before her, but they seemed to sense someone watching and as they glanced toward the window she hastily moved on. What next, she wondered. The twenty minutes were nearly up, so she returned to the bus and boarded it for her return home. Willy was already there.

"So, this Jessie is caught between her dad and her mom's boyfriend? Sounds like her mom has a few tough decisions to make." Willy glanced out at the passing panorama of downtown Miami and then back at Ethel. "If you're tuned in to reality TV, you might as well watch the ending, Ethel. I'm sure you can bring it up through a window somewhere along the way." He settled back in his seat as he added, "If you don't mind, I think I'll stay for the next episode." He didn't have to wait very long.

In the middle of the block, again caught in heavy traffic, the bus stopped next to one of Miami's popular indoor/outdoor cafes. There, inside but at a table close to the window, sat the woman Ethel had seen in the apartment and drug store. This time she was seated opposite a handsome, middle-aged man, intensely arguing with him over some dispute. He was not her former husband.

"But you can't possibly believe that I would 'come on' to Jessie – as she puts it. She's just a kid, for God's sake!" He reached across the table and took one of her hands in his as he peered deeply in her eyes. "Jessie is lying, Laura. I swear to you that I never touched her – nor even tried to. I know she's your kid, honey, but I can't understand how you can take the word of a troubled teen-ager over that of the man you profess to love. We're engaged to be married, Laura. Doesn't that mean anything to you at all?" He shook his head and repeated, "Jessie is lying."

She gently slid her hand from under his and pushed her chair slightly back from the table. "I can't handle this, Jon. I don't know who's telling the truth and who isn't. Why would Jessie make it all up? Of course, I want to believe you, but I can't let Jessie go. She said that if you move in, she's moving out. And guess who'll be there to take her? David has already made it clear that he's just waiting for the chance." She pushed her chair back further and rose.

The bus started to move away before Ethel could hear her last words. With a characteristic shrug of her shoulders, she turned toward Willy to get his reaction. But Willy wasn't there.

The next day Ethel was driving slowly down the same route the bus had followed, intently searching in every window she passed. She had told Roscoe that she wanted to do some shopping, knowing he wouldn't want to go along. What did she hope to see? She couldn't answer her own question. All she knew was that the story wasn't over – somehow she had to find out how it ended. Passing the same drugstore where she had seen Jessie and her mother, she now spied Jessie and Jon. She parked the car around the corner and returned to the window, carefully hiding herself behind a cardboard display.

"Why did you make that all up, Jessie? You know it isn't true. I thought we were becoming good friends – you and I – and then you pull this kind of crap. Why?"

She shrugged, but then answered softly, "I don't know. Maybe I wanted it to be true, Jon. I never wanted to be 'good friends.' I wanted you to look at me the way you look at Mom." Her voice quavered as tears glistened in her eyes. "I love you, Jon. You can't marry Mom. I couldn't stand living there with the two of you – sleeping together, having sex – right in the bedroom next door. I couldn't stand it!"

Jessie rose to leave, but he grabbed her arm and pulled her back into her chair. "Listen, Jessie. You can't do this. You're basically a decent kid and you know it isn't fair. Your mom deserves better. You know how your dad treated her, and now that she's found me, it's just not fair to take that away from her. I like you, Jessie, but I don't *love* you – at least in that way. I love Laura, and I want to live with her and be a good husband to her and a good father to you. A father, not a lover."

"She has a father, you son of a bitch!" Ethel had seen him coming, but Jon and Jessie were caught off guard as David towered over their table, his fists clenched as if to strike. Jon rose to face Jessie's father, while Jessie herself ran out from the drug store, nearly bumping into Ethel as she flew out the door.

Though she wanted to stay, Ethel reluctantly turned from the window and hurried back to her car. She had promised Roscoe not to spend the whole day "shopping," and his patience was easily strained by too much waiting. But when she returned to their hotel room, he was comfortably settled, watching one of the reality TV shows that had become so popular. She had never really liked them, but somehow the voices caught her attention. They belonged to the same people who had appeared in her window visions!

Now sitting on a sofa next to Laura, her mother's arms around her, Jessie was sobbing as she choked out the words. "Oh, Mom, I'm so sorry. I did make it all up, but I didn't mean to hurt you. I overheard Dad telling you that Jon had that record as a child molester and I thought that if I said he had also come on to me, you wouldn't see him any more. I was just trying to get back at Jon. I couldn't bear the thought of him not loving me. So that's why I said all those things about him. It wasn't true, Mom – not any of it."

Laura hugged her and kissed her on the forehead. "It's okay, Jessie. It's okay. I know it wasn't true -- and that you're sorry now. And I know you didn't want to hurt us. Jon just called me on his cell phone and told me all about your talk at the drug store and about Dad bursting in on you like that."

"That's what was so awful. Jon started to explain how he felt and I think I was beginning to understand. Then all of a sudden Dad came out of nowhere and started yelling at Jon. I just got up and ran back here. Oh, Mom, I'm so miserable!"

Laura lifted Jessie's chin and looked into her eyes. "It's going to be okay, Jessie. Jon said that it took a while, but Dad finally calmed down and they agreed to let the courts handle the whole thing. So, if you tell them that you don't want to live with Dad, you won't have to."

She paused before continuing, "But you also have to understand what Jon was saying to you. He does care for you, Jessie, but not in that way. He and I are truly in love, Jess, and we want to be a family – with you as part of it." She hugged her again before she asked, "Will you at least try? We can put all this behind us, honey.

We can start out fresh – the three of us. I know it can work – if we all just try."

Jessie nodded. "I'll try, Mom. I do want to stay with you and I want you to be happy. I want us all to be happy. But are you sure that Jon can forgive me? Can you?" Laura kissed away her daughter's tears and dabbed at her own with her sleeve. "We already have, honey. We already have."

The next day was their last in Miami. Roscoe had two morning appointments and took the car while Ethel finished her packing. She still had two hours before his return and decided to visit the museum she had noticed down the street when they first checked in. Her thoughts tumbled about in her head as she waited for the elevator. Maybe Willy will find me, she hoped. And when she stepped out into the bright sunlight, there he was.

As they made their way to the Impressionists' Gallery, she glanced over at Willy and grinned, "I suppose you already know that our windows story appeared on reality TV, don't you?" She didn't even wait for him to give his consenting nod of the head. I don't know about you, Willy, but this 'reality TV show' is beginning to get to me."

"Why? Don't you like the story line? You can always change it, you know."

"No, I'm glad Jessie confessed to all that she made up about Jon – and that her mother was so forgiving. But I wonder if everything is as okay as Laura seems to believe. Not that I think Jessie should go to live with her father. With that temper of his, I'm surprised that he and Jon didn't get into a brawl right there in the drug store. Still, it might be better for Jessie to be away from her mother and Jon for a while -- maybe just a long summer vacation away from home. Give her some time to get over her crush on him." She chuckled as she added, "I'm almost curious enough to want to see the ending – whether on TV or through another window."

Cocking her head, she looked at Willy again. "What do you think?"

"Why Ethel, you know better than to ask me. After all, they're all your windows we're looking through, aren't they?"

THE EMPRESS DOWAGER

When Eskimo died, Ethel felt an emptiness and grief she had not experienced since the passing of her mother and father several years before. "Constant companion" was too trite to describe the daily walks, grooming, hugging and petting, and games she had played with him over the years. When his arthritis became so bad that he could no longer walk by himself, the decision to put him to sleep was the hardest she had ever made.

Roscoe had never bonded with Eskimo as Ethel had, but as he comforted her in his arms she could sense the deep sympathy he felt. "You won't be able to think about this now, sweetheart, but eventually you'll want to get another dog. Not to replace Eskimo – I know you won't be able to do that – but a dog that you will come to love as much as you have loved him." Though he hugged her again, her tears continued to flow.

But Roscoe was right. A few months later they bought Leo – the friendliest and biggest six-week-old puppy in his litter. Leo was a 50/50 mixture of Shitzu and Bishon Frizee, sporting the soft white fur of the Bishon, but the more handsome head and face of the Shitzu. They named him Leo in recognition of the fact that Shitzu means lion in Chinese and the Shitzu breed was the court dog of the early Chinese emperors. Leo soon became a permanent member of the Matson family.

What particularly intrigued Roscoe was that Ethel seemed to be able to talk with Leo in a way she had not been able to do with Eskimo. Her friend, Ilse, was a recognized animal communicator and had patiently tried to explain, "It's not like actual words – at least not usually – but more like feelings or thoughts that can be sent telepathically from one to another. You're being too intellectual about it, Ethel. Just relax. Sit down next to Eskimo and concentrate on what he's trying to communicate. He tells me that he tries to speak with you all the time, but you just don't listen."

Ethel remembered that it was only shortly before his death when she had actually talked with Eskimo for the first time. It was during a snowstorm when they had slid off the highway on a patch of ice and landed In a huge snow-covered ditch on the side of the road. She had managed to open the window on the passenger side and, pushing Eskimo out, she kept telling him to "get some help." He had finally rescued them both by jumping out the window and running to the road; attracting the attention of a passing truck driver, he had led him to their snow-buried car.

For a few weeks after that she and Eskimo had periodically "talked" together, but then his arthritis had really deteriorated. And then -- well then they had said goodbye. "Don't cry, Ethel," his eyes said. "I know it's time for me to go. I understand." And he had laid his head on her lap as the vet gave him the shot. She would never forget that day and their last goodbye.

Ethel was determined to start out talking with Leo right from the very beginning – and she succeeded. He was so excited. "My last human never even tried to talk with me! She was the Empress Dowager of China, you know. I guess she felt it was below her station to talk with a dog." Leo was obviously not impressed with the Empress. "Oh, she was nice enough. I was a pure Shitzu then – we were the court dogs of Chinese royalty, you know. She petted me on her lap when she held court and even had me sit with her at fancy state dinners. But she didn't really love me like you do, Ethel." And he would jump up on her lap and lick her face. The dowager story sounded a bit much, Ethel thought, but she was fascinated enough to raise it with Willy the next time she saw him.

Willy always managed to visit her, at least briefly, when Ethel became involved in one of her strange adventures. Though Willy never appeared when Roscoe was present, Ethel figured he'd be curious enough about Leo's story of the Empress Dowager to check it out. And it wasn't more than a week later when Willy suddenly joined them while Ethel was taking Leo on his daily walk around the park.

"I thought it wouldn't be too long before you appeared, Willy. What do you think of our court dog here?" She smiled as he bent down to pat Leo on the back and then scratch behind his ears – just the way he liked it.

"Well, the Shitzu was the court dog of the imperial palaces – that's a known fact. There are even several paintings showing them with the emperors and empresses of the mid-nineteenth and early twentieth centuries." He cocked his head and shrugged his shoulders. *"But whether this guy here was one of them, I just don't know. They all look like pure Shitzu to me, and Leo here is definitely more handsome!"* He winked at Ethel as Leo perked up his ears and strutted regally along next to Ethel.

"So what's the story on the Empress Dowager anyhow?"

"In brief," Willy now assuming his professorial airs, *"Empress Dowager Xiao Qin Xian – known as Cixi for short – served as a Regent of the Manchu Qing Dynasty from 1861 to 1908. Under the nominal rule first of her son and then of her nephew, she exercised de facto control for forty-eight years."* He frowned slightly as he shook his head, pulling a sheet of paper from his pocket. *"I googled her name and wrote this down: 'Though some portray Empress Cixi as a villain responsible for the fall of the Qing Dynasty, in recent years professional historians have suggested that she was a scapegoat for problems beyond her control...' The article concluded that Cixi had actually been 'a leader no more ruthless than others, and in fact an effective if reluctant reformer in the last years of her life.' Fascinating, isn't it?"*

"It is fascinating, Willy. I only wish that Leo could tell us which version is the true one."

"*Well, why don't you ask him, Ethel? You can talk to him now, can't you?*" *And with that, he sauntered off down a side path into the park.* "*And if you decide to visit Cixi, let me know. She's one historical character I'd really like to meet!*"

When Ethel awoke, she was completely disoriented. She found herself in a darkened room resting on the floor on a soft brocaded pad. She was covered by a silk shawl and Leo was sleeping at her feet. Pushing him gently with her foot, she tried to rouse him. "*Leo – wake up!*" *He stretched and yawned, but was about to go back to sleep.* "*Wake up, Leo. Open your eyes and look around. Where in heck are we?*"

At that moment there was a soft tapping on the door and Willy stepped into the room. "*I think we're in China, Ethel – in Beijing. I'm right next door and when I woke up a few minutes ago I scouted around and, if I'm not mistaken, we're in the Imperial Summer Palace.*"

"*But how in the world ---?*" *She stopped in mid-sentence as a young serving girl entered with a tray and, bowing, set down two cups of tea on a low table next to Ethel and a bowl of cold water at the foot of the bed next to Leo. She then left the room.*

"*Willy, you've got to tell me what's going on here. I know some of my other trips were weird enough, but this one's a lulu!*" *On the other hand, she thought, was it really any stranger than her visit to Tibet or her meeting with the Lake Ness 'monster?'*

Willy sipped his tea in that slow deliberative manner of his before answering. "*I think that Leo knows more than I. How about it, Leo? What are we doing here?*"

The dog crawled up next to Ethel and licked her cheek. "*Now don't get upset, Ethel. But I'm not really Leo. That is, I am Leo to you, but I'm also his great, great, great, great, great, great grandfather and my name here in China is Shi-Shi.*" *He snorted,* "*It's kind of a play on Cixi's name – she's my mistress, but she let me sleep in here with you last night. You just arrived yesterday.*"

Willy was frowning as he stared at the dog. "*If you're really Leo's ancestor by at least seven or eight generations, what year is this?*"

"It's 1898," a voice came from the open door. A uniformed officer stood at attention and bowed. "We have just succeeded in a coup d'etat against the ill-advised reforms by Emperor Guangxu. We have isolated him on an island off the Forbidden City where he will have no opportunity to enforce his proposed reforms. The Empress Dowager Cixi has reassumed full control. She awaits the pleasure of your company in the imperial stateroom. May I lead you there?"

As they followed him, Willy whispered softly in Ethel's ear. "There was a coup in 1898, Ethel. Four years before, the Chinese suffered a humiliating defeat in the Sino-Japanese War when their navy was crushed by the Japanese. After that, the reformists wanted to modernize the government. But the suggested reforms would have limited Cixi's power and she supported the coup against the Emperor and returned to power after what many thought had been her retirement. It was only later when she actually enacted some less drastic reforms of her own."

"But what has all this to do with us, Willy? How did we get here? How did…?" She was interrupted by the officer who announced, "You may enter. The Empress Dowager will see you." He opened the massive carved door to the stateroom. At the far end sat Cixi on a throne, her hair piled high on her head and a brocaded gold robe wrapped over her shoulders extending to the floor. Leo – or Shi-Shi – trotted over to her and jumped on her lap.

Both Ethel and Willy approached the throne and bowed. An interpreter stepped forward. Cixi spoke, "Welcome. Please be seated." She gestured to some chairs in front of the throne.

"Yesterday when we found you wandering about the Forbidden City, you seemed to have no idea of how you got there. But we did learn that you are American scholars who seek to know more about the Qing Dynasty. It is my pleasure to assist you — if you, in turn, will assist me in learning more about your country, its government and this strange system of 'democracy' that you espouse. Does that sound like a fair exchange?"

Before they could reply, Shi-Shi jumped down and ran over to them with his tail wagging. "Why not give it a try? You both might learn something -- right?"

When she told Roscoe about her dream, Ethel omitted any mention of Willy. Roscoe still regarded him as her imaginary friend and her dream was weird enough in itself not to complicate it further. "The Empress Dowager really wanted to learn about democracy and I wanted to know more about her views on reform – so we had an even exchange." Ethel paused to scratch Leo's neck. "And Leo -- or Shi-Shi -- would fill me in on some of the details that Cixi sometimes omitted.

"Consciously or unconsciously omitted?"

"Oh, I don't know, Roscoe. The Empress seemed straight-forward enough and really interested in learning what some basic political and economic reforms might be able to do. She evidently wavered between favoring reform initially and then feeling that the Emperor Guangxu had gone too far and too fast when she realized that her own powers would be limited. I've done some research on her since our return – well, not a return really, but since what must have been a long dream – and contemporary historians now believe that Cixi ended up to be a real reformer in her later years."

Roscoe laughed, "And I suppose that you and Leo here want to take the credit?"

Ethel only smiled in return. "Well, maybe not Leo – but his great ancestor Shi-Shi might want to take some bows." But to herself she thought, "I wonder what Willy will say about all this – fact or fiction? Or maybe a little bit of both?"

NIGHTMARE IN NEW YORK

Ethel couldn't wait to tell Willy. She had told Roscoe about her weird dream as soon as he picked her up at the airport. But neither of them had been able to decide what to make of it all. When she finally saw Willy a few days later she was practically bursting.

"Willy, you'll never believe what happened! I had the strangest dream – or actual experience - I've ever had." Before he could even ask, she continued. "I went to the board meeting at noon, took in the Frick museum in the afternoon and then attended that reception and speech I told you about. After that, Roger took a few of us out to dinner at his club, and I got back to the Roosevelt Hotel at about 10:00 PM. I locked the door and got ready for bed. I was wearing some pearls that have a real difficult clasp to undo, and I couldn't get them off."

She noted his grin and shook her head, "No, I only had two glasses of wine, but those pearls are devils to take off. Anyhow, since I was going to wear them again the next day, I just decided to leave them on overnight. I turned out the light and went to sleep. Now, here comes the weird part. The next thing I knew I was standing in the hotel corridor outside my room across from the elevators – in my silk pajamas, barefoot, and wearing my pearls! I was completely disoriented, but I did know which was my room and tried to get back in. But the door was closed and automatically locked.

"Willy, I simply didn't know what to do. I couldn't very well take the elevator down to the lobby barefoot and in my pajamas!" She added with a snort, "Even though I was wearing my pearls. I checked my watch and it was 2:30 AM so it was unlikely that anyone else might be wandering about the hallway. But I had to get back into my room."

Though Willy first had that irritating grin on his face, when he realized how upset Ethel was, he patted her shoulder and asked with a worried frown. "So what did you do?"

"Well, there just didn't seem to be any alternative but to knock on the door of the room next to mine and see if whoever was there would call down to the desk and get someone to let me in. I tapped lightly at first but no one came, so the second time I just pounded on the door. I was really getting frantic!"

"It finally opened slightly and a man in his pajamas peered through the narrow slit and asked me what I wanted. He didn't look particularly sleepy, but he certainly was understandably suspicious when he saw me there in my pajamas and bare feet."

"I told him that I knew that what I was going to say would sound absolutely crazy, but I was locked out of my room and needed someone from the desk down in the lobby to come up and let me in.

"Someone inside his room was asking him what was going on and he whispered back that it was okay. But then he asked me what I was doing out there in the corridor in my pajamas in the first place. He seemed terribly nervous and kept the door almost closed. He obviously took my 'crazy' remark at face value, and frankly I couldn't blame him.

"I told him that I honestly didn't know why I was there. All I knew was that I went to bed at about ten o'clock and then just woke up out there in the hallway. I must have been sleep-walking. I said I could give him my name and if he called downstairs they could check it and would know that I was registered in 1701. By this time I was almost in tears and I practically begged him to call.

"He finally turned to go back in his room, but first said, 'Don't come in. You just wait right there.' I couldn't have gone in if I'd wanted to, because he then shut the door behind him. It seemed like an hour, but

he finally came back out with some pants slipped on over his pajamas and walked to the elevator. He said that he had to go down – that no one was answering. He rang for the elevator and when he stepped inside he warned me to stay right there – that he'd be back."

Ethel was winding down. She shook her head again and then shrugged. "Well, once again, the wait seemed forever, but he finally came back with a policeman and a uniformed hotel man. The hotel guy took my name, checked it with a piece of paper he held in his hand, and then walked me over to my room and let me in. I did try to thank the man next door, but the policeman had gone with him back to his room and I doubt if he heard me. Once I was safe inside, I piled a bunch of pillows in front of my door so that if I did sleepwalk again I would stumble against them and wake myself up. But I slept okay the rest of the night.

"So what happened then? The next morning I first thought it might have been a strange nightmare, but the pillows piled up by my door seemed to indicate that I really had been sleep-walking. To my knowledge, I never walked in my sleep in my life! I checked Google and none of the usual 'causes' was relevant: I wasn't under stress; I was not on drugs or taking any weird medications; I only had two glasses of wine; and I certainly am not a teenager who will grow out of this." Ethel finally paused. "What do you think, Willy? Why was I sleepwalking at two in the morning in the Roosevelt Hotel in New York City? What was I looking for? What did I want?"

Ethel had always counted on Willy to explain the strange episodes she frequently experienced. But this time he seemed as uncertain as she was. Finally, he grinned at her and quipped, "Hopefully, it was a once in a lifetime experience that will make a good story 'about the lady in pajamas and pearls' for your next door neighbor to tell – when he gets out of jail, that is."

Now she was completely confused. "Jail? I don't get it, Willy. Why jail?"

He pulled a newspaper from his briefcase and handed it to her. "I brought this along because you had mentioned that you were going to stay at the Roosevelt Hotel and I thought you'd get a kick out of the coincidence. But now it does more than that. It proves that you weren't just having a nightmare. You were definitely sleep-walking, Ethel, and you did have that conversation with the man next door."

She looked at the headline he pointed out to her. "Drug Ring Exposed in Roosevelt Hotel."

"I still don't understand, Willy. What does that have to do with me?"

Willy took the paper back and read from it: "The drug buyer was picked up in the lobby of the Roosevelt Hotel with the cocaine in his possession. The dealer who had made the sale was later identified by a hotel clerk who had seen him in conversation with the buyer. The clerk said, "I didn't know which room he had checked into, but recognized him when he came down to the lobby in the middle of the night at the request of some lady who had been walking in the corridor in her sleep. Our resident police officer accompanied us up to the 17th floor and made the arrest. I escorted the lady to her room."

Willy grinned as he gave her the paper back. "Here, Ethel. You might like to keep it as a memento of your sleep-walking adventure. Not everyone can solve a mystery in their sleep!" He then added as he left, "But in general, I wouldn't make a habit of it!"

THE DOPPELGANGER

"Hello, Ethel?"

The voice was familiar, but she couldn't quite place it. "Yes, this is Ethel. But who's calling?

"It's Judy, Ethel. Judy Nelson – your cousin."

"Well, for heaven's sake, Judy. What a surprise!" Why would Judy be calling her at ten-thirty at night? "It's been ages since we've heard from you. Is everything all right?" Roscoe was asleep, so Ethel went into the hall, taking the phone with her.

"Yes, everything's okay." A slight pause. "Oh, I know it's strange, my calling so late at night. But I just watched the ten o'clock news and had to find out if you were back from China or not. And how the Olympics were?" When Ethel didn't respond, she went on. "I saw you on TV, Ethel. At the closing ceremony. Oh, it must have been so exciting to be there in person. I watched almost all of it, and then – at the end – there you were!"

"Judy, I hate to disappoint you, but I haven't been to the Olympics and I haven't been to China – at least not since Roscoe and I went there maybe seven or eight years ago. I had actually wanted to go to the Olympics, but Roscoe wasn't too interested and I hated to miss all my classes. Anyhow, whoever you saw on TV may have looked like me, but it wasn't." She tried to soften her voice. "But how nice of you to call. Maybe we can get together with you sometime this fall, Judy. Why not send me some dates that would be good for you – you know, in the next couple of weeks?"

"I would swear it was you, Ethel. The same hair-do, your smile – even that blue briefcase you carry around. I'd swear it was you." She snorted an embarrassed laugh. "Well, if it wasn't, it wasn't, I guess. Yeah, it would be nice to see you and Roscoe again. I'll send a note or give a call. Okay? Sorry to bother you so late. I know you and Roscoe turn in early." Another pause. "Well, guess that's all. Will be in touch."

"Yes, please do, Judy. We'll look forward to hearing from you." The line was already dead. She quietly returned to the bedroom, but as she placed the receiver in the cradle, Roscoe turned over and grunted, "So, who was that?"

"Judy. You know, my cousin, Judy Nelson." She grinned as she shook her head. "She thought she saw me in Beijing – at the Olympics of all things. She was really quite insistent that it was me. I invited her to come and visit. You don't mind, do you?" But Roscoe was already back in dreamland.

By the next weekend Ethel had already forgotten about Judy's call as she fell into the routine of the day. On Saturday she always treated both Eskimo and herself to a long walk on the country road running past their house. As Eskimo sniffed the early dew, she waved at the car approaching her from her neighbors' house up the way. It pulled over to the side and Amy Lawrence leaned out the window.

"Hey, Ethel. Been meaning to tell you -- we saw you on TV! Maybe a couple of weeks ago. You were walking down one of the gates out at Mitchell Field Milwaukee Airport. Actually, they were covering the departure of that tall Chinese basketball player and you were walking right next to him." She laughed as she added, "Our local TV star! Was going to call you the next day, but then forgot. Did you know you were on?"

"Wasn't me, Amy. Haven't been flying anywhere for a couple of months." Deciding not to mention Judy's call about the Olympics, she shrugged with a quick grin. "Had to be someone else who maybe just resembles me."

"Ethel, it had to be you! She looked exactly like you. She wore a goldish-orange jacket like that one you have, carried a briefcase, and was grinning from ear to ear – your grin! Maybe it was a clip from the last time you were at Mitchell? But that basketball guy left for the Olympics week before last, so it couldn't have been from an earlier trip, could it?" Her husband revved the motor and she pulled her head back into the car. "Well, I don't know, but if it wasn't you, you sure must have a twin somewhere! See ya around."

Ethel had just settled down in her aisle seat on the plane to Beijing when the tall Chinese basketball player tapped her on the shoulder and motioned to the empty middle seat. "Oh, is that one yours?" she smiled up at him. As she began to get up, she paused for a moment and asked, "Would you prefer this aisle seat? I mean, being so tall, you could at least stretch your legs out in the aisle once we get going."

He smiled back and replied haltingly, "Thank you much. That is very kind of you. You do not mind?"

Ethel wiggled over to the middle seat and moved her purse and briefcase to the floor in front of her. "No, it's okay. We have a stop-over in Anchorage – I can stretch out a bit then. No matter how we do it, it's going to be a long haul. I've never understood why some of these flights go way up through Anchorage, do you?" She usually didn't like to chat with strangers on planes, but this young man intrigued her.

"I believe," he again hesitated, "I think it is to do with the curving of the earth? Like what they call polar routes."

"Oh, yes, I suppose." Now that she had his attention, she felt she had to continue. "I couldn't help but see all the reporters and photographers taking your picture when you boarded. I assume you're headed for the Olympics? Are you on the Chinese team?"

"No," he shook his head quickly. "I am on the American team! I am from China, yes, but I am in the States two years now and am American citizen. Then I hurt my ankle in practice and was not being able to go

with rest of team. But our coach said -- if I get better and Doctor say okay -- that I be able to come later." He grinned broadly. "And yesterday Doctor said ankle okay. So I phone – to China – and they said I should come. So..." He shrugged and smiled again. "I am going." Then he put out his hand. "My name is Tien Zhang – you may call me Zhang."

Ethel shook his hand and replied, "Good to meet you, Zhang. I am Ethel Matson – you may call me Ethel."

In the long hours that followed, Ethel and Zhang chatted about Zhang's life in the States, Ethel's previous work in the State Department, and American and Chinese politics. Ethel learned that Zhang's team would be playing while she was there, and she promised him that she would definitely attend his game. They parted at the arrival gate where Zhang was met by members of his team, while Ethel looked around for Tom Richards, her friend from the American Embassy who had invited her to the Olympics.

"Hey, Ethel." She finally saw him on the other side of the conveyer belt. He came around and hugged her as she searched for her suitcase. "What are we looking for?"

"Just a small one, Tom. Blue -- with a big pink ribbon tied to the end handle." She grinned. "You know Roscoe. He wanted to make sure I'd be able to identify it." Ethel had first met Tom when she worked on a two-year scholar/diplomat exchange program at the State Department for INR -- the Bureau of Intelligence and Research. She and Roscoe had become close friends with Tom and his wife while Tom was stationed in Washington. That was over five years ago, but they had kept in touch. "How's Doris?"

He grabbed her bag and led her toward the exit. "Oh, she can't wait to see you. She's planned a big party for tomorrow night. We've invited some of the embassy staff and a few of the American athletes who will be competing later this week. But tonight we thought you might like to turn in early, so it's just going to be the three of us. Actually, Doris has become quite a chef of Chinese cuisine. Hope you like Beijing Duck?" It was as if the past five years had evaporated, and Ethel settled back comfortably in the embassy limousine as they chatted animatedly the entire way back to the Richards' flat.

Ethel slept the next day until noon — and by seven the party was well under way. In addition to embassy staff, a few other Americans and four members of the American basketball team had been invited; Ethel was delighted to see that Tien Zhang was one of them. She and Zhang immediately gravitated toward each other and resumed the discussion of Chinese politics they had begun on the flight over. Before he left, he handed her a ticket to the game. "I think, maybe, Mr. Richards, he will have one for you, too, but these are special seats — just for relatives and friends of the players." He was so proud to be able to give it to her that she didn't have the heart to tell him that the embassy seats were also "special" — front row boxes reserved for the diplomatic corps in Beijing.

The game had been a close one -- each side struggling for every point. At the end, though, when the United States won out over China by the slight margin of 45 to 42, the American crowd went wild. Ethel thought that Zhang might be torn between his love and loyalty to his own team and adopted country and his equally strong attachment to the land of his birth. But when she met him briefly after the game, he was all smiles. "Did you see me make that free throw, Ethel? I maybe didn't run so good. My ankle was still not good. But I can throw."

"Yes, you sure can throw, Zhang. And you proved it at your game." She declined his invitation to join him at the closing ceremony which she planned to attend with Tom and Doris Richards. "I could meet you near Tienanmen Square, though — after the ceremony. I have to catch my flight back to the States the next morning." They agreed to meet in front of the Great Hall of the People at one side of the square.

The closing ceremony at the end of the Olympics was spectacular -- more than Ethel had ever expected. She knew that holding the Olympics in China was symbolically the stamp of acceptance, if not approval, of China's new role in the world community and a global recognition of its great power status. But the triumphant music, the marching with flags and banners, and the final passing of the torch were more the attributes of a Greek or Roman festival of yore, than an international athletic event of the 21st century.

Even after the formal ceremony was over, the crowds lingered on. The news media were everywhere, and photographers for the press and for TV were having a field day both at the ceremony itself and afterwards among the swarms of people crowding out to the walks and streets surrounding the Olympic stadium. Tom and Doris accompanied Ethel to the Great Hall and waited with her there until Zhang appeared. Tom fell into his official hosting role with ease. "Now, don't forget that the embassy car will pick you up promptly in about an hour. That will still give us time for a late supper and for you to pack before your departure tomorrow morning."

Ethel and Zhang wandered slowly around the perimeter of the vast square which had been cordoned off during most of the Olympic games. The area in front of the Great Hall was open to limited foot traffic, however, and several small groups of students and workers had gathered there, many carrying signs of protest – some for Tibetan independence, some for the Falun Gong, and some simply for "Democracy in China."

As the two of them watched, Ethel suddenly spied a familiar face in the Tibetan group. "Willy!" she shouted. The short white-haired man in the baggy trousers and blue Mao-type jacket smiled, waved his hand, and immediately walked over to them.

"Hello, Ethel. Fancy meeting you here." But then his smile faded. "I'm a little surprised that Mr. Richards didn't warn you about not getting too embroiled in these street protests. Even with all the police around, there could still be a clash."

"Well, we're hardly embroiled in them, Willy – we're just watching."

But Willy was watching, too. Looking more closely at the small group of students who were now approaching the steps leading to the Great Hall, he suddenly grabbed Ethel by her arm, yelled at Zhang to follow, and pulled them away in the opposite direction. Just before the bomb exploded, he shoved both Ethel and Zhang to the ground and covered them as well as he could with his own body. The thud of the bomb reverberated across the square and the screams of those hit by the flying shrapnel permeated the air.

Willy took Ethel's hand, grabbed on to Zhang's jacket, and pulled them both along behind him as he led them to the waiting embassy car. The limousine screeched away down the wide avenue before Ethel realized that both Willy and Zhang had stayed behind. In thirty minutes she was safely back at the Richards' residence, relating her story to the anxious concern of Tom and Doris. The next day she flew home.

"You know, Willy, I was just going to dismiss the calls from Judy and Amy -- Judy is kind of flaky to start with and Amy is always imagining things. There must be hundreds of people who have gold coats and carry briefcases. But when Dr. Janz phoned from the University and said that he had seen me on a special TV report about that terrorist bomb that went off in Beijing yesterday – well, frankly, it gave me the goosebumps. Supposedly, I was walking right there in Tienanmen Square – where the bomb detonated."

They sipped coffee in the little shop across from the University library where Willy had found Ethel immersed in the huge Random House Dictionary she had dragged over to the library table. "Doppelganger," she pointed to the definition as she read, refers to "a ghostly double or counterpart of a living person." It went on to say that in medieval Germany many people believed that such Doppelgangers sometimes led separate lives from those of the persons whom they reflected as a double or "doppel." Ethel knew that Willy would find her there. He always appeared when she embarked upon one of the strange experiences which so often beset her.

"We only have a small Webster's at home," she explained, "and it doesn't even include the term. But I remembered from my long-ago German classes that the ancient Germans believed in these doppelgangers." She frowned as she stirred the Cappuccino and licked the foam from her spoon. "I also looked it up on Google. Here's what it said."

Willy read aloud from the paper she handed him: "Doppelganger is German for 'double walker' – a shadow self that is thought to accompany every person. Traditionally, it is said that only the owner of the doppelganger can see this phantom self, and that it can be a harbinger of death. Occasionally, however, a doppelganger can be seen by a person's friends or family, resulting in quite a bit of confusion."

"I still think it's some kind of bizarre coincidence," Ethel continued, "but I have to admit that it's downright weird that three people swear they saw me on TV. And all over the place – at the airport, at the Olympics, and in the middle of Tienanmen Square. But I wasn't there! What could it possibly mean, Willy?"

"I don't know, Ethel. I'm not sure, but I think it's a variation on the reality versus imagination theme that's been plaguing you these last few years. Up to now, most of the subconscious happenings or "dreams," as you often refer to them, have affected you directly. That is, you've experienced them directly -- as yourself in your own body."

He could see that he was losing her. "What I think is happening now is that this "doppelganger" was experiencing certain events for you – kind of in your place." Willy paused. "What surprises me is that others have seen whatever it is – myself included – but that you have no memory of it or of your visit to Beijing. You see, I was there with you in Beijing – or with your doppelganger!"

Before she could interrupt, he continued, "What I'm not sure of is whether you will eventually remember it now, or perhaps even 're-live' or 're-experience' the same happenings all over again."

Ethel shook her head as she stared at him. "Willy, you are absolutely blowing my mind. It's bad enough that I'm not really sure if you are real or not – and whether all these other things happened or not. Like that trip to Tibet or the episode with my cousin's brain. But now you're trying to tell me that I have some double out there somewhere who is living part of my life for me? And that I may or may not be able to plug back into it?"

Willy patted her on the shoulder in that somewhat condescending way that she so disliked. "Let's just agree with Hamlet, Ethel: There are more things in heaven and earth, than are dreamed of in our philosophy." Before she could reply, he was gone.

Ethel put down the New York Times as Roscoe entered the room. "So, have you figured out what it all means, Ethel? You know, all these doubles of you that everyone seems to be seeing. Everyone but you and me, that is."

"Well, that's what is so annoying about the whole thing. According to what I've read, I'm supposed to be able to see these doppelgangers, but not anyone else. At least, not usually." She had told him about Dr. Janz, but made no mention of Willy.

"Evidently," she pointed to the Times, "Tien Zhang – you know, that Chinese basketball player whom I supposedly accompanied on the departure ramp at Mitchell Field? Anyhow, reportedly, Tien Zhang was in Tienanmen Square when the terrorist bomb went off. Exactly where and when Dr. Janz said he had seen me. And Zhang stated to the Times reporter that both he and an American woman had been pulled away from the explosion by some man in a Mao jacket who, he insisted, saved their lives. He called the lady 'Ethel,' but said he couldn't remember her last name." Ethel waited, but Roscoe said nothing. "Well?" she asked.

"Well, what?" he replied.

"Well, what do you make of it all?"

"Ethel, if you can't make sense of it, don't expect me to. I must admit, though, that it seems more than a mere coincidence when three people all swear that they saw you on TV – all within a couple weeks of each other. Still, you yourself said that both Judy and Amy Lawrence are a bit flaky, and as for the person Dr. Janz saw, it simply could have been another case of mistaken identity. You don't really believe that you have some kind of double existing out there, do you?" His eyebrow raised, he added, "Or do you?"

"I don't know, Roscoe. I just don't know." She hesitated before she continued, "But I do believe that I haven't heard the last of my doppelganger – whoever or whatever it might be!"

As she tried to fall asleep that night, Ethel's mind was still plagued by a myriad of questions about the appearances of her doppelganger. If we do have these doppelgangers, she wondered, do they live different lives from our own? And if they do exist separately from ourselves, can we ever experience their alternate lives? More important, she thought, will we ever meet them? In the quasi-reality of dreamland she found the answers.

"Willy!" Ethel's shout echoed from the cavernous walls of the Great Hall of the People where she saw him seated across the room. He was embedded in one of the over-stuffed chairs that had been pulled together with two others in a conversational grouping. Next to him sat a middle-aged lady with a briefcase on her lap. She looked a lot like Ethel. No – not just "a lot" – she looked exactly like Ethel!

"Come here, Ethel. I want you to meet someone." He stood. "Ethel, meet Ethel."

Two hours later they said goodbye. In parting, her doppelganger tried to sum up the gist of her lengthy explanation. "As I said earlier, all humans have doppelgangers or doubles who will occasionally appear in their lives in order to attend some event or live out some occasion that they would otherwise not be able to experience. That's how it was with so many of your adventures – Tibet, the terrorist attack on 9/11, the Indians in the diorama – all of them. And it was the same thing with the Olympics. You see, you had really wanted to attend the games so badly that your subconscious mind had to find a way to get you there. If not in person – that is, if not in your regular, ordinary, everyday body – then in some other way. That's where I came in."

During their two hours together, Ethel had peppered her with questions. But, as was the case so often with Willy, each answer raised another question of its own. Finally, after her doppelganger's summary of what had happened, Ethel tried to explain her own continuing frustration: "What I really want to know is whether you exist as a kind of alternate me – separate in a way, but yet existing in a sort of parallel life? Do I – or will I – experience everything you experience? And how does all this relate to time as we know it? Did your experiences at the Olympics occur at the actual time of the games and why did I only learn about my supposed presence there after they were all over?"

She paused for breath. "And most of all, which is real? I mean, was I the real Ethel back in Madison, just hearing about these things from my cousin, my neighbor and Dr. Janz? Or was – is the 'real Ethel' you -- my doppelganger?"

At that point the doppelganger rose, smiled at them both, and said softly, "Ethel, we're both real, aren't we? And now, I have to leave." She took Ethel's hand in hers as she continued, "We will meet again, I'm sure. But for now, I have told you all that I can." She nodded her head toward Willy. "Maybe Willy can explain some of the rest." She took her briefcase and walked quickly to the nearest exit. When Ethel tried to follow to thank her, she was gone.

Two days later, Ethel and Willy met for coffee once again at the little shop across from the UW library in Madison. "But why hadn't I met – seen – her before? At other times, I remembered my experiences either as dreams I had had or as some kind of subconscious state of mind in which I existed for a short period of time. Now, that you and she have told me, of course, I do remember flying to Beijing with Tien Zhang, attending the Olympics concluding ceremony, and running from that explosion in Tienanmen Square. But I remember it as if it were happening to someone else. As if I were there, watching it all, but not really experiencing it." She shook her head and sighed, "Does that make sense, Willy? Does any of it make sense? What do you think?"

He smiled as he patted her hand – not the condescending smile he sometimes had, but an understanding one. "Yes, Ethel. It does make sense. You just have to keep opening up that mind of yours – let it expand a bit. You've come a long way, you know. You really have. Not everyone could handle this doppelganger idea – or even the other experiences you've had in the last couple of years." He sipped the last of his coffee and rose to leave.

"As for what I think, I believe that we all have doppelgangers out there – some are mere images of ourselves who mirror our lives, while others lead their own separate lives as parallel experiences. Not too many of us can see these doppelgangers, but when we do, they can enrich our existence and sometimes even give us guidance along the way. So, I wouldn't fret the details, Ethel. After all, she did say she'd be seeing you again."

FEAR NO EVIL

As she clung to the jagged rock some forty feet from shore, the waves lashed out at her face and pulled at her arms as if to wrestle them down into their watery embrace. They seemed to assume a will of their own -- an evil intent to end her life.

"What a stupid, asinine thing to do!" Ethel thought, gulping in the air before the next deluge submerged her head and shoulders beneath it. When she swam out to the rock formation earlier, she had even noticed that most of the native swimmers remained close to the shoreline, as if in deference to the whitecaps at the greater depths. But she had ignored that obvious warning. Though a good swimmer, Ethel was tired now and beginning to panic. If she left the safety of the rock, she feared that the strong undertow would carry her even further from the shore and deep below the surface of the waves.

Hoisting herself higher on the rock, she peered over the top and glimpsed two black figures in the water. She wiped the water from her eyes and looked again. Yes, there were two men wading out at waist depth on the other side. If she could attract their attention, they could help her. All she needed was to get her footing; she hadn't swum that far and the water was only a foot or so above her head. Still, that was a foot too deep.

"Help! Help! Over here!" The shorter of the two heard her and pointed her out to his friend. "I'm afraid to get off the rock. The waves are too strong." They cupped their hands behind their ears, but the crashing of the waves obliterated the sound of her voice.

She beckoned then for them to come out to where she was stranded, but the taller one spoke to his friend and turned toward the shore. "Don't go! Help me, please," she shouted. "I can't ..." Then another huge wave engulfed her and drowned out the rest.

Ethel's head went under and she couldn't get her breath. But she clung to the rock until the wave receded and when she blinked again, she could see the shorter man motioning for her to hold on. His companion had returned and was hurrying out to him with a coiled rope, one end of which he secured to a large rock closer to shore. He tied the other end around his waist, and started swimming toward her, while his friend gradually let out the slack. It took maybe five or ten minutes for him to reach her, but it seemed an eternity. He too would have been swept out to sea, Ethel felt, if he hadn't had the rope tugging at his waist. He held out his arm, she grabbed hold of it with both her hands, and the two of them were pulled in toward the shore by the other man.

When her feet touched the sand she gradually loosened her grip, but her legs failed to support her. "Wait," the man said. "Hang on to me. We're almost there."

Though he had no accent, Ethel assumed he was of native origin. But neither of the men were the golden-brown color of most of the Bali natives; their skin was coal black.

Ethel nodded then, and gave him a weak smile. "You saved my life, you know. I don't think I could have held on much longer." He shook his head, but she repeated, "I just don't think I could have held on. I really don't."

Reaching the shore, all three dropped breathlessly to the sandy beach where the only sounds were the rush of the wind and the lapping of the waves. Ethel's brows knit together as she stared at her two companions, vaguely feeling that she had seen them before. Comfortable in the silence, the two black men smiled back at the American tourist, but when she regained her composure and her voice, her profusion of thanks seemed to embarrass them. Nodding to her politely, they started to rise as if to leave.

"Oh, don't go." Ethel scrambled to her feet and reached for their arms to detain them. "Please. I want to give you something -- just a little something -- as a reward. And

I must have your names and addresses." She squinted down the beach toward the cabana where she had left her book and towel when she took her swim. "Just wait a moment. I'll be right back." She hurried over toward the beach fronting on her hotel, grabbed her purse from the cabana, and raced back toward her rescuers. They were nowhere in sight.

"But whatever possessed you to swim out to that rock in the first place?" Roscoe had passed through his first reaction of concern and sympathy, and was now angry. "The 'danger -- high waves' signs are posted all along the beach, and even now with the wind died down there aren't any swimmers in the water." This was only the second day of their two-week vacation at the all-inclusive Excelsior Resort in Bali, and already Ethel was in trouble. "My God, Ethel, you could have drowned!"

Ethel knew better than to argue. When Roscoe was this upset, common sense explanations wouldn't do any good. Besides, she had to admit to herself that she hadn't shown very much in the way of common sense when she had taken off alone on her swimming adventure. It had been a spur of the moment whim, not tempered by thought.

"Oh, Roscoe, don't scold. I've told myself the same thing a hundred times. It was dumb -- and I'm sorry." Though she knew it wouldn't really mollify him, she flashed her best little girl smile at him nonetheless. "But I'm even more sorry that I couldn't find those two young men who rescued me. I didn't have enough in my purse to give them a proper reward, but at least I could have taken their addresses and sent them something when we got back home." She shook her head with a puzzled frown. "I wonder where they went?"

Ethel also wondered where they had come from. She did not remember seeing any black natives when they drove from the airport to the resort. Later, at the pool she surveyed the employees behind the poolside bar and the chambermaids who scurried from room to room -- they were all brown-skinned or a golden brown. None were black.

Well, maybe Willy would have some idea of who they were. He always had logical explanations for her strange adventures, and she was sure that she'd run into him sooner or later.

The next morning Ethel decided to go for an early dip before breakfast, while

Roscoe browsed through the paper he had picked up at the desk -- yesterday's edition.

For her part, Ethel was happy to be spared the details of the war in Iraq and the growing number of American casualties. That's what vacations were for -- to get away from it all.

She spied Willy sitting at the edge of the pool, a floppy shade-hat perched on his head and his skinny legs dangling in the water. "Hi, Ethel," he grinned.

"Hi, Willy. Thought I might find you here." Ethel sat down beside him, and without any further explanation, she told him her story.

"So, that's the long and short of it," she concluded. "I guess it was one of those near death experiences, though I didn't see much of my life flashing before me." Ethel laughed as she added, "I was too busy just trying to keep my head above water." Then, more seriously, "I was really scared, Willy. The pull of the waves was so strong and so incessant; almost as if they were driven by some force beyond themselves -- an evil force.

I don't think I would have made it if it hadn't been for those two men. But I can't understand where in heck they came from. I mean, I don't think they were Bali natives.

And why did they disappear like they did?"

"Well, maybe they were figments of your imagination, too." Willy had never quite forgiven her for once placing him in that category -- long

ago when they had first debated the question that always plagued their relationship: What is reality?

"No, they were real enough. I grabbed the arm of the taller guy when he walked me into shore; his skin was a shiny black and I could feel the muscles beneath it. I could even describe them to you, Willy -- their faces and the way they talked. Somehow, I had the feeling that they were familiar, that I had seen them before." She fell silent as she remembered the deja vu impression she had while sitting with them on the beach.

Willy didn't interrupt her reverie. He seemed to be waiting for her to say something more. Finally, when he saw Roscoe approaching down the pathway from the resort rooms, he patted her on the shoulder as he rose. "Have to go, Ethel. But keep that thought -- maybe you did see them before. You just have to remember when."

That night as she lay in bed, just before drifting off to sleep, Ethel remembered. It was when her mother had died, over ten years ago. She had written about it to her best friend: When the nurse told me that Mom probably wouldn't live until morning, I decided to stay with her overnight. Roscoe drove home with our car, but arranged for me to use his sister's car if needed. I sat by her bed until about ten o'clock, just talking about when

I was a kid and the things we used to do together. I felt the strong compulsion to remind her of all the good things she had experienced in her life -- all the happy memories.

Then, I held her hands in mine and said a few prayers out loud. Ones that she knew and would recognize. You know, like "The Lord's Prayer" and "Now I Lay Me

Down to Sleep" and that part of the 23rd Psalm -- "I will fear no evil." My mother wasn't hung up on religion, but she attended church regularly and certainly believed in

God and the hereafter. I don't know if she even heard me, but if she did, I think she would have been comforted -- just by the sound of my voice if nothing more. At least, I like to think so.

There was an extra bed in her room, so I finally lay down to rest; I must have dozed because I was kind of disoriented when I heard a noise from her bed. She had opened her eyes and was trying to sit up. I rushed over, put my arm around her shoulders and helped her to a sitting position. She didn't say anything and I'm not sure if she really saw me, but I'm pretty certain that she knew I was there. She squeezed my hand, sneezed, and then she died. In my arms. I thought the sneezing was strange, but maybe she was "giving up the ghost," as they say. My sole comfort is that I was there with her.

After I eased her back onto the pillow, I went down to the nurses' station, they called the doctor, and -- well, you know the routine. What happened then is what really frightened me. It was almost three in the morning when everything was taken care of.

Roscoe's sister had brought over their second car and left it in the parking lot. It had started to snow, and since I wasn't used to the car, I drove very slowly. When I reached the highway, I tried to accelerate, but the car wouldn't go more than forty miles an hour.

It seemed as if the gasline was clogged, because it kept stalling on me and I had the damndest time getting it started again.

From the time I left the lot, I had the strongest impression that someone, or something, was following me. The snow was swirling around so heavily by then that I couldn't see anything behind me, and the headlights of the car only illuminated the road for about five yards ahead. The sense of this "presence" was the sense of evil -- the presence of evil. I don't really know how else to describe it. I became terribly frightened as the belief welled up in my mind that this evil being was following me because I had said those prayers with my mother, warding off any harm to her as she passed beyond.

Now, it was trying to get me. I know it sounds crazy, Jenny, but I really felt as if the devil himself was after me. So I started praying again -- this time for myself.

The car was acting up again, slowing to twenty miles an hour. Then it completely stopped. I hadn't had the time (or the forethought) to pull over to the side of the road, so there I was, parked directly in the traffic lane. Right at that moment, I looked in my rear view mirror and saw two headlights coming down that lane straight at me. As the lights drew closer, I could see that they came from a huge semi; it was speeding towards me and blasting its horn in short, loud staccato beeps. That fool must have been traveling over 70 miles an hour!

For the first time in my life, I faced death head-on, but what scared me even more than that truck heading for me at top speed was my sense of some kind of malevolent evil behind it all. My hands were shaking and I felt entirely helpless. Suddenly, an old rattle-trap of a car appeared out of nowhere -- right in front of my car -- and two black guys ran back to my window and yelled for me to pump the brakes. They were telling me that the only thing I could do to warn the truck driver was to keep tapping my brake pedal so the brake lights would flicker on and off. I pumped like crazy! At the last moment he must have realized that I was stuck there, and he veered over to the other lane just in time. There probably weren't more than a couple of yards to spare.

Now, the odd thing about it all was that there are no blacks around Millford,

Jenny -- it's pretty much a lily-white town. But there they were. Those fellows couldn't have been nicer or more helpful. They pushed the car off to the side of the road and then drove me all the way home. Later on, when I told Chris about the whole episode, she said that they might have been my guardian angels. Well, I don't know about that, but if there was a black Madonna, why not black angels? I wonder if I'll ever see them again?

It wasn't until years later, when Ethel learned the answer. Her room was quiet now that Chris and Kathy had left, after hugging and kissing her goodnight. They were such good kids. Well, not kids anymore, what with grown children of their own. But she still thought of them that way. She was so proud of both of them. She wondered if they knew how much she loved them. Oh, Roscoe had loved them too, of course, but he had never said it very often -- never quite able to express the affection he felt so deeply.

She began to feel drowsy. The medication had taken away the pain, and had even numbed the fleeting bouts of anxiety that touched her mind whenever she thought about the death that she knew was fast approaching. As she reached up to turn off the light, she heard a light tapping on her door. "Come in, I'm still awake," she called.

The two black orderlies entered together. "Hello, Ethel," they said in unison.

"How's it going?" They looked so familiar -- reminding her of the men who had saved her from the speeding semi and, later, from the watery depths of the Balinese seas. But, no, they weren't just familiar. They were the same.

"So what are you going to rescue me from this time?" she smiled. "I don't think that even you two can quite pull me away from the grasp of death."

"No, but we can remind you of something you almost forgot." And as they sat on either side of her and held her hands, she heard them repeat the 23rd psalm: "Yea, though I walk through the valley of the shadow of death, I will fear no evil – for Thou art with me." She was peaceful now -- warm and secure and all at ease. Then she sneezed -- and closed her eyes.